eternity

LAURY FALTER

First Edition: August 2011

The characters and events portrayed in this book are fictitious. Any similarity to real persons, living or dead, is coincidental and not intended by the author.

Falter, Laury, 1972-
Fallen: a novel / by Laury Falter – 1st ed.

Summary: Maggie prepares for defense against the world's most evil creatures while uncovering the truth behind her identity and why their enemies will never give up.

ISBN: 978-0-615-53342-1
ISBN-13: 978-0615533421

For Babs – whose endearing love and astonishing insight in to this story made it possible to be written.

And thanks to my husband, Brian, for his fortitude and understanding during the many late nights it took to finish this novel.

And thanks also to Jill for her honest and motivational reviews.

∞

CONTENTS

∞

PREFACE

London, England, 1350 AD

Night was arriving quickly now. The shadows were creeping longer, like gnarled fingers reaching for each other and intertwining across the city. Dampness clung throughout the narrow cobblestone streets, aided by a thick fog that had begun to roll in from the River Thames. Along the streets, windows were now lit with flickering yellow candles warding off the darkness and the cold. In the distance, harsh coughs mingled with the howls of loved ones lost to the mysterious condition overtaking London.

As I turned the corner, my feet scuffed across the stones making a noise that I knew was too loud. I kept the flap of my cloak tightly wound to me, doing my best to minimize my appearance. I was just five feet tall but even at that height I was too conspicuous. Ducking lower, I kept moving. My eyes scanned the buildings ahead of me, and as best I could, behind and to the sides. I hadn't seen them yet but there were still a few streets to go before I reached my destination.

A howl rose above the rooftops and I stopped. It was a sound familiar to me and it caused the hair at the back of my neck to stand up. My hands began to shake and small beads of perspiration rose up from my brow.

It was close. Very close.

I began to run, paying special attention to quieting my footsteps as I made my way through the labyrinth of London's corridors.

The street that would take me to safety was only a few yards away and then my skin prickled worse on the back of my neck, the hair there standing straight out now.

Glancing up I found it perched on the roof of the building ahead. What appeared to be claws dug into the edge, its body cocooned in thick, black wings. Its head was tilted down so that it could watch me better.

I didn't stop this time. My pace became a sprint and suddenly the gas lamps dimly lighting each side of the street blended in to one and the moist air on my exposed face collected and fell like raindrops down my cheeks.

The thing gave a brief shudder – a sign of excitement at the prospect of murder – and unraveled its broad wings. With a single pump, the wings lifted it into the night sky. It hovered for only a moment and then dove towards the earth, towards me. It made no sound other than the wind whistling over its fluttering wings.

We were now on a collision course unless one turned and fled the other direction. This, I knew, would not happen.

Fleeing, at this point, was not an option. I leaned forward, the balls of my feet barely touching the ground as I increased my speed.

I looked at my attacker, watching as a wicked smile of stained, jagged teeth stretched beneath its gleaming, eager eyes. My own eyes were now narrowed, mustering every conceivable prowess I had in me. I would need it.

The collision never came.

From a side street emerged a movement so blindingly fast it was indistinguishable. The winged being and my defender slammed into a building wall, becoming a mesh of entangled limbs, crumbling brick dislodging from the force.

"Eran," I screamed, though it came out a whisper.

"Stay…back…Magdalene," he struggled to warn me.

Without thought, I tore the cloak from my shoulders and joined the fight.

1. THE ARRIVAL

New Orleans, Louisiana, 660 Years Later

The day before school started I woke up to a quiet house.

This is good, I thought. Easier to sneak out.

I slipped out of bed and quietly walked across my room to the closet, opening it to a row of T-shirts and jeans. I'd never given much thought to what I wore and today was no different. Everything I owned was made of cotton and denim so I pulled out a Cottage Cheese Band T-shirt, the closest one to me, and a pair of jeans. After dressing, I picked up the only pair of shoes I owned – black leather biker boots with steel tips – and headed for the door.

Passing by my standing mirror, I caught sight of my reflection and paused.

Standing at just five feet, my image barely filled the frame. But what I lacked in height, I made up for in other areas. I've been told that I look like an oversized fairy and, to be honest, I could vaguely see the resemblance. With a long mop of curly cocoa-colored hair falling to my hips, a slim waist, rather meager legs, and super-sized hazelnut eyes I fit that description fairly accurately. I just wished I had wings…to help make my escape a little easier.

Opening my door, I cautiously peered outside. Still no sound. Good. I slipped out into the hallway and crept passed the only other door on the way to the stairs.

In the dim light of the second floor, I stared at it, partly hoping for it to open and partly hoping it remained shut.

Behind that door was my guardian, Eran Taylor; someone who had dedicated his life to protecting me and had proven already that he would go to extremes to do it. He'd risked his life more times than I knew in order to keep me from taking my last breath. More than that, he was also my one true love, my best friend, my eternal confidant, the reason for me to fight for that last breath. Therein lays the problem and why I was torn between the door opening or staying shut.

That door wasn't the only thing separating Eran and me.

It was also Eran.

As my guardian he made it clear that he would not allow himself the luxury of intimacy with me. His responsibility as my guardian came first. He'd explained in a way that left no room for argument that while he loved me unconditionally and without end that love would not distract him from his sole purpose in keeping me safe.

I disagreed wholeheartedly and had not been able to shake the disappointment that – to him - our love was a distraction.

Because of this disagreement and because my entire being ached at the sight of him, I was doing my best to avoid him – which hurt me as much as it frustrated him.

So as I crept down the stairs, I avoided the floorboards I knew to be loose. This was a challenge. Living in a historic Victorian house on Magazine Street in New Orleans meant that the house was old and therefore – it creaked.

While I loved the house, I did not like the fact that it was Eran's accomplice in notifying him when I was leaving.

To my surprise, I landed at the base of the staircase without a sound and quickly made my way to the kitchen.

That was where my sneaking out ended.

From inside the kitchen, a hearty Irish voice asked, "Whatdoya call that mess?" It belonged to Rufus, a giant, heavily tattooed man who always reminded me of a Viking warrior with a secret sensitive side.

His answer was a mere sigh and it came from Felix, another housemate. Felix was the exact opposite of Rufus – bony, flighty, and as vibrant as his bright, rust-colored hair. A moment later, as if not wanting to be outdone, Felix replied haughtily, "Licorice mayonnaise, if you must know. Widely liked in Europe until the eighteenth century."

"Couldnta been that widely liked…if they stopped usin' it."

I entered the kitchen to find Felix's already thin lips pinched closed. He was clearly trying to prevent an argument but I strongly doubted it would help.

The moment he saw me his mood changed. Drawing in a sharp breath, he exclaimed, "Good morning, Mags!" Clearly he was using me as a change of subject. "Are you leaving for Jackson's Square so soon?"

I hesitated in answering. They sided with Eran so any mention that I was leaving would be their cue to wake him. "It's seven o'clock in the morning, Felix."

"Right," he nodded, his entire body shaking as he furiously whipped his licorice mayonnaise. "Right…" It looked as if he wanted to say more but didn't know how to phrase it. So it was Rufus, who didn't follow social etiquette, who asked the question.

"Tryin' to get outta here 'fore Eran is up?"

I considered these people my family, having parents who passed on at the time of my birth and an aunt who took her photography more seriously than she did me as my only known blood relatives. Yet, if there was any question who my housemates were more loyal to, this little spat that Eran and I were going through made it clear.

Because of this, I ignored Rufus – even though I knew my silence would be a declarative 'yes'. There was really no way around the truth. Not that I cared to lie. I never understood the need to. I was going to do what I wanted regardless of their opinion. It was just easier for me if I kept them questioning.

"Smells good," I replied instead.

He nodded, understanding I wouldn't give myself up. As a peace gesture, he scooped his scrambled eggs on to a plate and set it in front of me before turning to stroll back to the stove and remake them for himself. He narrowly missed Felix, who was now approaching me with a suspicious grin. I couldn't help but wonder what would have happened if the two were to collide. Since Felix reminded me of a scarecrow and Rufus resembled an ox there shouldn't have been any guessing who would be left standing.

Felix reached me and quickly slopped a dollop of pinkish congealed glob next to my eggs. "Just try it."

I stared at it warily. Felix had built a reputation for his interesting culinary skills so I wasn't surprised that it was the licorice mayonnaise he'd been mixing before I'd entered the kitchen. Curiously, I dabbed my fork into it.

Something made me wonder whether they were using their food to keep me here until Eran woke up.

"It's meant to eat, Maggie, not to stab," said Ezra, entering the kitchen. As a robust swarthy woman and the oldest member of the house, she brought with her an air of authority. She patted my shoulder passing by me to pour a cup of coffee – of which I knew was the fourth cup so far today.

"Morning Ezra," I replied. Felix beamed a smile at her and Rufus simply gave her a gruff nod.

"Good morning, dear friends," she said pleasantly, inhaling the aroma of her steaming coffee and smiling to herself. "What a beautiful one it is too. I see we are all up early, with the exception of Eran."

As if on cue, the three of them looked in my direction.

"What?" I said shrugging, knowing full well they were questioning what I thought of that and whether I'd make another attempt to leave before he was ready.

In truth, I could leave whenever I wanted. Ezra watched over me while my aunt, whom I typically live with, toured Europe on a photography excursion while I spent my senior year in New Orleans. So, Ezra and I had an unspoken appreciation for the fact that she (nor Rufus nor Felix) had any right to enforce rules. Yet, she knew that I respected her and wouldn't overstep my bounds by blatantly ignoring her wishes. If she asked me directly to wait for Eran I would have, but I think she'd avoided that request simply because she didn't want to interfere. She was letting Eran and I work it out, which I appreciated.

Still, it was Rufus who saved me by changing the subject.

"Was a good mornin' till ya look at what Felix's makin'," Rufus muttered.

Felix sighed heavily. "There's no need for that type of comment."

Rufus ignored him and countered with a far more appetizing side as he slid sausage patties on to my plate.

Ezra peered at me over the edge of her cup, the words "Today is the last day of some of your life" glaring back at me. If I didn't know Ezra better, I would have wondered if she'd positioned her mug so that those words sent a silent warning to be extra diligent.

The kitchen grew quiet with the exception of Rufus, whose fork clanked against his plate while hungrily shoveling his breakfast into his mouth, and a frequent, disgusted sigh by Felix. Neither one of them noted the silent communication sent between Ezra and myself.

I quickly ate what was on my plate – licorice mayonnaise included because it wasn't as bad as I'd thought and it gave Felix his pride back – and then laced up my biker boots.

Leaving the three of them at the table, I said a hushed goodbye, glanced down the hallway to make sure Eran wouldn't see me leaving through the back door, and snuck out.

My bike was in its usual place, inside the back shed, but I didn't bother starting it. Given that it was a big and beautiful Harley Davidson Sportster, the exhaust noise would definitely alert Eran. Instead, I pushed it out of the shed and along the driveway towards the street.

The morning was unusually warm for a January, with the sun already beating rays of light through the shadows of the trees surrounding the yard, and I was looking forward to a peaceful ride to Jacksons Square. That, unfortunately, would be delayed.

I was just beyond the backyard when Eran's voice came up behind me.

"And just where do you think you're going?" he called out with his English accent that, despite my efforts, still charmed me.

I ignored the excitement burning in my stomach, a reaction I always seemed to have when he was around, and looked for something to do so I didn't have to turn and face him. Strapping my book bag to my bike was a good enough diversion.

"Avoiding me again? Really, Magdalene?" His voice was laced with disappointment.

Get used to it, I thought.

"We've discussed this," he reminded me, though I didn't need any reminding.

"No, you discussed it." I leaned my bike back on its kickstand and spun around, staggering a bit at the sight of him.

He stood before me handsome, arrogant, and charismatic. Beneath his wavy brown hair, he smirked with clear aqua eyes teasing me. Long, powerfully built arms crossed his chest and his legs, covered in jeans and accentuated with muscles, stood apart.

I struggled to regain my composure and was successful - a little.

"I'm sorry you feel that way," he stated, unsympathetically, his haughty grin remaining. "Sneaking away is not going to help. I'll simply come find you."

"Look, Eran," I hated the way my tone was whiny. I paused and began again more declaratively. "I won't abide rules that I had no input or agreement in establishing. That is just the way it is."

His grin faltered slightly but his tone remained cajoling. "It is one rule and it is for your benefit. And there is no denying it…You need me."

"I do not," I said a little too briskly.

He tilted his head down, looking up at me through his lashes, waiting for me to assess that statement.

"Well…" I stuttered. "Not in that way. I need you in other ways…Oh, you know what I mean."

Eran approached me, stopping just outside my reach, which didn't feel fair. His voice was quieter, kind this time. "I understand why you're avoiding me. I don't blame you. This is just the way it has to be until…"

He didn't finish his sentence but he didn't need to. We both knew what he meant. Not until I was safe, until my enemies were eradicated, until his job as my guardian was no longer his primary objective. Until then, everything else, including me, was a distraction.

"Fine," I said, disliking myself for surrendering. "Fine. This is the last day of holiday break so...let's get on with it. I have work to do."

Silently, and with a good amount of tension, we slipped on our helmets, got on my bike, and rode to Jackson Square.

The Square, as I call it, is a famous New Orleans landmark surrounded by historical buildings. Because it is a treasured site by both tourists and locals, street vendors congregate there to sell their talents. I have a regular spot just outside the St. Louis Cathedral, which is where Eran parked the bike.

The remaining street vendors had already set up their areas with colorful artwork hanging from makeshift wooden walls and tables piled with New Orleans trinkets. The stores and restaurants bordering the square had thrown open their weathered wooden shutters and doors too, beckoning in regular patrons and sightseers. Since a mist had rolled in over night from Lake Pontchartrain to blanket the city the day looked a little dim but the sun seemed to be successfully baking the dullness away. Today, as mentioned, would be unusually warm for January so the trees encircling The Square would offer relief to both the vendors and the sightseers.

Felix arrived with Rufus in his lime green Camero and began setting up their tables. Felix, being a tarot card reader, was often times quicker than Rufus in setting up, who was a talented caricature artist and needed various drawing instruments laid out. My area consisted of two chairs and a sign that read simply:

Send & Receive Messages
to Dead Loved Ones

Payment Due on Proof of Delivery

Eran helped us, which made it faster. He then stood in front of me as I took a seat in one of my chairs.

"I'll be close by."

"Yes, I know," I said. My anger had dissipated by then.

Eran recognized it and knelt down in front of me. He then waited until our eyes were locked so that he could convey what he wanted me to know: That he was equally as disappointed we were put in this position.

As quickly as he'd knelt, he stood and moved through the crowd; far enough that I could perform my work undistracted, close enough to keep me in sight.

New Orleans tourists were beginning to filter into the brick-paved area around Jackson's Square now. It was mid-morning and yet most of them appeared blurry-eyed, in need of caffeine, and interested mostly in making a beeline for Café du Monde. However, my sign did catch the attention of a few college girls who gave me an inquisitive stare.

The time passed quickly with most of those stopping by being regular customers. I'd been performing this service for several months and had acquired 'regulars' who kept up ongoing conversations with family members and friends on the other side.

When the daylight began to fade and The Square emptied, I collected my sign and folding chairs, giving them to Felix to drive home. Watching Felix's lime green Camaro disappear around the corner, I turned and found Eran leaning against the gate behind me. His arms were crossed over his chest again highlighting the curves of his muscles, making my breath catch.

He broke his typical arrogant grin to ask, "Good day?"

"Fairly good." I shrugged. "Most of the messages were about family gossip. Only one is holding a heated argument that doesn't look like it will end any time soon…about whether their dog should be groomed. "

Eran stifled a chuckle and then turned serious. "I have an errand to make before we get you home."

"You do?" I was a little suspicious. "Okay, should we use my bike?"

"We should," Eran confirmed, handing my helmet to me.

As we headed through the streets of the French Quarter, I couldn't deny its magnificence. Passing colorful, weather-beaten buildings decorated with black wrought iron balustrades, neighbors chatting on the sidewalk, and restaurants with lines spilling from their open doorways, I realized that my enamor with this city hadn't weakened since I'd arrived a few months back. Before that point, I had traveled across the country, staying in each place no longer than three months at a time while my aunt worked on her photography collection. No place before had captivated me like New Orleans.

Eran took us to a quieter part of town and a narrow street alongside Lake Pontchartrain. I'd never been to this area of the city and could quickly see why. It was made of warehouse stores and I'd never been very interested in shopping.

By the time we reached our destination, it was nearly dark and the buildings were mostly hidden in shadows. The shopkeepers in this area had long since closed their doors and gone home for the evening.

Only one window was illuminated.

We removed our helmets and I followed Eran towards that window. We stopped at the door next to it where a simple wooden sign had been nailed at eye-level.

"Phillip Howell…Antiquities Dealer…" I read it aloud.

The door opened then and a quiet, gruff voice replied, "At your service."

The voice belonged to a man who looked old enough to be in his nineties. He stooped over a gnarled cane that looked about the same age. His eyes were kind and gleaming as if he had a secret to tell.

"Mr. Howell," Eran said, extending his hand.

"Pish," was the reply. "I'm an old man and have no time for pleasantries. Come in."

We followed him through a small room which may have been a pleasant storefront at one point. Now it was cluttered with statues, paintings, and boxes. Aisles had been cleared to allow us to reach Mr. Howell's office in the back.

"Sit." He pointed to a brown leather couch across from his desk and we did.

Mr. Howell continued on behind his desk but didn't sit down. He instead hobbled to a scuffed but sturdy safe in the back corner of his office. After a few brief dials, he opened the door and removed a thin envelope.

Returning to his desk, he sat down and shoved the envelope toward Eran.

Eran reached for it, opened the flap, and peered inside. A quick glance told me inside was a cashier's check from Mr. Howell and written for four million dollars. I gasped. Unfazed, Eran winked confidently at me and closed the flap. He tucked the envelope in his jeans pocket before addressing Mr. Howell.

Speculatively, he said, "I'm surprised at how quickly it sold. Who bought it?"

"A new collector…here in town."

Eran nodded.

"Beautiful piece. And with the history behind it…" Mr. Howell exhaled a reflective chuckle. "Bids flew in from around the world once I set up the silent auction. But don't worry. It's confidential, just as you wanted. No one knows the name of the seller but me."

"Ah…" I mumbled to myself, drawing their interest. "That's why the check came from Mr. Howell."

Mr. Howell smiled, his skin folding over itself as his face lifted. "She's quick."

"You have no idea," said Eran, and then asked again, "Who was the collector?"

Mr. Howell appeared slightly perturbed at the question. "Just as you had, he asked to remain anonymous. In fact, he sent an assistant to pick it up."

Realizing I was missing much of the story, I asked, "What was the it you are referring to?"

Mr. Howell smiled like a child in a candy store. "A renowned diamond necklace missing since the American Revolution. I was asked by several bid submitters where it was found but your boyfriend here won't give that up."

Eran grinned and stood up as if on cue. "Mr. Howell, thank you for mediating the sale."

"For that piece? My pleasure." Mr. Howell stood also and escorted us to the door. With a quick, courteous nod, he closed and locked the door behind us. The office went dark a moment later.

"Renowned necklace missing since the American Revolution?" I said with a curious lift of my eyebrows.

Eran nodded. "Thought I should store it for a rainy day…That rainy day arrived."

"But where did you store it?" I didn't bother to hide my amazement.

"There's a little place in the Appalachians."

The realization hit me quickly. "The cabin…"

Eran nodded again. He didn't seem interested in sharing information so I figured it was up to me to ask.

"But how did you get it? You've always been here with me. When did you find the time?"

"Magdalene," he said, subduing a smile. "Have you forgotten how fast I can move?"

I rolled my eyes and replied, "Not in the least." I knew full well that Eran could make it around the world in a single day. A trip to the Appalachian Mountains would be a quick jaunt for him.

"Still, I had a friend watch over you as you slept." He paused briefly, struggling to decide whether to disclose more. In the end, he allowed himself a brief reprieve from his typical aloof behavior. "I would never leave you alone. You are far too important to me." He struggled with those words, releasing them gruffly. Listening to them made me feel an overwhelming sense of compassion for him. Our distance was challenging him too.

Only a second passed before his expression changed and he grew concerned. "What, Magdalene? What's wrong?"

He saw the reaction in me before I recognized it myself. Suddenly my hands were shaking, perspiration broke out across my forehead, and – most distinctly – the hair at the back of my neck stood up as if I'd been shot with electricity.

A moment later I heard a young, male voice state, "Ah…now isn't this sweet, boys? Ill-fated lovers meeting again."

Eran moved to face the street, his expression changing to stone. I did the same while desperately trying to calm my reaction to those who now stood in front of us.

A ripping sound began, drawing my awareness towards Eran where I watched as his T-shirt tore away from his body. From the back of his shoulder blades, two gashes opened and from them grew a pair of brilliantly white wings. They expanded until they could easily have surrounded us but remained outstretched and ready for flight.

A single line of eight men scowled back at us, their stances much like ours – ready for attack. Each one looked to be just older than teenagers, each one was shirtless, and each one had massive grey wings spanning from their thick, brawny backs.

13

I looked at Eran and realized that we were alone, we were outnumbered, and we were suddenly facing the enemies that Eran had been trying to warn me were coming.

2. FOREWARNING

Eran lifted his arm and gently tried to push me behind him as the group of eight winged men took a unified step forward. I swiftly moved around Eran's barrier.

"I'm not afraid of you," I called out, almost daring them to advance, so angry I nearly wanted them to attempt it.

"They know that, Magdalene," Eran muttered, his voice calm but tense.

"Still haven't lost that vigor, I see," reflected the one who had stepped out in front earlier.

I noticed he was addressing me, which caught me off guard. Without diverting my gaze, I quietly asked Eran, "Do I know him?"

"Yes," Eran replied stiffly and then called out, "What do you want, Marco?"

Marco appeared to feign offense. "So much time has gone by and this is your greeting? I mean…it has been…what? Three hundred years or so since we've last seen each other. We have much to catch up on."

Marco's choice of words seemed peculiar to me at first. Then I realized that he, and most-likely his winged accomplices, had spent several centuries on earth and had become a blend of what they'd experienced. Their language, their mannerisms, even their accents were no longer distinct. They belonged to no culture and could no longer identify any roots. They were wanderers – or more precisely – nomadic hunters.

"We have nothing to say to each other." Eran kept his guard up and his stance in place.

Marco clucked his tongue at us. "Not cordial, Eran," he said. It seemed to be a warning. "And you, dear sweet Magdalene. Miss me?" He grinned then, an evil, mocking expression that made the hairs on the back of my neck stick straight out.

To my surprise, Eran growled. It was slight but loud enough to reach me. I'd never heard Eran react that way before.

Marco was intentionally provoking Eran, and doing it successfully.

"You're just as beautiful as I remember, Magdalene." He paused, reflectively. "When we first met your name was Marie. Do you recall that, Magdalene? When we first met? But, of course you wouldn't…I heard somewhere that you remember very little of your past lives…You have no recollection of any of us…Do you?" He shook his head in what seemed to be mock pity. "Why ever would you choose to return here as a human? By doing so you've left yourself vulnerable, weak…"

"Marco," Eran said impatiently, sending an unspoken warning. "What…do…you…want?" he continued through teeth clenched against his rising anger.

Marco ignored him. "But, dear Magdalene…how I've missed the curve of your-"

Eran immediately stepped forward and in reaction three of the men behind Marco advanced, wings widening their span in preparation for an assault.

"All right…All right." Marco brought up a hand in a gesture to calm the situation. "What do we want? Only to watch. We won't intervene. Promise."

I couldn't tell if Marco was insane or still playing with Eran.

"Watch what?" Eran asked the same question that was perplexing me.

Marco's eyebrows lifted in surprise. "You mean to tell me that no one has told you? All mighty, all powerful, all knowing Eran is the last to learn?" He scoffed.

"Watch what, Marco?"

"The upcoming battle, of course." Eran and I glanced at each other, both of us wary. When we didn't respond Marco went on. "Not with us. No, no. But I do hear that quite a few of us will be arriving shortly as spectators. You'll have an audience, it sounds…from all over the world. We wouldn't miss this for…well, for all eternity." He paused to snigger at his own joke.

Eran's patience was thinning and he showed this by sighing loudly. "If the battle isn't with you, who is it with?"

Marco opened his mouth to answer the question but he was only toying with us, which became clear with his answer. "Hmmm…No…No. I think you should figure that out for yourselves." Marco spun around to face the others, chuckling at our expense.

The remaining men broke in to smiles, relaxing their wings somewhat.

"Let's head out, boys," said Marco and then sent Eran and me another warning. "We'll be seeing you two around."

Almost in unison, each of their wings made a powerful flapping motion, and their bodies were lifted into the inky night sky. They became a single gray line against the black background, a dividing line. One more flap and they faded out of sight.

Eran's own wings sunk without a sound into his back as we stood quietly for a moment. Without taking his eyes away from the sky, he did a quick, thoughtful assessment. "Marco's untruthfulness is legendary. He could be fabricating the possibility of a battle. But the fact that he didn't engage in an attack tonight makes me slightly leery that he believes one is coming. If he does decide to attack, I can handle him and his cronies. But if more Fallen Ones start flocking here we'll need to get you out of New Orleans."

"You know I won't leave," I said, determined.

Eran frowned. "We'll discuss your leaving New Orleans if the time comes. For now, I'm going to get you home."

Instantly, my thoughts fell back to when I'd been first introduced to the Fallen Ones. Given that I had moved every three months since birth, I'd been able to evade them. Then I landed in New Orleans and they caught up with me. From that point forward, my life had been at risk.

Fallen Ones for the most part are cold, calculating instigators and equally sinister avengers. Having been shunned from the afterlife for causing a malicious act against humanity, they've been committed to an eternity on earth where they've subsequently kept up their treachery.

They especially do not like anyone who assists humans and that included me and any guardians sent to protect us. Because of this, a war has been raging between Fallen Ones and guardians for centuries, a war that I was now embroiled in whether I liked it or not.

Eran had bent down and was now collecting the remnants of his T-shirt.

Despite the gravity of what had just happened, I noticed his muscles stretching as he pulled a spare shirt from his book bag and slipped it on. I also noticed that the gashes in his back had completely healed.

"They're stunning," I said.

He glanced at me. "My appendages? They're good to have in times like these."

"Are they…painful at all?"

"I barely notice them," he said sympathetically, knowing I was concerned without having to say it.

"Good."

"Come on…Time to get you back home."

Unlike our typical leisurely pace, this ride was fast and sharp. Eran was nervous but he didn't show it in words. It came through in the maneuvering of the bike.

We arrived at the house and parked the bike in the shed with neither of us saying a word until we were inside the house. Our other three housemates were playing a fairly heated board game when we entered but they greeted us briefly before returning to it.

"Dinner's in the fridge," Ezra said, her head bowed towards the game.

"Thanks but I'm…I'm just not hungry," I said. I didn't bother adding, not while knowing that my enemies had arrived just as Eran predicted and had threatened a looming battle. For some reason, food just didn't sound good.

Eran simply shook his head. Apparently, his appetite was gone too. "I think we'll call it an early night."

Felix snickered, moving a piece on the board, to which Rufus slapped his hand away. "Ain't your turn," he said briskly and then fell back in silent contemplation over the board. Felix huffed.

Ezra was the only apprehensive one. She seemed to have an innate ability to know when something was wrong but allowed you to bring her in on it when you were ready. "Then good night you two." She paused and added, "Keep the doors open."

Since Eran began living with us three weeks ago, Ezra had allowed him to stay on one condition: The bedroom door needed to be left open if Eran and I were in the room alone. She worked with troubled teens so she had a preexisting condition that she acknowledged and called suspicious tendencies. She knew she couldn't help what happened outside the house but was dedicated to preventing anything from happening inside it. Out of respect we obeyed her one wish.

At the top of the stairs, I knew that Eran expected that I follow him to his bedroom. Without a word, I deviated and went to my room.

A warm night like tonight would ordinarily find us on my balcony overlooking Magazine Street, chairs tilted back, our feet propped on the railing. I went directly to the French doors leading to it and opened them wide.

"What are you doing, Magdalene?" Eran came up behind me, attempting to suppress his irritation.

"I know I'm being irresponsible by leaving us exposed but I will not live in fear."

"Acts of self-preservation are not a reflection of living in fear." I could guarantee that he'd said this line many times before.

"It is to me." I said firmly, taking a seat in my chair, tilting it back, and propping my feet up.

Eran groaned but dropped into the chair next to me. "You're never easy on me…"

We sat in silence for several minutes, listening to the squeak of my chair as it complained against my rocking motion.

My rocking was meant to be more of a diversion from my thoughts than to pass the time. Eran's proximity to me posed a challenge. His very presence pulled me to him and it took a defined force inside me not to stand, slide into his lap, and lift my lips to his – damn his worries of distraction.

In truth, though I would never admit this to him, he'd been correct about my enemies finding me again and he'd been correct about avoiding affection with me. It was our brief moment tonight when his eyes were locked on me that Marco and his gang appeared – and we hadn't noticed them until they made themselves known. We would have been easy prey.

Despite it all, there was an undeniable part of me that refused to let go of the notion that life without love – or at least exploring that love - is an empty one.

When I looked at him sitting stoically in the chair next to mine, I knew that I would die for him just as he would die for me – and that risk of death didn't deter my love for him in the least.

Eran's face was still impassive, his body was motionless. His entire being appeared to be absorbed in thought.

Then he spoke suddenly, catching me by surprise. "I won't let them near you. They won't touch you, Magdalene." His tone was self-assured, a trait that Eran radiated.

I reached out and laid my hand on his arm. He sucked in his breath, clearly fighting the same urges as me. "I know…" I said, softly, to both circumstances.

Then his mood changed, hands curling around the armrests of his chair, his muscles flexing beneath my hand. I glanced up to find his eyes narrowed at some distant memory coming to the surface. "Not this time…"

That gave me a jolt but I didn't think now would be the best time to ask what he meant. I got the sense that he wanted to jump up and preemptively attack them and I'm not sure he wouldn't have if he knew where they could be found.

He was clearly struggling with his thoughts so I changed the subject. "Should we tell Ezra what happened tonight?"

Eran took a moment to recover before answering and then said in a slightly less troubled tone, "I've been considering it. But there's no need to upset them when we have no proof of Marco being truthful one way or another."

I agreed with a nod. "If Marco is telling the truth and there are others coming for us, who do you think they are?"

Eran drew in a deep breath and shook his head, confirming my assumption that he wasn't taking Marco's prophecy lightly. "We have so many enemies, Magdalene, it's impossible to know at this point."

I didn't want Eran wrapped up in protecting me. I had never asked for it and I still didn't entirely believe it was needed. But it was comforting to hear him use the word 'we' and to reaffirm that we were together.

I opened my mouth to ask a lingering question, one that kept pestering me since our brief interlude with Marco, but I wasn't sure if it would upset Eran further.

"Go ahead," he said, noticing, encouraging me. "What's on your mind?"

"Well…Marco."

Eran again grew tense.

"Are you sure you don't mind me asking?" I hesitated.

Despite his overwrought appearance, he said, "No, I don't mind you asking about Marco. If he stays – and it sounds like he plans to – it's important for you to know what to expect from him."

I shook my head, irritated now. "Sometimes I can't stand being a reborn." Most of those on earth are considered reborn, having come here for an educational experience and intentionally forgetting their past lives so as not to impede their learning in this life. I had chosen this path too and it had prevented me from remembering anything at all about our enemies. Why I had chosen to come back as a reborn - and without my memory or the powerful assets that others had brought back with them, others like Eran and Marco - had always been a mystery to me. It was one that no one seemed able to answer which was a cause of deep frustration for me.

"You came here for a reason," he said drawing my attention. Supportive of me even when I wasn't, he added, "You always do."

I smiled my appreciation. "I'm trying to work through the ambiguity, to remember anything I can, and Marco hinted at a past…So I'm wondering how we know him."

In reaction, Eran's lips quivered in anger but thankfully it seemed to be fleeting. He then drew in a breath and cleared his mind. "As you are aware, you've been to earth multiple lifetimes. Each one introduced new risks to you as Fallen Ones found you and then…" He paused, stiffening, and then continued, "…and then attempted to slay you. Only Marco has differed from that…rhythm. Marco didn't start out as other Fallen Ones do. While others fall as a choice or are required to fall as punishment for their sins, Marco…well, he was fooled in to it."

"Fooled?" I repeated, allowing that understanding to sink in. "That sounds awful."

Eran grimaced, though I couldn't understand why my pity would cause that reaction. "Yes. I'm sure it was," he concluded.

Even though Eran's answer sounded dispassionate, I made an effort to comfort him. "I only meant that he's now required to live an eternity in a place he didn't necessarily choose," I explained, hoping the odd disappointment I saw in Eran would subside.

"I understand," Eran said serenely. "I'm not offended. I just don't enjoy recounting it because, at that time, he tried to assume my role."

"Your role?"

"Yes…Marco was your bodyguard."

"My what?" I said, loudly. I couldn't have been more surprised if he'd told me that I'd been a cat in my past life.

"Your guard. You hired him to protect you during the French Revolution. They were chaotic times, Magdalene. No one knew who they could trust. Even relatives were suspect. In retrospect, you made the right choice but chose the wrong person."

"Okay…" I muttered, allowing the realization to sink in. "So I hired him to be my guard. What happened after that?"

Eran dipped his head and when he looked up, his lip curled. "After that…he fell in love with you."

I didn't quite believe what I was hearing. "Fell in love? With me?"

"Yes," Eran replied, his lips thinned in resentment at the memory. "Marco fell in love with you." Eran turned to look at me for the first time. "But it doesn't mean he won't hesitate to kill you. He is enamored with you superficially. It can't be compared to-" He stopped himself then.

"To us," I finished. "It can't be compared to us."

Eran turned away again. "No. It cannot be compared to us in the smallest sense."

I paused, realizing a little conquest had been won. Each time Eran, who kept me at a distance, admitted his true feelings for me under any circumstance I felt placated. It was a small victory but one I savored. I tried to hide my joy but wasn't sure if I'd succeeded. "So…he was my guard and he fell in love with me."

"Yes," Eran grumbled. "He then proceeded to try to protect you from Fallen Ones without fully understanding his predicament. At the time of his death, at the hands of a Fallen One, he was told by that Fallen One if he were to die and return to join their ranks, that he would be able to have you for all eternity."

I gasped. "I find that incredibly offensive."

"You should," Eran replied, clearly satisfied with my reaction. "As you know, he did return but…clearly he did not win you over."

"No, and he never will."

Even with Eran's head facing away, I could see him respond with a content smirk.

"So did time heal old wounds or is he still in love with me."

"Slighted…would be the word I would use to describe him."

I absorbed all that Eran had told me for a moment and then a somewhat pertinent question came to mind.

"So as my eternal guardian, where were you when Marco was sacrificing his life for me?"

For the second time, Eran turned to me. I could see in his manners that he was hurt by my inference. "He did not sacrifice his life for you. To clarify, he nearly plunged himself into the sword in order to be given the powers to defeat me."

"Defeat you? So you were there, protecting me."

Eran responded, equally firm and passionate, "Always…Magdalene."

I had never – to my recollection – seen Eran jealous for me. But at this moment, it seemed to flow from every pore in his body, and it surprised me.

He looked away again. "As it is, he has since found another squad to run with…one he can influence and dominate."

I reached out and placed my hand on his arm again. "Thank you for telling me."

"It is important that you know. He won't stay hidden in the shadows while he's here. That much I can guarantee. Marco enjoys your attention."

With that affirmation, I couldn't help but sigh in frustration. If Marco did start interfering with my life (again) I would be living as if I were perpetually walking around with my finger stuck in an electrical outlet. As was the case when any Fallen One was nearby, I would be alerted to his presence by the hair standing up on the back of my neck and often times a rapidly increased heart rate, a sudden gush of perspiration, and clammy, shaking hands. This helped to alert me that my enemies were nearby – which I appreciated - but it was also a real irritation.

As if reading my mind, Eran said, "You're going to need to control that radar of yours."

"You know…I'm not sure I can."

Eran considered this for a moment. "I saw it flare up tonight when Marco arrived."

"Yeah, it only hurts when a lot of them are nearby. Usually it's just an annoyance."

"Good…Then maybe there is a way you can control it."

"You think so?" I was immediately interested. Anything to overcome the unpleasant feeling of panic in their presence would give me some peace-of-mind. "Being so wrapped up in trying to calm my reaction leaves me open…vulnerable."

"That is exactly what worries me," replied Eran. He shifted in his seat to face me. "Have you tried concentrating on something else, anything else, when one was nearby and…clearly…unable to reach you?"

I shook my head.

"You have an amazing ability to focus, Magdalene. I've seen it. Attempt to concentrate on something other than your reaction to them."

I shrugged. "I can try."

Eran sat motionless and then I watched as his face fell in distress. "As much as I try to protect you…" His voice trailed off as he became lost in thought.

"I know," I said, trying to draw him back to me. "I know. There are some things I just need to handle myself."

His eyes rose and stared at me with such determination it frightened me a little. "If I could, I would absorb all the pain you feel."

"I wouldn't want that, Eran."

"I know you wouldn't."

I was overwhelmed then with the feeling that he was fighting every urge to take me into his arms, to wrap me in his protective embrace. I watched his breathing grow shallow and staggered as his need to shield me from the world shared his need to feel my touch. He wasn't alone in the struggle.

"Eran," I whispered.

He drew in a quick, tense breath. "Magdalene..."

Then he stood. His head tilted back to avert his gaze from me, regaining his strength and sense of purpose.

"We have to get up early."

"Right," I grumbled recalling that holiday break was now over and school started again in the morning. Knowing that I'd be required to return to a private school run by a principal who hated me and students who'd built my reputation up to rival the Wicked Witch of the West, I was entirely unenthusiastic.

My only consolation was that Eran had enrolled too.

"And we'll need to be extra diligent," said Eran.

His words were a good reminder that I had enemies and that they seemed to be flocking here at this very moment.

We closed the French doors behind us, turning the locks in place. I watched him leave and cross the hall to his room. It was painful to be so close and yet so far from him, but we did leave our bedroom doors open. It gave me some consolation, not that he could come to my rescue if I needed it but that he wanted the same thing I did: to prevent any more barriers from keeping us apart.

3. MS. BEEDINWIGG

We woke up the first day of school to a thunderstorm pummeling New Orleans.

A loud crack resonated through the house just as I opened my eyes. From my place on the bed I could hear a hurried downpour of water outside my French doors. I imagined that a swift, steady flow had already filled the gutters, spilling out on to the streets and the ferns hanging from balconies around the city had become waterfalls.

A rumble of thunder resonated through the house, rattling the windows. Soon after, a bolt of lightning flashed and I knew by timing that the storm had just arrived.

From the sounds of it, Ezra was not going to like what it would do to her vegetable garden.

"It seems we'll need an umbrella today," Eran reflected.

I was overjoyed to hear his voice but it surprised me that it didn't come from the direction of the door.

I sat up in bed and found him slumped in the wingback chair in the corner of my room. His eyes were swollen and bloodshot and his clothes were disheveled.

"How long have you been there?"

"All night," he replied nonchalantly.

I gawked at him.

"I did keep the door open," he informed me.

I rolled my eyes. "That's not really what I'm thinking about…Why didn't you lay down with me?"

"That may have allowed for a more restful night but I'm not sure it would have been a good idea."

My shoulders slumped. "But why?"

He drew in a breath and pushed himself up from the chair with a groan. "Because…I'm not sure I could have contained myself," he admitted. Without allowing me to respond, he added, "See you downstairs in thirty."

I felt a smile stretch across my face. The moment Eran left my room my feet hit the floor running. I showered, dressed, and slipped on my biker boots in record time.

Downstairs I found Ezra and Rufus reading the newspaper, the kitchen smelling of freshly brewed coffee. Felix was at the stove concocting asparagus waffles and herbed syrup.

"Good morning," I said loud enough to be heard over the rain.

After a muttering of greetings they each returned to what they'd been doing. Judging by the amount of energy in the room, it seemed that no one had gotten a good night's rest.

I took a mug and poured coffee to the rim, then refilled everyone else's cup in exchange for thankful expressions from each.

Within a few minutes, Felix's mystifying waffles and syrup were placed on the table. Rufus clearly was not cooking his regular eggs and breakfast meat today and, given my inability to even boil water, I didn't have much choice but to pull a few waffles on to my plate.

Felix gleamed proudly at me.

After a few bites and hefty swallows of straight, rich coffee, they didn't seem so bad. I was chewing without face contortion by the time Eran entered the kitchen.

He mumbled "good morning" and received the same response I had. Then he too poured himself a cup of coffee, although this one was into a jumbo mug.

"No prerequisite meeting with the principal today?" Ezra inquired.

Mr. Warden required all new students to meet with him prior to beginning classes. I'd gone through it myself and considered it an interesting little introduction in to his demented, narcissistic world that the rest of us would call school grounds.

Eran swallowed and said, "It's scheduled in a half an hour."

"Ah, that should be fun..." Ezra mused, knowing personally what Mr. Warden was like.

Eran repressed a smile.

Felix dangled his keys in front of Eran and nodded towards the window, a motion that said it was too dangerous to drive a motorcycle today.

After a quick chuckle, Eran said, "Thanks. I was going to ask."

"We won't need it. No chance of visitors in The Square today."

I grinned my thanks to Felix and finished my entire plate of waffles just for his sake. Then I picked up my book bag and we headed out of the kitchen towards the front door.

Eran stopped at the opening to say, "By the way, I thought it would be appropriate if I were to start helping with the rent."

They each shook their heads but it was Ezra who spoke. "That is not necessary."

"I knew that would be your response but...I feel I should contribute. And...I have a little extra money."

Felix, who strayed from his usual behavior and broke the rules of social etiquette, cocked his head and asked, "Well, how much extra money?"

"Four million dollars," Eran replied earnestly, without a hint of conceit. "It should give us some peace of mind…"

Felix and Rufus' mouths dropped open but no sound came out, jaws dangling, shocked in to silence. Ezra was the only one to respond, her eyebrows, her tone showing solemn amazement. "Well, we could all use a little of that."

I giggled after we'd ducked and ran for Felix's car. "Felix is right now making a mental list of his birthday wishes."

Eran responded by throwing back his head and releasing quiet laughter.

For the remainder of our drive to school, neither of us spoke. We each kept our focus on our surroundings. I half expected Marco to drop in front of the car as we drove through the streets against the pouring rain. That was dramatic, I knew, but I also knew that I had to be prepared for anything.

As it was, we made it to school without any incident and parked in the empty lot at the opening to the central foyer. We got out and ran down the middle of the U-shaped quad to the main entrance, reaching it nearly soaked through our clothes. Even while shielding myself from the storm, I noticed the school grounds. While typically they looked so manicured, now they resembled green blobs floating on lakes of muddy water.

We entered the foyer, shook off the excess water, and headed for Mr. Warden's office. The hallways were already decorated with signs for prom, various clubs, and reminders about campus rules. I fought the craving to reach for Eran's hand as we walked quietly side by side. He seemed not to notice; instead he was observing his new surroundings, searching for escape routes and potential hiding spots, no doubt.

We turned the corner to the South Hall where Mr. Warden's office was located and only then did I realize we weren't alone.

The hallway was vacant but the same reaction I'd experienced last night in the street came over me.

I stumbled, nearly tripping over myself. Eran saved me with a quick arm cutting in front of me and steadying me all in one fluid motion. "Are you all right?" he asked, his expression suddenly concerned.

"They're here."

His concern swiftly changed to vigilance.

"Where?"

"In the warden-I...I mean Mr. Warden's office."

As if the world had turned slow motion, we watched as the door leading to Mr. Warden's office opened. From it emerged our principal followed by eight young men.

Marco and his accomplices had beaten us there.

They were fully clothed this time in matching blue polo's and light khakis. Their wings were gone, retracted into their bodies as they attempted to pass themselves off as actual human beings.

They filtered out to the hallway where Mr. Warden's voice carried over to us.

"Ordinarily, our school is very secure. We have very few internal threats. There is only one incident I can recount which occurred last semester when a student blew up the biology lab."

Marco nodded, serious and appearing official with his hands clasped behind his back.

Mr. Warden continued, apparently not aware that Eran and I stood a few feet away. "Yes, Magdalene Tanner is the student's name. Her antic nearly cost the lives of several of our students. Luckily, no one was permanently injured."

"I see," said Marco. "Were any charges brought against her?"

"No...no." Mr. Warden looked disappointed. "There wasn't enough evidence to support it. But there is no doubt in the minds of the faculty or the students who was to blame. Indeed, you'll need to keep your eye on that one. " He drew in a heavy breath and shook his head. I wasn't surprised he'd just condemned my reputation to apparent strangers even with the claims being baseless. The warden had never liked me. "Anyways...we've hired you as security more because of external threats. We only became aware of these threats recently but we wish to take every precaution."

Security? Now if that wasn't ironic... And recent external threats? I could tell the warden who had concocted those threats in order to win their way in to the safety of my school, though I was certain he wouldn't listen.

My anger flared, which Eran must have sensed because he reached out an arm to hold me back. With my fury rising and without any way to release it, I tried to refocus and that was when it happened. I realized that the reaction I had to these Fallen Ones – the raised hair on my neck, the perspiration, the nervous shaking – it all had dissipated. Not very much, but enough for me to notice.

Eran had been correct. I only needed to change my thoughts and their impact on me lessened. Of course, I would need to learn to replace that nervous terror with something other than anger – more along the lines of a calmer, more astute reaction. Nonetheless, this was a significant leap for me.

As I tried further to concentrate on things other than my radar sounding off, it soon became clear to me that only Mr. Warden remained unaware of us. The others began glancing in our direction, fidgeting, and shifting their feet irritably. It reminded me that, when I was in their presence, the Fallen Ones felt the same sense of panic as I did.

Eran never flinched or took his eyes off them.

The warden was pointing down the hall, away from us, directing Marco's team to their posts around the campus. He then he swung his arm in our direction.

There he paused and a frown rose up. He finished his sentence and said, "Gentleman, this is Ms. Tanner. You'll recall her name, I'm sure."

The eight of them stared in our direction, expressionless, except for Marco. He wore the same demented, mocking grin as the night before. I got the odd sense they were waiting for us to attack them.

"And who is the boy with you, Ms. Tanner?" asked Mr. Warden, without a hint of cordiality.

Eran answered though he didn't approach them. "Eran Talor. I'm happy to reschedule our meeting as I see you are busy with-"

He confirmed my thoughts: Eran had no intention of leaving me, at risk, in the hallway with the Fallen Ones.

Mr. Warden wasn't going to make it easy though. "No, no. I've just finished and your new student meeting is a requirement."

The warden wasn't going to budge. Both Eran and I knew it. That left us in a conundrum. There didn't seem to be a delicate way to refuse the warden.

Eran looked at me and said almost inaudibly, "I'd like you to join us."

It seemed that the warden had good ears because he immediately rejected that idea. "Absolutely not. These are private meetings. She will not be included."

Apparently, the warden wanted Eran all to himself. I wondered what other malicious lies he'd planned to tell.

The Fallen Ones hadn't moved, which I guessed was because they were interested in seeing how this struggle would play out. I desperately tried to think of some way for Eran and I to stay together but couldn't come up with a single plan. The nervous terror was creeping back stronger, I noticed, which upset me and as a result it yielded again.

"Mr. Warden," said a woman coming up behind Eran and me. Her pleasant persona was in direct conflict with the whirlwind of negative emotions surrounding the rest of us. "I'm terribly sorry to bother you..."

I turned to find a slender woman approaching us, smiling widely and without any realization that she was disrupting a battle of wills. My first opinion of her was that she would have a challenging time fitting in with the rest of the snobby faculty. The ankle-length dress she wore hung without shape from her boney shoulders and was made of a pattern that resembled drab, faded, green window curtains. She wore wire-rimmed glasses that were clasped to a simple chain around her neck. Her auburn hair was curled in a thick bun piled on the top of her head. She wore no makeup and no jewelry. The only pieces of her wardrobe that gave her any air of edginess were the black combat boots sticking out from beneath her dress.

I liked her instantly.

She had reached the warden and was hurriedly discussing something about a missing key that opened her classroom door. She'd spoken with the custodian but they couldn't seem to locate the spare.

With the first day's class starting in less than sixty minutes this set the warden in to a panic.

"Marco, scatter your team around the grounds and find that key. Go...go...go!"

Marco and his staff, disgruntled to be shooed away, left begrudgingly, sulking down the hallway and out the exit doors.

"Thank you, Mr. Warden, I-"

"You must be more careful, Ms. Beedinwigg. Situations like this just won't do...They just won't do."

Properly chastised, Ms. Beedinwigg complied, "I absolutely agree. It won't happen again. Thank you...Thank you...Oh, are you Maggie?"

Her change of pace caught me off guard. "Yes, yes I am," I answered, perplexed. "How do you know me?"

"Oh, I recognize you from the student database. Mr. Warden has put together an exemplary background on each of his students," which didn't surprise me, "with their educational history...accomplishments...indiscretions..."

"Yes, yes..." Mr. Warden turned, not wanting to be called out on his own unethical indiscretions, and snapped his fingers at Eran. "Come. We have a meeting."

Eran didn't move.

"Maggie," said Ms. Beedinwigg. "Would you be so kind as to help me look for my key?"

Eran clearly thought this was a good idea as he leaned down to whisper, "Stay in her presence. They won't attempt anything with witnesses."

"I will," I said, enjoying his proximity and the way his breath caressed my face.

Eran and the warden disappeared into his office as Ms. Beedinwigg and I slowly walked back towards the main entrance.

"What does the key look like?" I asked, scanning the ground.

"Oh, silver, small, like nearly every other key. If we come across it, we'll know." She didn't seem as interested in finding it as she had a moment ago. "So...Maggie...you're new to this school, is that right?"

"Yes," I said, figuring she'd learned that from the warden's database.

She confirmed it by mentioning, "Your file said you were only here as of last semester and that you moved quite often before that. Every three months, in fact. That must have been challenging."

"Sometimes." I saw something glint in the corner of a row of lockers and approached it only to find it was a silver gum wrapper.

Ms. Beedinwigg didn't appear to notice. She kept on with her inquiries. "You seemed to take well to fencing. Do you enjoy it?"

"Actually, yes." I hadn't considered it before, having only taken the class for semester credits, but it might come in handy against a Fallen One.

"Good," she seemed genuinely pleased with my response.

"I enjoy fencing, too. I'm a fencing master capable with both foil and epee."

"Oh, are you the new fencing teacher," I asked, surprised they would replace Ms. Valentine.

"No...I'm the new biochemistry teacher," she announced.

I stiffened, wondering whether my reputation caused by the explosion in last semester's class had reached her yet.

"Don't worry," she said, confirming she'd heard. "Judge not lest ye be judged, right?"

I smiled up at her, liking her even more. "Right."

I hadn't realized it before but we'd unconsciously strolled directly to the Biochemistry room door.

Ms. Beedinwigg drew in a surprised breath then and pulled a key from the pocket of her dress. "Well...how about that? I had it with me the entire time..."

Something beneath her self-critical laugh, made me wonder whether she'd known it was there all along but I couldn't be sure.

"Well, good thing we're here," I said. "You're my first class."

"I am?" she asked, fitting the key into the door and opening it to a darkened room. "Well isn't that convenient..." she murmured.

As Ms. Beedinwigg entered and arranged her desk before drawing her name on the whiteboard. I took a seat at the back of the room and dropped my book bag over the chair in front of me, saving it for Eran.

Biochemistry was also Eran's first class so he should be arriving any time. I was happy that we'd be able to spend an entire hour together because, as luck had it, we wouldn't be together in the remaining ones.

He came through the door within minutes, an arrogant grin spread across his stunning face. At the sight of him, butterflies began battering my stomach. I mouthed a hello and he broke his grin to mouth it back, causing the butterflies to flap harder.

Other students were filtering in by then so he had to sidestep a few before reaching me. He was back to grinning, which made me curious. I'd never known anyone to leave the warden's office in an upbeat mood.

I was in the process of removing my book bag for him when he picked it up in mid-lift and effortlessly placed it on the ground for me.

"I believe I have made it on to Mr. Warden's delinquent list," he proclaimed quietly, sliding into his seat facing me.

"Is that what your grin is about?" I asked, unable to hold back my own smile.

Eran chuckled. "Each time he tried to criticize you I wouldn't allow it. After cutting him off in mid-sentence for the fourth time, he told me I had a bad attitude and that the teachers would be alerted of my behavior."

He and I shared a private laugh together as Ms. Beedinwigg closed the classroom door to start the session. I quickly looked around the room, recognizing very few students, with the exception of two girls. Bridgette Madison and Ashley Georgian. It took a conscious effort to hold in a groan. They were sharing a private giggle, their expressions contorted in snobbery, while glancing in Ms. Beedinwigg's direction.

They were the wealthiest students in school who had been trained from an early age to flaunt their upper crust heritage, so their immediate dislike of Ms. Beedinwigg was not surprising to me.

They would be the first to ridicule Ms. Beedinwigg for her appearance and from my experience with them last semester I knew they would enflame her infamy as much as possible.

Ms. Beedinwigg didn't appear to notice. Instead she leaned against her desk set in the middle of the room, her combat boots projecting from beneath her dress, her slim arms used to prop herself against the desk's edge.

She didn't bother to call out the attendance list. Instead, she swept her gaze over the classroom, making note of each student. I realized she must have memorized the faces, and likely the history recorded in the warden's database. I was impressed. She was obviously a quick study.

After a brief pause on Eran and me, she began the class. "Biochemistry is the study of chemical processes in living organisms. Understanding what makes them tick, what makes them strong, what makes them weak. How they reproduce. How they die…I've dedicated my life to understanding how certain creatures do these very things. That is the knowledge that I will pass on to you." She then launched in to a review of the syllabus.

I'd never had passion for this area of the natural sciences but Ms. Beedinwigg seemed to have enough for all of us. She moved around the room, never bothering to sit, with her arms flapping wildly to illustrate her descriptions. She caused several eruptions of laughter over the course of the hour and at the end I believe the only two people who didn't enjoy Ms. Beedinwigg were Bridgette and Ashley. Their disgusted scowls left no delusion.

For the most part, I was kept enthralled but every once in a while my attention would drift to Eran's hair curled around the base of his neck and I would need to fight the urge to run my fingers through it. I also didn't miss how his shoulders shook when he laughed or how his ears rose slightly when he smiled. It was the first class he'd taken in over a hundred years and he seemed to enjoy it.

When the bell rang and we stood to head to the next class, Eran turned to me. "You know, I've missed this," he said simply. He then picked up my book bag for me and we headed for the door. I felt Ms. Beedingwigg's eyes on us and a quick look back confirmed it. She tilted her chin up as a quick nod to me and then returned to her syllabus.

Eran escorted me to my next class, as I knew he would. He was going to keep me in his sights as long as he could. But along the way, his mood changed to serious.

"Was anyone in the last class a-" he paused and realized he couldn't be as open as he'd like while in the middle of a busy hallway. "Did anyone draw your attention?"

I knew what he was asking, "No, no one to be concerned about."

"Good..." he said thoughtfully. He relaxed for a moment and I thought he may be suspecting Marco lied after all. Then his defenses rose again. "If you do suspect or encounter trouble, I'll know it and I'll be right at your side."

I smiled at him. "You don't have to tell me."

Eran had an uncanny way of knowing what I was feeling and in turn I could often feel his reactions in me. We knew when each other was nervous, excited, or sad. I had never been able to explain it other than to assume it came from lifetimes of knowing each other. Amusingly, I'd seen this sometimes in others when people have met and share an instant connection with one another and I often wonder whether they knew each other in past lives as well.

I then added teasingly, "I know what you are capable of..."

He gave me his trademark arrogant smirk and replied, "You haven't seen anything yet." There was a glimmer in his eyes that told me that I hadn't and I had to calm my stomach from its flip flops. In truth, I wasn't sure I wanted to ever learn what he was referring to; knowing he only used his exceptional abilities when they were needed to defend. If he were to use them, it would require a scenario in which fighting was involved and that I never wished to see. "We're here," he pointed out.

I noticed the sign over the door reading Calculus II and said slightly disappointed, "Yes, we are." I wanted more time with him.

"Don't worry, Magdalene. You've lived your youth without me. You can make it through another hour."

But that was before I knew you existed, I thought, watching him turn and head towards his next class.

He peeked over his shoulder, saw me still standing in the doorway, and shooed me to enter.

This was the routine for the next few classes. Eran would meet me outside the door, escort me to my next class, and then gesture me to stop ogling him and go inside. Clearly, he had no idea how challenging it was to do it or he wouldn't have asked.

My classes would have been far more interesting if I hadn't been acutely aware of the clock's impossibly slow movement and the fact that each lingering moment was agonizingly keeping me from seeing Eran again. I hoped, for the sake of my sanity not to mention my grades, that this desire would dissipate some as time went on, but I doubted it.

I was beginning to feel confident that Marco had been wrong or untruthful and that no more enemies would be showing up any time soon. Against Eran's wishes, I relaxed some and simply enjoyed the time I could spend with Eran between classes, becoming more oblivious to my surroundings with each hour.

Then lunch break arrived...along with the familiar prickle of hair standing up on the back of my neck.

4. A TEST

There were two areas to the cafeteria, an inside seating area and a patio. With the thunderstorm pummeling the patio and grassy area beyond, every student congregated inside. I didn't know whether it was because of lack of seating or because it was the first day back and group cliques had lessened over the weeks away but those who wouldn't ordinarily share their table were doing it today.

Eran and I made our way through the lunch line where we bought ham sandwiches, chips, and sodas before making our way to a table across the lunch room. Because of the rain, it hadn't been possible for me to bring my preferred sandwich, a muffaletta which I bought at the same deli every day, so we had to settle for stale bread, processed meat slices, and near-plastic cheese.

"So you like your classes?" I asked weaving my way around a chair left in the middle of the aisle. Eran smoothly moved it out of the way for me.

"I do," he said, diligently keeping himself aware of all the potential threats he saw, which went virtually unnoticed by me. "The teachers are capable. The lessons are somewhat limited but for that I blame myself. I think that I'm aware of so much more than what they plan to cover that I'm slightly disappointed." It was admirable that he didn't fault the teachers for being unable to keep up with him. With centuries of knowledge, he would be a tough student to please.

"Yes," I replied, lowering my voice. "It would be hard to cover five hundred years in a single semester."

He glanced back to address my teasing with a suppressed grin. "And you?"

"I think I'd like them more if I could keep my mind on them," I admitted.

"Maybe we can work on that..." he suggested. The fact he used the word 'we' told me that he'd understood I was passing my time thinking about him.

"I'm not sure that is possible but I'm open to ideas." I drew in a breath to laugh when my nerves flared and my voice released a moan instead.

Without delay, Eran turned to me, aware of what had just happened. He waited for me to single out whomever it was causing the reaction.

I was already scanning the room when the cafeteria door opened and a boy and girl, each with bright blonde hair, entered. I noticed they had the same facial features with distinctly Swedish traits as they stopped just inside the door. Their eyes crossed the room slowly until they landed on Eran and me.

The irritation at the back of my neck spiked suddenly and I heard the silverware rattle on my tray as a result.

As arch enemies, we stared across the cafeteria, daring the other to make a motion. If something did happen, if someone were to take an offensive stance, I was certain that chaos would ensue and cause injury, not only as a result of the raging battle but from the stampede that would follow as students tried to escape the cafeteria. There was no telling how many people would be hurt.

"Who are they?" I asked Eran, keeping my voice low, which also helped prevent it from quivering.

"The Kohler twins. Haven't seen them since Germany."

My immediate thought was that if these Fallen Ones hadn't shown themselves in the last few hundred years and they'd suddenly walked through the door in to our lives now...Marco had been telling the truth. More Fallen Ones were arriving. If that part of his message were true, it also meant that someone was preparing for a battle against us, one that he'd forewarned was said to be vast.

I knew Eran was thinking the same thing. His expression was still glowering though, I noticed.

Very briefly, my nerves spiked and I knew the Kohler twins were projecting hatred our way. I dug my fingers further into my tray, trying to keep my soda from tipping. It seemed to help a little.

Concentrate, I thought. Concentrate on something else. My mind became erratic then and I noticed nearly everything in my close surroundings at once but locked on nothing in particular. I saw the half-eaten apple on the tray three tables over was browning already, that one of the girls to my right had dipped her sleeve in spilt chocolate milk, and that the vent across the cafeteria had just turned on and spewed a puff of dust into the room.

"Magdalene," Eran said, anxiously. "Magdalene?"

That seemed to break through to me and I refocused on him. "Let's sit down," he insisted, quiet and calm.

I raised my eyebrows at him.

"It doesn't look like they're interested in us," he mused. "Not yet at least."

Amazed, I refocused on the Kohler twins and found them moving through the lunch line, neither one addressing us any longer. They now appeared to be normal students interested in nothing more than their choices between black or refried beans.

Eran took my tray – before I dropped it – and led me to a vacant table near an exit door. Considering it led to the outside and into the rain, I figured it was probably locked but with Eran's strength he could push through it at any time if we should need it.

"It wouldn't be good to leave right now," he was explaining, setting our trays on the table. Luckily, no one else seemed to want this particular table as it was in the far corner and beneath a broken light fixture. That gave Eran and me more privacy. "It'll make us look unprepared and we don't want to appear that way. I can handle them should they attempt anything. They're not very skilled in the art of fighting so they can be easily overcome."

I was trying to process all that he was telling me but having difficulty with it. My hands were still shaking.

He paused and his voice grew soft, warm. "Magdalene, are you all right? If not, we can leave-"

"No...no." I drew in a deep breath, settling myself. "This is good practice...to calm my nerves."

He watched me steadily, not quite believing what I said. "It's your call. We can go any time you want."

I shook my head, taking a second to pause in the Kohler twin's direction. They'd taken a seat at a table close by, on the route out of the cafeteria, and were now sneaking peeks at us too.

"How..." I shuddered and refocused myself. I was determined to control these nerves better than they controlled me. "How do we know them?"

Eran was taking a sip of his soda and trying to appear at ease. He swallowed before answering. "They found us during the Germanic Peasant Wars or rather we found them," said Eran matter-of-factly. "They were drawn to the strife the peasants were encountering to prey on the defenseless. We thwarted them and they retaliated – though not well. I'm not certain, but I wouldn't doubt that they still hold a grudge regarding it."

"Well…how did they prey on them?" I persisted, my food remaining untouched, mostly because I was still battling my nerves.

"They entered the wars under the pretext that they sided with the peasants and would then take the lives of the peasants while no one else was present, blaming their murders on their adversaries."

"Hmmm…" I said, thoughtfully. I shook it off and added, "How did we find out they were murdering the peasants?"

Eran lifted his eyebrows. "Through you."

"Me?" I asked, stunned.

He shrugged as if it wasn't surprising. "Yes…Well, actually, through your messages. You delivered a message from one of the dead notifying us to what they were doing. That message instigated the only manhunt for someone from the same side of the battlefield in the history of those wars." Almost without a break, Eran added, "We should eat or it'll appear odd."

Following his own suggestion, he took a bite of his sandwich and grimaced. "This is the food they serve in school nowadays? It's…It's…"

"Atrocious, or was horrid the word you were looking for?"

"Both," he said, chewing slowly. "It's no wonder dropout rates are a concern." He shook his head.

We nibbled at our food from that point on until nearly the end of the lunch hour. Conversation was limited to superficial topics such as whether we'd been burdened with homework already and when our first exam would be. The Kohler twins barely ate as well, I noticed. They were probably having the same reaction to the food as Eran but they did remain in their seats and continued their surveillance of us.

When the bell for the next class was about to ring, Eran stood and suggested that we get moving.

By that point, the cafeteria crowd had thinned with most students preferring to carry their lunch break into the halls. Yet, it was still fairly crowded so when the incident happened a good sized audience was watching.

One moment we were walking unassumingly towards the door and the next a chair came sliding across the tiled floor so rapidly that I didn't see it until it was nearly at my side. Made of a wooden back and metal framework, anywhere it had hit would have hurt. As it was, Eran intervened, fluidly stopping the chair before it reached me.

He asked tensely, "Are you all right?"

I almost asked why when I saw his palm against the chair's back, where he'd placed it to break its slide.

"Yes, thanks."

"You're welcome." He hadn't moved his eyes from the Kohler twins.

It only took a second for me to realize the chair had come from them. They sat at the end of the open aisle where the chair had slid, each wearing a smirk.

The cafeteria was now still. No one spoke. No one moved. The sound of the rain hitting the pavement outside seemed to have increased in decibels. All eyes were either on us or the twins. I was certain their surprised expression would have deepened if they knew they were viewing the extension of a conflict that had started five hundred years ago.

From my position, I could make out Eran's tightened lips and narrowed eyes. The message he sent was simple: That...was a mistake. He didn't seem to acknowledge anyone else in the room but the twins.

Then, with an almost undetectable jerk from Eran's palm, the chair slid back towards its original direction, at a speed far greater than which it had come. The twins barely escaped its path, each throwing themselves in opposite directions just before the speeding projectile reached them. The chair slammed into the table where the twins had been sitting, shoving it and ejecting all remaining chairs around it several feet away.

Gasps resounded throughout the cafeteria as all eyes turned on Eran. His retaliation had clearly sent a signal that he shouldn't be provoked – by Fallen Ones or by humans.

We left the Kohler twins picking themselves up off the ground and the rest of the crowd scrutinizing us as we walked out the door.

From the corner of the room, Marco and his cohorts studied us too but didn't make a move.

Eran was shaking his head as we made our way toward my next class, his anger still riled, making me reconsider twice about asking my question. It wasn't until his paced slowed some that I voiced it.

"I thought they wouldn't attack if others were present?"

"That wasn't an attack, Magdalene," he explained almost inaudibly, bowing his head towards mine so others wouldn't hear as we passed them in the hall. "They were playing with us."

We didn't speak again until we were just inside the classroom door. What he then recommended I immediately rejected.

"I feel it is necessary for you to leave the city."

"Eran," I scoffed. "That…that…whatever you call it…playing around back there did not scare me."

We paused until two students passed by on their way to their seats.

Before giving him a chance to respond, I continued, keeping my voice low, "And it wouldn't have happened if you hadn't been there. We stayed because you were there to protect me, remember? If you hadn't been there, the moment I sensed them I would have left the cafeteria, giving them no opportunity to…to play with me." He and I both knew that wouldn't have happened. I would have stayed, refusing to be run off. He opened his mouth to oppose me so I added, "This isn't the time. I think you would agree."

The class was settled now and the teacher, Mr. Gomer, was approaching us by that point.

"I'm safe here," I whispered quickly.

He shook his head again in frustration, this time at me, but he gave a courteous nod to Mr. Gomer and slipped out the door.

"Ms. Tanner," said Mr. Gomer tightly. "Would you mind taking your seat so we may begin our study of the Spanish language?"

"Sorry," I replied, swiftly moving passed him to the only open desk left.

Only after settling in and pulling my writing pad from my book bag did I notice that Bridgette sat directly beside me. She rolled her eyes at me and I knew that she'd either seen or heard about the incident in the cafeteria.

At that point, I wasn't sure this day could get any worse.

As it turned out, once I was able to ignore Bridgette I found the class was nearly as interesting as Ms. Beedinwigg's, though without the charismatic musings and regular strolls around the room. I actually began to enjoy myself by the time the end of class arrived, my excitement rising also because I was about to see Eran again.

He was waiting for me before the bell rang and the students could spill out into the hallway.

He was eager to talk, I could tell, but the number of other students in the hallway seemed to have doubled and prevented it.

Keeping close beside me, we strolled silently towards the West Hall. There was talk of prom night, college acceptances, and unbearable course loads. There was also talk of the cafeteria clash. More than a few students ducked their heads and whispered as we passed them, reminding me of the lab explosion last semester in which I became the notorious student with a reputation for causing destruction and injury. I was once again in familiar territory.

Eran seemed to have overheard because the only thing he said before leaving me at the door was, "Don't pay attention. It'll die down."

I wasn't so confident.

The last class, which happened to be another elective course in sculpting, was painfully long. It wasn't because of the few students who sent frowns in my direction to condemn me again for something that wasn't really my fault but the fact that no sculpting could begin until the clay arrived the following class. So, we spent the hour talking about the many different types and nuances of clay. It was a very long hour.

The only positive was that there were no Fallen Ones or Bridgette Madison's in this class.

Most of the time, I spent cogitating on how to handle Eran's determination that I leave the city. This was a logical option, I knew. Clearly, Fallen Ones were arriving and a fairly significant attack was on its way. However, there is a part of me, a rather large and vocal part, which adamantly detests running. Eran calls this trait stubbornness. I call it rational. Running only encourages and emboldens enemies, something I refuse to allow. By the end of the class, I had found no resolution that would appease my needs and Eran's simultaneously.

The bell rang and I found Eran, once again, waiting for me outside the door. Despite the Fallen Ones arrivals and our disagreements on how to handle it, my interest in seeing Eran had not been tempered. I couldn't stop the smile now lifting my cheeks nor did I really want to.

"Good last class?" he asked, cordially. He seemed far more relaxed than before.

"It's good to see you," I said.

Then my smile faded.

Out of the corner of my eye, a flash of blonde hair halted directly in front of Eran. Instinctually the muscles in my back tightened.

"Bridgette Madison," she said, holding out a bejeweled hand in greeting.

Eran hesitantly reached for it. As slight as it was, he'd noticed my reaction to her and was therefore guarded.

Watching now as she gazed up at Eran through thickly covered eyelashes, I suddenly realized that I'd been wrong. Bridgette hadn't rolled her eyes at me in class because of the cafeteria clash. I got the suspicious feeling she was interested in Eran.

"What can I do for you, Bridgette," he asked, amiable but unsmiling.

"Well…we have a group planning prom night. I manage it," she said with artificial modesty. "We wanted to know if you'd like to join us."

"In going to the prom?" asked Eran, innocently.

"No, no. I'm…I'm not asking you to the prom."

Clearly, I thought. She wouldn't lower herself to break tradition. She was going to wait for him to ask her, and that annoyed me.

"I meant," she continued, "in planning it."

"In planning what?" he asked, retaining his oblivious expression.

I glanced at Eran, found that he was playing with her, and had to stifle my laughter.

"In planning the prom." She seemed flustered. Evidently, she didn't know her simple question would be so confusing for him. For good measure she added, "Would you like to join our group in planning the prom?"

Eran thought this over for a few seconds, though I'm certain it seemed much longer than that to Bridgette. He finally answered, "No, I don't think so…but thanks for the offer."

Her face contorted in to a mixture of confusion and offense. "Oh…all right." Bridgette was rarely rejected and it showed.

Agitated, she finally turned to me and muttered with downturned lips, "Maggie," before turning on her heels and headed down the hallway.

"She was flirting with you," I said, between clenched teeth, trying to contain my anger.

"I believe she was," Eran replied simply.

We didn't speak again until we were inside the car, a fair amount of tension lingering between us – which was likely a combination of the looming argument to come and the flirtation I'd just observed. As we slammed the car doors closed, he didn't move to insert the key into the ignition. The sound of rain hammering the roof enveloped us, giving the false notion of being concealed from the outside world. Eran was watching me, a slight, affectionate smile warming his handsome face. "I didn't get a chance to say it earlier…" He intentionally waited until I looked at him and then his smile softened. "It's good to see you too."

My breath caught as he admitted it and my smile returned.

He started the car and pulled into traffic on the side street outside the school, leading us back to the house.

"If you still refuse to leave the city," he stopped to sigh in frustration at my decision which he knew remained unchanged. "I have a solution."

My head snapped towards him, excited that an argument wouldn't ensue after all. "You do?"

"I do."

"Well…what is it?"

"Oh…" A smile played on his handsomely curved lips. "You'll find out shortly…"

My brow creased in curiosity. "When?"

"The moment you get home," he stated.

From then on, until we reached the back door of our house, my eagerness increased exponentially.

5. ALTERUMS

As Eran parked the car at the back of our driveway, I noticed two things at once: our kitchen light was on, glowing like a beacon against the darkness of the stormy day, and a stranger stood under the eaves against the window, frowning.

The man was tall with a slender build. His closely cropped bold white hair, silky smooth swarthy skin, and clear blue eyes stood out in direct contrast to each other. He would be hard to miss.

I didn't sense any measure of panic so I determined he wasn't an enemy. Eran didn't offer any explanation but simply got out of the car and moved towards the man. I followed.

"Campion," said Eran, genially.

"Sir," he replied in a more submissive, respectful tone.

My curiosity was clawing at me from the inside.

"Enjoying the rain?" Eran held back a smile at some private joke.

"Not very much, sir," Campion grumbled.

"Sir?" I inquired but it wasn't until we were inside the kitchen with the door closed against the rain did Eran clarify.

"Magdalene, as your memory won't allow it, I would like to reintroduce you to Campion, my first lieutenant."

My eyebrows rose. "Your..." I heard myself trail off as I was left in bewilderment.

"Campion will be watching over you while I am away."

"Away?" That thought I understood immediately. "You're going away?" I asked a little too loudly.

"Intermittently."

That didn't help much.

"You're leaving?" Ezra's voice came from the doorway. She seemed nearly as distraught as I was.

"Ezra, I'm glad you are here. I'd like you to meet Campion."

Campion stepped forward and extended his hand. Ezra took it, hesitantly. "What's this all about, Eran?" Her ability to see beyond the situation was coming out.

"I'd like to explain it to Felix and Rufus as well."

"Explain what?" Rufus said entering the kitchen. Unruffled at seeing a stranger standing in our house, he gave Campion a quick look up and down and a cordial nod. No introductions were needed with him. He pulled a soda from the refrigerator and popped the top before leaning against the sink intending to wait for Eran's answer.

"We'll need Felix-"

Rufus bellowed for Felix, prompting a shudder from Ezra and me. It worked and Felix fled down the stairs and into the kitchen, stopping just as his eyes landed on Campion.

"Well..." he said, surprised. "A dinner guest?"

"More along the lines of a new roommate," said Eran.

That made everyone's eyebrows rise.

"Shall we sit?" Eran offered.

We each took our seats and Eran went in to explaining that we'd learned of the Fallen Ones arrivals and of the impending battle, keeping his briefing in chronological order and succinct. Listening to him, I saw the military leader in him emerge, a persona he felt completely at ease in. It left me in awe.

In the end, Eran summed it up with, "I have strategically placed my army with you at all times. You won't see them or hear them but they will be watching over you should you need their protection."

Ezra was nodding her head thoughtfully. "So...you've given each of us our own guardian," she summed it up.

"Correct."

"Blimey..." Rufus leaned back with a distained scowl. "I don't need a guardian. What I need's a pint o' beer."

Felix rolled his eyes in response. "That's...thoughtful," Felix condoned. "Although it's also unnecessary."

Eran was not going to be dissuaded. "I'm sorry if you disagree. It is in your best interest. More so, it is done. They are in place and carrying out their orders as we speak. They will not be a disruption, I assure you."

Ezra, Rufus, and Felix exchanged looks that conveyed their reluctant agreement.

"While I will watch Magdalene throughout the day," Eran continued, "Campion will need to watch over Magdalene during the evenings. This requires him to take up residence here."

Campion watched, slightly doubtful, of what their reaction might be and appeared relieved when Felix and Rufus shrugged, untroubled by the idea. Even Ezra agreed.

"I believe we have a cot in the downstairs closet we can prepare for you," she offered.

"I would appreciate it," said Campion graciously.

The discussion seemingly over, I leaned towards Eran and spoke softly into his ear. "Where will you be going?" I asked, nervous about what his answer might be. With his army watching over us, who would be watching over him?

"I need to gather intelligence, know who's coming for us, how many, where they're coming from, when they'll be here. There are a lot of unanswered questions."

His plans sounded treacherous. "Can I speak to you alone?" I whispered to him, unsure my voice could rise any higher.

"Yes," he replied, as serious as I felt.

He then followed me down the hall and into the parlor where we found ourselves standing next to the hearth. A fire had been lit to warm the house, sending dancing shadows across the walls. I vaguely noticed that it gave the room the scent of cedar.

Eran stood close to me, far closer than usual. I soaked up the image of him and felt every inch of his presence just inside my reach.

"Stay," I pleaded.

He drew in a shaky breath and then for the first time that day, Eran reached out and touched me. His hand gently pressed against my cheek, his thumb caressing me. It sent a shudder through my body so vehement that I had to close my eyes against it.

I was on the verge of tears, struggling to contain myself, when I felt his lips softly brush against mine. They lingered there, pliant and welcoming as I tilted my head to meet him.

Then our passion, all the weeks of tense distance, came roaring to the surface. He wrapped his arms around my waist in an iron hold, pressing me to him. My fingers dug into the contours of his back. Our bodies clung to each other, our lips crushing against one another.

The next thing I knew, he was holding me by my hips and the back of my head, my body limp against him.

"Did I…" I started, still getting my bearings straight. "Did I…faint?"

"You did," he replied, bemused.

I was appalled.

"Don't be embarrassed. It's happened before…"

My humiliation deepened so he restrained his smile for my benefit. "You probably don't remember it."

I didn't and I wasn't interested in recalling it at this moment either. Instead, I concentrated on standing.

"Careful," he warned. "You're still ashen."

I groaned, and placed my feet under me, but Eran kept his arms around my waist for safe measure.

"I'm sorry that I ruined…"

"You didn't ruin anything," he reassured me. "It was beautiful. It'll keep me company while I'm away from you."

"Do you really have to go?"

"You know I do," he muttered.

"Can't you send someone else?" I whispered.

Eran's face contorted in insult. "Magdalene, this is my job."

"I know but isn't your job also to protect me?" I reminded.

"Protecting you is what I am doing."

His arms were still around my waist, our hips intimately pressed together. He pulled me even closer. It was a significant and unfair distraction and he knew it. The grin on his gorgeous face told me so. Then he grew solemn. "I hate the thought of leaving your side. I know your safety won't be in question, but it's the fact that I won't see your stunning face until the morning or be able to listen to the sounds of you getting ready in the evening."

My mouth fell open. "You do that?" I hissed.

His grin returned, mischievous, and he continued on, "The opportunity to hear your melodic voice will be cut short, your beautiful voice which is such a comfort," he sighed, "…when you're not opposing me."

I drew in a quick breath in insult and he chuckled, pulling me closer. My forehead landed softly against his chin where he murmured into my hair, "Trust me."

"I do...implicitly. It's who you might encounter that I don't."

He moved his lips across my forehead, leaving an arc of feather-light kisses in their wake. I struggled to catch my breath. Then, he slowly leaned back. "You have nothing to worry about, my love. They aren't expecting me. They'll never see me coming."

The inherent confidence in him settled my nerves, somewhat.

I placed my cheek against his shoulder, nestling my nose against the curve of his neck, settling into him. I could hear his heartbeat, powerful and defined. His breathing was steady and calm. We stood this way for a very long time, neither of us willing to move away from each other. It wasn't until dishes began clinking in the kitchen and Felix peeked around the corner to ask if we'd be interested in pork chops brined in fish sauce did we leave each other's arms.

Eran's absence was not brought up at dinner, though we sat as close as possible. My concerns weighed heavily on my mind, knowing that Eran would leave as soon as dinner was over.

I attempted to keep my mind off Eran's departure by trying to engage in conversation and watching others around the table. Although it went unmentioned, we all secretly wondered how Campion might react to Felix's cooking but, to everyone's surprise, Campion eagerly finished his plate and asked for another. Felix was supremely delighted.

When the plates were cleared, Eran stood and I followed. We stepped out under the eaves where the rain had become a drizzle now.

"Promise me that you'll be safe," I said.

"I will."

"Promise."

A flicker of a smile rose up and fell away. "I promise."

Because I still couldn't find the words to convince him to stay, I remained silent.

"Try to get some sleep tonight," he suggested.

"Come home tomorrow," I whispered.

He lifted his hands and placed them on each of my cheeks, his warmth comforting against the chilly air, and then he guided our lips together. Unlike before, this kiss held a different passion. It was full of purpose and reassurance.

When he pulled away, his eyes were intense; leaving no doubt that he wouldn't leave me unless he knew it was necessary.

"I'll need to speak to Campion alone. Will you-"

"Yes," I sighed. "I'll send him out."

Our hands never separated until I stepped inside and left his reach.

The moment Campion closed the door behind him I headed for my balcony.

Despite three other individuals in the room, the house seemed unbearably empty now.

Once in my room, I flung open the French doors and leaned over the far edge for any sight of Eran. Then, through the broken clouds, the silhouette of massive, powerful wings moved through the moon's rays. I watched them lift Eran higher and farther across the horizon, amazed at his virility. Suddenly, a boom reverberated through the sky and Eran disappeared. To anyone listening, it would have sounded like a clap of thunder but I knew it was Eran moving at nearly the speed of light.

"How did you know Eran needed you?" I asked, sensing Campion standing behind me.

"He called out to me."

"Called out?" I asked, unable to move or take my eyes from the sky.

"Yes…" he paused and I could feel him evaluating me. "We can hear you on the other side. You simply need to call out our name and we listen."

I considered this and wondered how many customers would stop seeing me if they knew this to be the case.

"So…" I said, taking a seat in my chair. "How long have you been on earth?"

Campion answered so quickly it made me think he was counting the minutes. "In your time, just under five hours."

I froze, knowing that my casual conversation had just taken a serious turn. A realization had come over me so quickly I didn't have time to process it before muttering to myself, "You fell to watch over me…"

"Yes," he replied, and I groaned.

"No…"

"I fell because Eran asked it of me, Magdalene."

I appreciated him trying to absolve me from my guilt but his admission told me something more. The declaration of that statement, the sacrifice he had made reinforced in me the strength of the relationship these two shared.

Still, I couldn't shake my culpability and felt compelled to ask, "How often can you fall? I mean…you must be able to die and fall…as often as you'd like, right?" I asked, hoping this would be the case.

Campion explained, "Once we are on earth, we stay on earth until our bodies give out."

I cringed at hearing those words. They meant that Eran and Campion were now here, locked in this dimension and unable to return at will – and both were here because of me. It was too much, they had given too much. They had chosen to forgo the feeling of comforts the afterlife offered, the familiarity, the relationships with loved ones there. It felt like so much time away, so much to sacrifice, and never before had it been so evident to me that my ability to visit the afterlife at night was a gift - a gift that Eran and Campion had come here to protect.

Campion shuffled restlessly.

"There's another chair here," I offered.

He accepted it and quietly gazed across the rooftops before adding, "Falling is excruciating, nearly unbearable. It can be compared to the process of birth from what I understand. Though I've never personally experienced birth as I've only come here in...other forms...but I've been told of its agony. Falling is similar and thus we try to avoid falling if possible. Had Eran not come down as an Alterum, I would not have followed."

I looked at him, perplexed. "An Alterum?"

His eyes squinted back at me. "You don't remember anything at all do you?"

"No...I seem to hear that regularly."

"Hmmm, that's a good reminder never to be reborn," he muttered before continuing. "The fallen come to earth because they have either been banished from the afterlife for committing an act against humanity – for which they have been given the name Fallen Ones. Or, we come to earth by choice, as is the case with Eran and myself. We are called Alterum's, which means the other life."

"So there are Fallen Ones and there are Alterums..." I mused. "How do you tell the difference?"

"Well...both have capabilities far beyond ordinary humans and both retain the appearance of a human – commonly taking on the same facial features and body structure across lifetimes."

I groaned. "Oh, I understand...That must be how Marco identified Eran and me...because we have the same face as when he last saw us."

Campion pointed a quick finger at me. "Correct, but that is where the similarities end. While Alterums attempt to live peacefully, Fallen Ones are intent on satisfying their own malevolent needs and will destroy anything that inhibits them. Most humans are unable to detect them...You are the exception, able to identify them within a few yards away."

"Campion..." I waited until he looked in my direction. "How do you know so much about me?"

He tilted his head back to release a quiet laugh. "I've known you for some time now," he explained, not bothering to elaborate further.

"I see," I said plainly.

We fell silent, him diligently keeping his attention on his surroundings and me still watching the sky where I last saw Eran.

"You mentioned that you wouldn't have fallen if it weren't for Eran. Why is that?" I asked, sensing there was something more behind his statement.

He grimaced. "It's the skin mostly. I can liken it to the feeling of being covered in burlap sacks and lugging them around. On the other side we are weightless...free and unencumbered. That...I miss already. But then there is the cold, the heat, the hunger, the requirement to use a bathroom..." he pondered further. "There are other reasons but the ones I've given are at the top of my list."

"Huh...I've never considered how it would feel for the fallen," I admitted. "For the Alterums." I was again amazed at the sacrifices Eran had made for me, and now that Campion had made. "Are there any perks? I mean...what's the impetus for other Alterums to fall if they aren't doing it to act as guardians to humans?"

"The powers we bring with us," he hinted, grinning broadly.

I smiled. "Of course...So what powers did you bring with you?"

"Telekinesis, regeneration abilities, flight, and…this one you may not like as much…the power to induce sleep."

I glanced at him confused. "Why wouldn't I like…" I began to ask but never finished my sentence.

Suddenly I was seeing Campion at the end of a long tunnel, his voice echoing towards me. "Sorry, Magdalene. Eran made me promise to put you to sleep so you wouldn't worry about him throughout the night."

I opened my mouth to protest and then the darkness closed in.

6. SLEEP

When I awoke I was no longer in New Orleans.

The arched hall surrounding me was made of white concrete and ornately designed. Countless pockets lined the walls containing rolls of parchment paper and concrete benches were strategically placed the length of the hall. Despite its beauty, the hall was vacant, filled with a quiet serenity.

It was daylight as it always was here.

I sat up, familiar to this place, which I knew as the Hall of Records. I'd been coming here every night for as far back as I could remember. Unlike others who brush their teeth, wash their face, and slip into bed for a solid nights rest, I spend my time here – awake in the afterlife.

A soft, warm breeze rustled my clothes – the same ones I'd been wearing when Campion had put me to sleep. The frustration I felt towards him for sending me in to a narcoleptic state had carried with me here but was quickly dissolving. I understood. He was simply following orders. I briefly wondered whether there was any way of preventing him from doing it again but I knew that would be a practice in futility. I couldn't deny Eran so how could I ask anyone else to?

I stood and considered what I could do to keep my mind off Eran for the time I would be spending here. Unlike others who exist in the afterlife permanently, my fears didn't diminish in this place and an active part of my mind was still worrying about Eran. I intentionally restrained horrid thoughts of different scenarios he may encounter that kept rising up from my subconscious but it was challenging. Those thoughts were accompanied with the aggravation in knowing that he was doing this for me – putting himself at risk to protect me - something I would end eternally if he'd allow it. Knowing this would happen and knowing I never slept, I figured he must have sent me here for a reason.

Ordinarily I would deliver messages for my customers, who visited me in The Square, but it was during the school week and I didn't work during the week. That left me with the challenge of finding something to fill my time.

Then I drew in a contented sigh, realizing what a precious gift Eran had given me…He'd intended me to make a visit to the only person who could keep my emotions steady.

I stood and walked down the hall to a specific pocket, pulling the parchment from within it. It unraveled on its own, flowing to the ground, resembling the movement of liquid paper, and piling at my feet. I found the name I was looking for and softly moved my finger over it. This was the same process I followed when I sought to find the recipients of messages that I delivered for my customers in The Square. This time, however, I'd be visiting a friend of mine.

As my finger finished tracing the name the world around me seemingly disintegrated, rapidly turning to dust, and fell away. My feet left the floor and I was suddenly being carried through the air, the ground below me moving along at neck breaking speed. On these journeys I always tried to catch a glimpse of what was below me. They were other people's heavens, designed to fit their interests and needs and it was as if I could peek in to other's desires without needing to disrupt them. Entire cities, remote tropical islands, even planetary clusters had been built by individuals. However, I was taken to an area known for gathering as a community.

I landed at the open doorway of a building resembling a Greek temple and glanced around. Groups of people from all cultures mingled around the colossal Doric columns and sat on the steps lined with decorative stonework. Behind me, down the hillside and across a vast gorge, a few of the winged populace congregated casually in the sky. From inside and across the cavernous meeting area, I found him.

Dressed in a toga, Gershom leaned against a column, his expression reflective. While he still looked about my age I knew that he, like everyone else here, had the ability to change their appearance. Evidently, he felt most comfortable at the age of seventeen.

After seeing me approach, he lithely stood and took broad, eager steps towards me.

"Maggie," he said, beaming. "It has been weeks…in your time at least. Where have you been?"

I laughed lightly at myself. "Working."

"Ah," he said, tilting his head back in thought. "Of course…The customers over holiday break kept you busy then." He leaned in to wrap his arms around me.

I returned his hug. "They did." Then I stood back and openly scrutinized him. "You look like you are adjusting well. Your eyeglasses are gone though."

"Yes," he chuckled. "No need for them here."

"Of course…"

"Should we sit on the steps?" he offered. "The view is impressive."

I agreed and followed him outside to take a seat overlooking the gorge. Groups of people still hovered there, some with pets circling their feet and others playing various games. It reminded me of a park setting, except that those ordinarily on the ground were now suspended in the air.

"Tell me," he said, "have I missed anything? How is the warden treating you?"

I rolled my eyes. "I wish you were still at school…simply because I miss you being there. But the warden…he is actually the least of my problems."

"Hmmm," he replied pensively. "That doesn't sound good."

I then recounted all that had happened, finishing with the fact that Eran has started on nightly reconnaissance missions and left me nervously wondering about his return.

Gershom smiled woefully. "Maggie, I appreciate that you are worried and if it were anyone else besides Eran going on these missions I would be just as concerned. But Eran's abilities, not to mention his legacy as an experienced fighter, are narrated in stories here and on earth. I mean, he's legendary." He paused to assess my mood and added, "I honestly don't think you have much to worry about. He's not going to put himself in harm's way because that would mean not coming back to you."

Gershom had made a reasonable argument, I knew, but I still couldn't shake the feeling that something was wrong.

"How does he like school?" Gershom asked, trying to change the subject and keep my mind from roaming.

I appreciated the effort. "Being that he recalls the last several hundred years, he knows more about the subjects than the teachers."

Gershom chuckled. "But he enjoys the actual practice of going to school. I think it's nostalgic for him."

"Maybe the teachers will run across some of his previous exploits…" Gershom suggested and we shared a laugh. "They may even run in to one of your previous exploits…"

"Mine?" I said, feigning offense. "All I've done is to deliver messages."

"True," Gershom replied sincerely, "and it caught the attention of others. You were known in London during the Black Plague, in Paris during the French Revolution…Newspaper articles have been written about you, your meetings with the upper crust of society have been documented. You do have a reputation on that side. But, on this side, well…you're even more renowned…over here you're more legendary than Eran."

I found that difficult to believe. Eran was extraordinary in every way I could identify, so I immediately discounted Gershom. And the messengers…well, we were all the same.

"How could I possibly be any different from other messengers, Gershom. We all perform the same job. We deliver messages between earth and the afterlife. It's actually pretty simple."

Gershom responded with mocking laughter. "Oh no, it's not that simple. Maggie, you are the last messenger on earth. That alone makes you special. But…it's more than that…What makes you different from the other messengers is that you were the one to mobilize them, train them to protect themselves. While Eran trained his army of guardians, you trained the messengers to defend themselves against the Fallen Ones."

"I did?" I was reserved now, amazed that I had absolutely no recollection, no intuition of having done the things Gershom was insisting.

"And then you hired families on earth to train messengers there too. Before you, messengers didn't last more than a few years and then the Fallen Ones would find them and murder them. Before you, they had no defenses. You stopped it. You gave them a fighting chance. You changed everything, Maggie."

My reaction to that news was subdued, to say the least. I sat quietly in awe of what I had just learned, trying to understand how I could have accomplished all that Gershom had said.

That type of work, that goal, wouldn't be complete for lifetimes, possibly centuries. In fact, instinctually, I felt that the training, the defenses were still being pursued. I had always been driven to do what I thought was right but this...this lifestyle I had pursued went beyond moral dedication.

"That must be why the Fallen Ones want me dead..." I speculated.

"It's definitely where it started. But I think you've acquired personal vendettas against you along the way."

"Hmmm...well...that explains a lot."

"It certainly does..."

"So I taught others how to exterminate them..." I said thoughtfully.

"Exterminate and imprison," Gershom corrected. "The ones you and Eran have been able to catch are living the remainder of eternity in a prison that you helped design. The ones you haven't caught yet know that or eternal death is what awaits them."

In response, I groaned. "Finally, I understand the vehemence the Fallen Ones have for me, Eran...and the other messengers."

Gershom sat beside me, pensive, shaking his head from side to side. Then, clearly hoping to change the subject to something more lighthearted, he asked about my housemates. It took our conversation on a winding course for several hours.

As was the case on this side, the daylight didn't fade and the number of winged visitors to the communing area remained unchanged. The hours passed unnoticed by everyone but me. I had been here often enough to sense when dawn was approaching on earth and knew enough to say goodbye to Gershom before I felt the sudden yank pulling me back to my bedroom in New Orleans.

I awoke more eager than usual, sitting up in bed, my eyes darting around in search of Eran.

"It seems that someone is ready to start her day," I heard his calm, confident voice before I was able to slow my eyes enough to find him.

When I could focus again, I realized he was sitting at the foot of my bed, watching me with a relaxed grin.

"Sleep well?" he inquired. "Maybe my suggestion to put you to sleep was a good one."

"Suggestion?" I countered. "That was an order you gave Campion and you know it."

His grin turned in to my beloved smirk. "It worked."

I sighed in irritation. "Still, it's uncomfortable enough not having control over where I go when I sleep. At least give me the option to choose when to go to sleep."

"I can't promise that…" he said. Seeing that I was about to protest, he added, "but I will promise that it will only be used when necessary."

I considered this and, knowing I was not going to win this dispute, I did as Gershom had and changed the subject. "Where did you go last night?"

He shrugged casually as if he were simply out of town for the night and not on a dangerous undertaking to discover our enemy's plans. "Germany, France. I made a stopover in London."

There was little I recalled of my past lives with Eran but I had learned that these were the places we had lived. "Why our old stomping grounds?"

"Information can be found if you dig deep enough."

"Were you able to dig deep enough?"

He tilted his head and lifted an eyebrow to accentuate the silliness of my question. "It takes time, Magdalene. This won't happen overnight despite your desire for it to be that way."

I felt my shoulders fall. "So you do plan to go out again tonight…"

"I'll be out every night until we learn what we need," he replied with an apologetic smile.

I was afraid that would be his response.

"But," he softened the blow of his confirmation by adding, "watching you sleep so peacefully this morning made me seriously reconsider it…"

"Good," I retorted quietly.

"So…how about you get dressed, meet me in the kitchen, and then you can tell me how Gershom is holding up."

I drew in a sharp breath. "I knew that was your plan…to send me to him to calm my nerves."

He stood up and winked as he turned towards my bedroom door. "And you are you correct. See you downstairs."

The kitchen this morning was bustling as usual. The door to the backyard was opened to allow the sweet scent of fresh air. Campion sat at the table, alert and quiet. Dressed in a button down shirt, plaid vest, and tweed slacks he looked more like a model from a men's magazine than a first lieutenant.

"Nice clothes," I stated, pouring coffee into a mug.

"Thank you. I flew to New York City this morning when Eran returned. I figure if I'm going to need to be here, than I'm going to do it in comfort."

"And style," Felix remarked approvingly, having a fondness for clothes.

Clearly, I was the odd one out, having no appreciation for fashion whatsoever.

"Mags," said Felix moving fluidly around Rufus firmly planted at the stove, "Campion would like ideas on what he should do throughout the day. Any suggestions?"

"How about going with them to The Square?" I asked Campion.

Felix drew in a quick breath. "Excellent idea. It is the quintessential New Orleans experience."

"No," I corrected him. "I meant to watch over you…for added protection…"

Felix didn't immediately respond, choosing to avoid me by pouring himself a glass of orange juice. I got the impression he was evading the suggestion.

"Campion? Do you mind?" I persisted.

He shook his head. "It's what I've come here to do."

Felix turned to Campion with a stiff smile. "Thank you."

If Campion noticed Felix's irritation, he certainly didn't address it, preferring to answer simply, "You're welcome."

Eran arrived in the kitchen a few minutes later when Felix's jovial mood had returned. He entered in jeans and a long-sleeved t-shirt fitting his body snuggly and making me catch my breath. He caught me staring and grinned before dropping his book bag on a kitchen chair.

"Campion," he said, firm but genial.

"Sir," Campion replied in nearly the same tone.

"We'll be back after her last class," he informed.

"I'll be here."

With plans for my evening protection in place, Eran and I took a few pastries from a package on the counter and headed for school. It came as no surprise that within a few minutes from school I began to feel the hair rise at the back of my neck.

"I feel them," I informed Eran as we pulled into the parking lot.

Sure enough, a few new Fallen Ones sat in cars and casually strolled along the school pathways. Marco and his men were in a group near the front door. Each one of them immediately noticed us just as we did them.

To my surprise, Eran parked the bike anyways and waited for me to stand up.

"We're safe," Eran announced when he had slipped off his helmet. "I have a few on my team nearby."

Even though he'd warned us that we wouldn't be able to see or hear them, I couldn't stop myself from glancing around as I removed my own helmet.

"Don't worry," he said. "You're covered no matter where you go."

"Oh really? And what if I need to use the bathroom?" I teased.

He didn't share my playfulness. "You're still safe. I have females in my army."

My eyebrows rose.

Noticing my reaction he added, "You'll be proud to know they are among my best fighters," he replied.

"I would expect nothing less," I stated to which he chuckled.

We'd made it to the path leading to the main doors by that point when I asked, "So do you think they are here only for the show?"

"We'll see," he said. "Remain alert."

"Ay, ay, Captain," I said and gave him a weak salute.

"Colonel…" he corrected. "I'm the equivalent of a colonel. And someday I'll show you how to correct that salute."

I scoffed and playfully jabbed him in the ribs.

"Alert, Magdalene," he reminded me.

"Yes, yes…colonel."

"Better…" he said with a wink.

Throughout the day, the Fallen Ones did not interact with us, keeping a reasonable distance whenever we came across each other. Oddly, this made me more anxious. While Eran was thoughtful in his approach, bent in collecting information to build a skillful defense, I was the exact opposite. I simply wanted to get on with this battle rather than draw it out any further.

I wouldn't get my wish.

The remainder of the week passed as I'd expected it would. More Fallen Ones arrived, though none were in my classes, which relieved Eran. They behaved like the rest of the student body and most of the faculty, watchful and suspicious of Eran and me. Bridgette and Marco even seemed to have backed off from us, although they did keep an intent eye when we were around.

The Fallen Ones made no additional attempts to taunt us. No one, not the students, faculty, or administrators, seemed to perceive them as anything different than what they portrayed. It made me realize that, despite their lack of humanity, ironically they blended in well with humans. I suppose this was because they'd originally started as one and after years, often centuries, on earth among us they'd either retained or learned our habits.

If it hadn't been for Ms. Beedinwigg we'd have lived in an almost complete void within the walls of our school. Only she went out of her way to speak to Eran and me, starting conversations in the hallways and including us in class discussions. More so, she retained her identity, refusing to exchange her draping dresses, hair bun, chained eyeglasses, or combat boots. She stood out among the faculty in style and in personality. I liked her more each day.

A routine began to develop whereby Eran watched over me at school during the day and Campion at night. In fact, everything seemed to be moving along predictably...and then Friday night arrived and things began to change.

7. ASSAULT

Friday evening started out quiet with only an occasional breeze stirring the leaves to break the silence. It felt as if someone had closed a lid on New Orleans, cloaking the city in darkness, and causing all living beings to fall into hibernation.

My feet were propped against my balcony railing with my eyes focused on the spot where I last saw Eran leave for his nightly excursion. I was pondering when he would fill me in on what he'd learned. When I had asked he seemed hesitant, telling me simply that there wasn't much to tell. I had a sense, however, that there may be something more but Eran was compelled – as always – to protect me, even if it meant keeping information to himself that he thought might alarm me.

From inside, I could see Campion reading, staying close by in case he was needed.

I sat, rocking my chair on the balcony, watching the sky, and missing Eran. Jazz music played in the distance and the smell of jambalaya floated up from a restaurant nearby.

Below me, the houses along the street were dark. Only the glimmering streetlight outside our house showed any movement.

Then, down the street, two headlights approached. They moved slowly, as if they were searching for something or someone. I followed them until the car stopped just outside our house. It was a black Rolls Royce with darkly tinted windows, shined and buffed until it looked like it had just rolled off the showroom floor.

It was close enough for my radar to sound off if a Fallen One sat inside it but I felt no reaction. Still, I remained in my seat, tilting forward just enough to see over the railing.

The door opened without a sound and out stepped a man. He wore a black suit, bow tie, top hat, and white gloves. I was not impressed by it. What did impress me was that his eyes were locked on me.

"Ms. Magdalene Tanner?" he asked politely.

I replied with a single nod.

"I have been asked to deliver an invitation to you," he stated simply.

I could feel my brow crease. I was being invited to something? I didn't know anyone in the city that would have any interest in inviting me anywhere. This sparked my curiosity.

I stood and entered my room.

Campion lifted his head.

"Good book?" I asked, walking by him.

"Excellent, I've forgotten how it ends," he said.

I was at the door before Campion realized I was heading for it. "Where are you going?"

I shouldn't have played with him. He was here to protect me and he took his job seriously. I just couldn't help myself.

"Downstairs," I replied, indifferently. "Someone just drove up."

I held in a giggle as Campion flew by me, the wind actually picking up my hair as he passed. He was at the front door, peering out the entryway window, by the time I reached the base of the stairs.

"I'm going out first," he informed me.

I ushered him towards the door.

He opened it and stepped out on to the porch, going no farther. I stopped beside him.

The man I had seen from my balcony was still there, standing a few feet away. He appeared unflappable despite the assertive stance Campion had taken.

"I bring with me an invitation for Ms. Magdalene Tanner," he announced.

"I'll take it for her." Campion moved forward but I placed a hand on his arm.

"Campion, it's all right. I would tell you if it wasn't," I said, starting down the steps.

He frowned but followed directly beside me, giving the man a good, sweeping inspection.

By the time we reached him, the man had withdrawn an elaborately designed envelope and was holding it out for me.

Before taking it, I asked, "Who is this from?"

"Mr. Duke Hamilton, who is also my employer," he stated leaving the invitation in his hand extended.

"And who are you?"

"Alfred Goodfrey, Mademoiselle. I am pleased to make your acquaintance."

"Pleased to meet you too, Alfred."

"Will you accept Mr. Hamilton's invitation?"

I took it and he stood straight again. With a quick nod, he spun on his heel and strolled back towards the car. He sat in the back seat and the car sped off much faster than it had arrived.

"An invitation?" Campion inquired, equally as curious.

"Yep...I'm wondering if it is safe to open it..." I joked.

He didn't find it funny. "May I see it?"

I handed it to him for a quick inspection.

"May I open it?" he asked.

"Campion…it is my invitation…"

He gave it back and I slipped my finger inside the envelope flap to peel it back. Inside was a silver card. Pulling it out, I noted how expensive it looked. Only one side had any words. They were discreet and embossed.

Mr. Duke Hamilton wishes to make your acquaintance as his private dinner guest. You will be handsomely paid for a confidential session to commune with a deceased loved one. I deeply apologize for the late notice. Regrettably, time is of the essence.

What appeared to be Mr. Hamilton's signature was signed, in ink, at the bottom, just below the address, time, and date.

"He's asking to meet you tomorrow night," Campion observed.

"Then he must be on his way out. Why else would someone want to commune with the dead when they're going to see them soon anyways?"

He reflected on my point and then said, "I've been told that some feel they need to make amends with those who have passed on before them in order to be accepted in the afterlife. A purging of sins if you will…"

That confirmation made me grieve for this stranger. Fear and inhibition were common during the passing process. I had seen it many times and had tried to relay to those close to their time that passing was a journey to the other side. With experience in attempting to calm fears, I was compelled to do the same for Mr. Hamilton, but I wasn't so certain Campion agreed with me. "You don't think he's safe so you don't want me to go…" I assessed.

"Not at all. It's the ones who don't feel they need to make amends that concern me." He evaluated me closely for a moment. "Are you interested in accepting the invitation?"

"It's what I'm here for, Campion."

He paused briefly, evaluating the scenario, and then said compliantly, "I'll accompany you. If you should need me, I'll be there."

"I know," I said with an appreciative smile.

Again upstairs and in my chair, I thought about the invitation now lying in my lap, my eyes skirting over the address. Mr. Hamilton's residence was across town towards the far end of the Garden District – where the wealthier residents lived. I was actually looking forward to Mr. Hamilton's dinner. It would keep my thoughts preoccupied while Eran was somewhere in Europe closing in on our enemies, alone, unprotected, and tenacious.

In truth, if it wasn't for the fact that I would be assisting the man...personally, I would have been of the mindset to prefer to be in Europe.

A lavish dinner at an exclusive residence with an affluent member of the New Orleans society was not exactly my idea of a good time. I felt more at ease in an environment that didn't require using the correct fork and keeping my elbows off the table. I preferred the danger, the thrill of the adventure, the inability to know what was going to come next, and the potential to meet up with the enemy who was at this very moment preparing to blindside us, just so I could blindside them instead.

Dwelling on it only made me upset so I dropped my feet to the ground, informed Campion that I would be going to sleep, and fell into my bed, eagerly waiting for the night to pass.

Eran was at my bedside when I opened my eyes the next morning, watching me inquisitively. I felt my cheeks stretch as a smile unwittingly rose up.

"Do you have any idea how gorgeous you look when you sleep?" He then added, more to himself than to me, "...Stunning."

"Thank you. Words like that make me eager to see you," I informed him playfully.

"Well then...I'll have to use them more often," he suggested.

"You should," I agreed.

We fell silent, staring back at one another, each wearing a slight smile. Instinctually, I slid forward on the bed, closing the gap between us. Eran didn't move, though his muscles tensed, and his breathing shortened. I slid closer. Still he didn't move. My knees now leaned against the arm he used to prop himself. Our faces were inches away and I could breathe him in, a mixture of sweet fresh air and an aroma that was distinctly Eran – something I likened to how sunshine would smell if it had a scent.

Since our moment in front of the hearth, he had again fallen back to his prudent behavior and had kept his distance from me. Unlike before, he hadn't even made an attempt to brush against me, which made me sad that he'd ever admitted to this in the first place. Feeling his touch was like a bolt of lightning coursing through me and I missed it.

I rested my knees deeper against his arm, my stomach performing flips inside me.

"You haven't touched me since your nightly missions started...Campion is here watching over me. You have your army in place to watch over Ezra, Rufus, and Felix," I explained. "But you still seem to have your guard up."

His expression, one of intense passion, deepened and then, like a fleeting cloud, it disappeared. In its place was sadness. "I do...I do..." he mused. "My inherent responsibility is to protect you. It is what drives me, Magdalene, to my very core. I'm doing this the best way I know how but there are times when I weaken..." His shoulders slumped and he briefly showed his regret. "There are times when I cannot help myself…"

"Neither can I," I admitted in a whisper, too overwrought with emotion to speak louder.

"And there are times when I don't want to…" he confessed. "I want to allow myself to express what I am feeling. I want to be free to watch you not because we have enemies but because the sight of you comforts me. I want to keep you close to me not only to protect you but because when we are apart I feel an emptiness inside that aches…"

In an effort to keep myself from crying, I put my hands to my mouth, while a single thought echoed inside me: None of this was fair.

"You and I…" Eran went on, still distressed. "Magdalene, we weren't supposed to fall in love. It's never happened before between a guardian and their ward. We are unprecedented. No one was prepared for it…"

"But we did fall in love."

"Yes…we did…and now we are figuring it out without any historical guidance, without anyone to offer us advice. We are figuring it out for ourselves…and it…it's been a challenge…" He pondered that admission quietly. "What an understatement…" He then drew in a deep breath, taking a moment to stare at the ground beyond me. He then returned to his customary behavior, confident but restrained. "There is one thing that I do know with absolute certainty…We cannot let our guard down, not once. It is imperative that your safety comes first. You come first, Magdalene. Not us…You."

"Which means any show of emotion towards me is off limits…" I said summing it up, absorbed in the unnerving feeling of hopelessness. "I just don't understand why…"

"Because it has happened before." His head dipped and shook side to side, as if he were trying to clear his thoughts. "A moment's distraction…just a single moment…and you're hurt." The ache of guilt he felt was evident in his voice, something that I felt just as clearly. He was beating himself up inside remembering it.

"But here I am," I pointed out softly, "without pain." When he didn't respond, his head still down, I added, "Campion…you trust him?"

That caused him to raise his head. His eyes gleamed unwavering confidence. "I trust him implicitly."

"Good, I knew that because you wouldn't leave me with anyone less."

His face lightened, a little. "Then why did you ask?"

"Because if you trust him so much to watch over me…maybe you can trust him to watch over me when I'm with you."

Eran laughed through his nose. "I should have seen that coming…"

"Nah, seeing things coming is Campion's job…"

"Only during the night," he stated. "I'm still your guardian."

He declared that with such devotion, it made my stomach tighten with pride.

Then, our progress was reversed. He slid back, away from me, to my grave dismay.

"I will put some thought in to it," he promised, standing and heading for the door.

As he reached the hallway I called out to him.

"Whatever happened when you let your guard down…it was only once and it was so long ago…You can't spend eternity feeling guilty for it."

"It wasn't just once," he said, his tone deep, intense regret brewing just beneath the surface. "It has happened every lifetime, Magdalene. Every one of them. I intend to ensure that it will not happen in this one." He started into the hallway again and stopped. Without turning, he finished, "And for me…for me it was not so long ago."

A moment later, I heard his door squeak closed but it did not click shut. My entire body ached to run to him and throw my arms around him, to hold him like I had in front of the hearth. But this was the exact opposite of what he wanted to accomplish. He needed time to recover, to withdraw from his emotions, to become stoic again so that his judgment would not be impaired and weaken his awareness or defenses.

I heard a knock on my door and found Rufus standing in the hallway, a sheepish grin across his face.

"I ain't goin' ta tell ya I didn't hear that," he said, his Irish accent tinged with reluctance. "'Cause I was listenin'." He came into my room and took a seat in my wingback chair. Leaning forward, he lowered his voice. It was firm and demanding. "'N here's all I'm gonna say...yer love's lasted centuries...it kin damn well make it through this."

My lips curled against themselves and, finally, the tears won welling up against my eyelashes. Rufus, not being one to handle tears, left the room but not before patting me affectionately, and with a tinge of discomfort, on my head. Then the tears fell, darkening my sheets with small dots, until I wiped them from my face.

Somehow, Rufus always knew how to say what I needed to hear. He'd given me a dose of hope, enough for me to get myself moving.

After a brief, listless shower and a change of clothes, I met up with Eran in the kitchen. He watched me cautiously yet kept his distance.

We spent the day in The Square, where I collected messages to deliver to those who had passed on. Eran watched over me, though I could sense that this time he was more interested in my mood than my physical safety. He knew I was struggling.

I couldn't seem to shake the dejected feeling, even with Eran so close to me or maybe because of it. I realized that if it weren't for the talk this morning I may never have known just how deeply Eran felt about his self-imposed detachment. There was nothing I could do to change it, I knew this and it made me feel worse. The only option I had was to keep from thinking about it. So, I focused on taking my orders during the busy times and pondered about the private dinner meeting I had scheduled tonight with the wealthy, elusive Mr. Hamilton during the slow times.

The day did not move quickly so I was glad when the sun set and the tourists dispersed from The Square. After stowing my chairs and sign in Felix's trunk, I slid on to my bike intending to head home.

Eran approached, strapping on his helmet without a word. He'd sensed my mood throughout the day and knew there was nothing he could do to change it – other than to retract his intentions which we both knew would not be done.

This time, Eran rode in the back. He wrapped his arms around my waist, allowing for plenty of space between us. Again, this tested me as I was torn between wishing he'd hold me and just not touch me at all. Every turn shifted him into me, teasing me, making me grow more frustrated.

Again he sensed this and, while at a stop light, he offered, "Maybe I should be riding my own bike."

"Why?" I shouted back to him, over the motor's sound. "You have wings."

Something came over me then, an indescribable urge to do something demonstrative of the anger coursing through me. Only one idea came to me.

Speed, I thought.

Maybe I was fleeing from my anger at our untouchable love; maybe I was fleeing from the unfairness that the Fallen Ones dominated our life to the extent we couldn't freely explore our love; maybe I was fleeing from my life overall.

All I knew was that I wanted to go…and I wanted to do it fast.

I kicked my bike in to gear, peeling the rubber from my tires as I crossed the intersection against a red light.

Night had fallen and the lights around us whisked by in a blur.

Vaguely, I heard the horns honking and the curses coming from those on the sidewalks. The smile on my face should have told them something.

I didn't care.

It wasn't until a car pulled out in front of us, the hood rapidly approaching, that I understood I had lost control.

There was no stopping our motion at this speed and with so little distance.

I braced for impact.

Our front tire was a foot away when we left the ground. The hood, which we should have been colliding with at the moment, suddenly seemed like one on the size of a toy car. The trees were now beneath us, the houses shrinking to miniature sizes.

The air up here was cool and damp, refreshing on my face, calming. We moved through the spattering of clouds, neither of us acknowledging what had just happened…what was happening now.

The bike was still with us, I noticed. Eran's hands were now on the handlebar grips, his feet beneath the foot pegs. He was holding on to my beloved bike for my sake, refusing to let it drop beneath us, and my anger instantly dissolved.

His shirt hung in tatters as his wings, now extended, pumped effortlessly to keep us aloft. I listened to the sound of them, their breathtaking strength propelling us above the city.

"Feeling better?" Eran asked into my ear.

"Slightly," I said, enjoying the feeling of him close to me despite my mood.

We were high enough now to see the entire city, its streets dotted with obscure yellow halos where streetlights reflected off the wet pavement, its cars moving like ants along the roadways.

We lifted higher still; breaking through a patch of clouds, into a land illuminated by the moon's light.

That was when I realized we weren't alone.

In the distance, directly in front of us, was another pair of wings.

The body was hovering; its arms and legs curling out as if it were floating in water; its wings pumping slowly and just enough to keep it from dropping. It seemed to be facing us, possibly watching us.

"Eran," I whispered unable to entirely finish calling out his name before we suddenly plummeted towards earth.

Eran's wings moved rapidly now, drawing up far above us to nearly touch at the tips and plunging down – working to gain as much speed as possible.

Impulsively, I turned to look back and wished I hadn't.

It was coming after us…and gaining ground.

Despite the wind in my ears sounding like I'd stuck my head out of an airliner's window and the feel of my cheeks flapping against the pressure, I told Eran, "It's almost caught us. We need to go faster."

"We can't," he called out to me. "Your body won't take the force."

I groaned. Once again, my human body was holding us back. "Do it anyways."

Though I couldn't be sure, I think I heard him sigh in frustration at me.

We were descending so quickly that I could make out people walking along the sidewalks now.

"Hold on," he warned and I braced myself against the bike and Eran's solid torso.

The next moment we were swerving through rows of tombs and statues made of concrete. The cemetery was vacant, thankfully, because at this speed a collision would have resulted in serious injury. I guessed that this was the reason Eran had chosen this particular location to lose our pursuer.

My attention was drawn to my right and I found that it had reached us, keeping pace one row away. The darkness hid its features, but I could discern that it was similar in size to Eran and with equally powerful wings.

Then it was gone, fallen away, and out of sight.

Its disappearance was followed by a resounding crash as it collided with the side of a tomb. I peered over my shoulder just in time to see crumbles of concrete roll into the aisle behind us.

I giggled, unable to contain it.

However, I sensed that Eran didn't share my enthusiasm over his victory. When we had safely landed at the back door to our house, he stepped off the bike, reserved and in thought.

It was oddly quiet now with the wind no longer in my ears.

Campion opened the back door in his typical fashionable attire. He saw Eran's demeanor and instantly stood straighter and more attentive. "Sir," he declared, appearing to wait for instructions.

"Magdalene, I will see you in the morning," said Eran firmly.

I hesitated, wanting to kiss him before we left each other. Knowing this was not going to happen, I settled for a meek, "Thank you…for tonight."

The sternness in him eased a little, though it was almost undetectable.

I entered the house and closed the door behind me, but I did not leave the kitchen. The other housemates were in their respective rooms so voices from outside could travel a good distance – even behind a closed door.

"There was an attack on Magdalene tonight," Eran notified Campion, going in to details about the assailant.

"Do you know who attacked her?" asked Campion with the same grave tone as Eran.

"I'm going back to survey the area. I'll keep you informed."

"Do you want me to accompany you?" Campion offered.

"No, just keep her safe."

"You know I will," replied Campion resolute.

I heard the leaves outside stir across the yard and then Campion opened the kitchen door.

My arms were crossed against my chest and I didn't bother to hide the discontent on my face. "You should be going with him. He'll need another set of eyes on his back."

"He's instructed me to stay with you."

"We'll go together than," I said, starting for the back door. "I know right where we left-"

"Magdalene," Campion said, moving to block me. "He also instructed me to keep you safe. Returning to the cemetery is not what he had in mind."

"How do you know?" I countered.

He gave me a face that told me not to be ridiculous.

I met his stare.

"Your dinner with Mr. Hamilton starts in an hour. You should prepare yourself."

I knew he was trying to divert my attention.

"I am prepared."

Campion glanced at me from head to toes, frowning.

I sighed and turned away, feeling helpless.

"Let's see what we can scrounge up from your closet," Campion proposed, laying his arm across my shoulders and spinning me to face the door, the one that led towards the staircase. "You'll go to dinner and in the morning you'll wake up to find Eran at your bedside…just as you did this morning…just as you had the morning's previous."

Campion prompted me up the stairs to my bedroom where he dug deep into my closet for something he thought would be more suitable to wear.

Yet, as I sat on the edge of my bed, uninterested in Campion's criticism of my wardrobe, I couldn't take my mind off Eran.

He was returning to the site where we'd last seen our attacker make a volatile attempt to harm us…and he was doing it alone.

It left me incredibly uneasy.

The irony was I had no idea that my acceptance to Mr. Hamilton's dinner invitation would turn out to be more treacherous than Eran's nightly mission.

8. THE RUSE

Campion and I arrived promptly at the time Mr. Hamilton was expecting me, stopping in front of what looked to be one of the oldest mansions on the street. It had been remodeled, of course, so that its columns appeared sturdy, its stained glass windows were no longer warped, and its paint looked as if it had been applied yesterday. The hedges lining the house and the grass around the estate appeared to have just been put in as well. It struck me as odd that he'd replace them all at once but I ended up shrugging it off. Maybe Mr. Hamilton was trying to give it curb appeal so that whoever inherited the house would have an easier time selling it.

Campion assessed it openly. "How much did he say he'd offer for a private session?"

"He didn't say."

"You should ask for at least twice your going rate."

"Campion," I hissed. "I don't use my ability to fleece my customers. I take this very seriously-"

"I know...I know...I was playing around. Sheesh..." He rolled his eyes at me.

I sighed lightly at myself. "Sorry, I'm…I'm just a little on edge."

Campion surprised me by taking my elbow. "He'll be just fine, Magdalene. You'll see."

I gave him a wavering smile of appreciation, thankful that Eran's commendation was coming from someone who'd known him for centuries.

We took the steps to the main entrance but before we reached it the door opened. Alfred stood just inside the cavernous foyer, soft light illuminating his stately butler uniform. Beyond him, two sweeping staircases curved along the side of the opposing walls, seeming to hug the elaborately designed chandelier hanging from the center of the foyer. The tile was imported black and white checkered Italian marble and the busts set on individual shelves along the staircase walls were carved from pure marble. Jazz music played from somewhere in the house.

"Mr. Hamilton is eagerly awaiting your arrival," said Alfred. "Please follow me."

Alfred took us through the first floor to a luxuriously appointed library. We found ourselves surrounded by shelves of books so that not the smallest bit of wall space could be seen. I noticed that oversized leather and velvet sofas were placed strategically around the room and that one of them was already occupied.

"Your guests, sir," said Alfred before leaving and closing the doors behind him.

Mr. Hamilton stood and turned towards us, welcoming us with a beaming smile. He could be described in a single word: debonair. His striking silver hair was immaculately groomed, his fair skin gleamed brightly, and his choice of clothes told me that he spent a good amount of money on his wardrobe. I could sense that Campion was impressed.

Something did stand out to me regarding Mr. Hamilton though. He didn't appear to be the least bit ill, which caused me to instantly wonder why he was in such a hurry to meet me.

"Ms. Magdalene Tanner, it is an honor to make your acquaintance," he greeted me, taking my hand into both of his as a sign of deep respect.

"It's a pleasure to meet you too, Mr. Hamilton."

"And you…" he turned his attention to Campion. "I haven't made your acquaintance."

"Campion. I'm Ms. Tanner's escort."

"Well…welcome, both of you…" he said graciously. "It is a late hour so I imagine you are hungry…"

Campion shook his head, attempting to be polite. I discarded that option right away.

"Starved," I declared without any hesitation.

Not a second passed when a door leading elsewhere in the house opened and Alfred emerged, pushing in a silver tray with matching plate covers. I noticed that he set four plates on a small table prepared for us by the lit fireplace.

"Will someone else be joining us?" I asked, as we made our way to the table.

Mr. Hamilton glanced at me, impressed. "You are astute." He said this in a way that made me think someone had foretold him. "Yes, one additional guest." He turned to Alfred and asked, "Would you mind informing Bronte," he asked and received a brief, silent nod in response. Alfred then quickly left the room.

"I understand that you perform your services in Jackson Square," Mr. Hamilton stated.

"Yes, it makes it easy for my customers to find me."

"But you also have repeat customers living here in New Orleans as well, I assume."

"Yes, that's right."

"But I gather that this is your first house call," he surmised.

"It is."

He smiled as if he already knew the answer to that question. Then the door opened and we turned to see who was entering.

"And I believe you already know Bronte..." he hinted, a grin lingering beneath the surface.

I turned and my mouth fell open in surprise.

I did know Bronte but by a different name.

"Ms. Beedinwigg," I said, bewildered.

She crossed the room looking very much the way I've seen her at school. Her dress had been changed to a deeper colored floral print but her bun was still in place, her glasses hung to rest against her chest, and her combat boots were still protruding from beneath her dress. As always, her entire demeanor reflected a self-assured, warm welcome.

"Maggie," she said affectionately. "I am so glad you could come."

"So glad you're here too," I retorted with a laugh. "Do you live here?"

"Yes, for...about a week now."

I tilted my head, more dumbfounded now. "Then, that means, you moved here just before classes started."

She and Mr. Hamilton glanced at each other, sending an unspoken message between them. I would discover what this message was a few minutes later.

"Eran wasn't able to make it to dinner?" she asked, changing the subject and addressing Campion.

I introduced her and Campion, explaining, "He's my escort for the night."

She seemed surprised by this but replied, "It's a pleasure to meet you." She then clapped her hands lightly and offered, "Shall we eat before it gets cold?" She was already taking her seat before anyone could answer.

I noticed that the covers had been removed and that on each plate the meal was different. Ms. Beedinwigg had a traditional jambalaya while Mr. Hamilton chose a pair of

Cornish hens. Campion had been given Eran's meal which was prepared as a succulent steak. My meal was a hamburger and fries and it was perfect. It made me realize that somehow, Alfred had known what we'd each prefer.

At that point, I began to feel as if Mr. Hamilton and Ms. Beedinwigg knew more about me than I assumed.

Despite my feelings, dinner conversation was casual, centering on school and whether I enjoyed it. While giving them an honest answer, I refrained from elaborating on my feelings for Mr. Warden and Bridgette Madison.

Towards the end of dinner, I began to question whether Mr. Hamilton had actually called me here to deliver messages to someone on the other side. In an effort to imply this, I asked, "Mr. Hamilton...I'm curious...Did you learn of my ability to deliver messages to those who have passed on through Ms. Beedinwigg or by passing me in Jackson Square."

Again, a glance was shared between Mr. Hamilton and Ms. Beedinwigg before he answered, "I'm glad you asked the question, Magdalene." He dabbed the corners of his mouth with his cloth napkin and set it at the side of his plate before leaning back in his chair and continuing. "I too have just arrived in New Orleans. Previously, I traveled, alongside Ms. Beedinwigg. In fact, it wasn't until I purchased a necklace...a very rare necklace...in a black market antiquities trade did I consider making myself a more permanent resident. The necklace is renowned, diamond, and had been missing since the American Revolution."

He paused, waiting for my reaction.

"Eran's necklace?" I asked more to myself than to him...and suddenly I was standing and my guard was up.

Campion, who had been listening intently, was standing too, positioning himself between me and Mr. Hamilton and Ms. Beedinwigg. His back was arched, ready to release his wings. I deduced that the only reason his wings remained hidden was because our hosts stayed seated and calm, despite our reaction.

"The necklace, Maggie," Mr. Hamilton hinted. "A necklace like that does not go unnoticed. When I found it on the antiquities market I knew where to find you. It's probably how everyone else is finding you."

"Who are you?" I demanded.

While my question was to both of them, Mr. Hamilton answered. "We aren't here to harm you. Quite the opposite, in fact. Allow me the chance to explain and you can decide for yourself."

I then focused in on my body's reaction, sensing whether the hair on the back of my neck was standing up.

Recognizing this, Mr. Hamilton confirmed, "You'll find no Fallen Ones here." He seemed almost insulted at the idea.

More than anything else, it was his choice of words that made me consider staying to listen. He had used the words Fallen Ones and he should have no knowledge that Fallen Ones even existed. "All right…but I'm edgy so you'll need to make it quick." I knew I was being uncouth but it wasn't as if they had been entirely honest with me.

"We've been looking for you for quite some time," said Mr. Hamilton. "Your traveling with your aunt for her photography business made it challenging. We've always seemed to be a bit late in catching up to you. It wasn't until Eran's necklace landed on the black market here in New Orleans did we know where you could be found."

"Why were you trying to find me?" I asked pensive.

"Well, to put a fine point on it…to train you."

My eyebrows rose in astonishment.

"That's correct…" he confirmed, noting my surprise. "We would like to train you in your pursuit against the Fallen Ones."

"We?"

"Myself and Ms. Beedinwigg. I have the financial resources needed to do so. Ms. Beedinwigg is an expert in all forms of combat and weaponry. She hails from a line of experienced trainers. Our families have dedicated themselves to these purposes for many centuries."

It dawned on me then who these people were. They were descendants of the families I had trained to teach messengers how to defend themselves against Fallen Ones.

Mystified, I asked, "So you knew who Eran and I were all along, didn't you?"

Ms. Beedinwigg grinned mischievously, stood, and pulled a photo album from one of the bookshelves lining the walls. Carrying it to us, she opened it to an archive of newspaper articles. Some were written in English, some in French, but each one had a drawing encircled by the text. Looking closely, I found myself and Eran in each of these articles. The resemblance was striking, with the same face and body structure as we did today. The only difference was our clothes and hairstyles, which reflected the fashion of that period.

"You...You collected all the articles throughout each of our lifetimes on earth?"

"My family did. I simply try to preserve them now."

"The articles were published without your permission and often times without your participation," Mr. Hamilton explained. "You've done a fairly adequate job staying hidden and thus out of the sights of Fallen Ones over the centuries. However, your unique ability hasn't gone unnoticed and the printed records of you have always been against your will and were commonly fabricated."

I stood there, unable to speak. Gershom had mentioned that I'd been revealed in articles and other documents throughout my lifetimes. It just never occurred to me that I would have the chance to run across them.

"You know, no one but the high school editor has approached me for a news article..." I reflected.

"She'll be the last," Mr. Hamilton reassured me. "I keep myself well informed of the media's intentions and have been successful in diverting the attention of news organizations."

I stared blankly at him, having had no idea.

"And you've done a fine job of it," commended Ms. Beedinwigg. "Keeping Maggie's ability hidden is no small feat."

"Yes." I was compelled to agree with her. Then it unexpectedly dawned on me that I made a spectacle of myself in The Square offering my service to complete strangers. "I won't stop my work in Jackson Square," I informed him.

"On the contrary, I recommend you maintain your usual routine," said Mr. Hamilton. "Any change from your typical behavior will only draw attention to yourself. I will keep your name out of the news."

I smiled my thanks and returned to flipping through the pages, scanning the articles. My eyes couldn't seem to be drawn away from Eran's likeness in each of the depictions. His handsome features never diminished or changed. Looking at him made me wonder where he was at that very moment and I felt a pang deep in my chest at his absence.

I gave no attention to Campion up until now but then I noticed that his stance had relaxed. He stood straight, a proud expression on his face. It looked like he wanted to throw his arms around Ms. Beedinwigg.

"Campion?" I asked baffled.

As if I'd given him a cue, he drew in a deep breath, his chest expanding out proudly, as he took two long steps to cover the distance between himself and Ms. Beedinwigg. "I've wanted to meet you…your family…since I witnessed your family in battle. Fantastic fighters…"

"Thank you," said Ms. Beedinwigg demurely.

I felt my mouth fall open. "Campion, you know about them?"

He turned to me, as if his grin were plastered on. "From afar…Only from afar until now."

Watching him admire Ms. Beedinwigg, I knew I couldn't have gotten a better testimonial than Campion's reaction.

Still, I was curious about their motivations and I wanted reassurance that their faith and dedication wouldn't lapse. "What's in this for you?"

"A sensible question," said Mr. Hamilton with a single shoulder shrug. "Some people volunteer for Greenpeace…Some build houses for Habitat for Humanity…We eliminate Fallen Ones."

"It is our act of service to humanity," added Ms. Beedinwigg, "and we've been performing the service since before you were born. You can trust us, Maggie."

In case her declaration weren't enough, Mr. Hamilton hinted, "Ms. Beedinwigg was, in fact, present in the training of your parents."

My breath caught in my throat. "You knew my parents?"

She flipped the pages of the photo album until it landed on a collection of old photographs and then she pointed to one in the middle. Standing between my mother and father was Ms. Beedinwigg in her early teens. They were smiling, with arms wrapped around each other's shoulders, squinting against the sun.

I released my breath then, not knowing I'd still been holding it.

"I've never met them you know…On the day of my birth, we all died. I was the only one to be revived."

"We know," Ms. Beedinwigg confirmed gently. "They were two of the best messengers I've ever had the privilege of meeting." She laughed quietly through her nose, recalling them during a moment of nostalgia.

"So you know they have the ability too…"

"It's why we trained them, Maggie."

"Of course…Of course," I muttered, still dumbfounded at all that I had learned. "I tried to find my parents, to locate them on the other side, but I saw in the scrolls…the scrolls that record each soul's history of their lifetimes on earth…"

"In the Hall of Records," Ms. Beedinwigg offered.

"Yes…I learned that they died exactly where I was told and yet they aren't there…They never returned to the other side."

Ms. Beedinwigg and Mr. Hamilton glanced at each other and I could actually feel the tension rise in the room.

"Maggie…" replied Ms. Beedinwigg. She seemed to be searching for the words to explain her thoughts. Whatever they were it was clear by her apprehension that they weren't good. "Messengers are different. When they die at the hands of a Fallen One…they perish. They suffer the ultimate fate…eternal death."

It took a few seconds for me to absorb what she was telling me. "They don't return to the afterlife like everyone else?"

"No…they don't," she said, placing a comforting hand on my shoulder. "We thought you knew."

I shook my head. "All I knew was that they died protecting me. They died…" I repeated and then began to piece the puzzle together. "And I died with them…at the hands of the same Fallen One…on the same night…in the same place…and yet I am here." My eyes met hers, demanding, questioning the truth to her statements.

It was Campion, however, that stepped forward to answer. "No Fallen One has ever taken your life, Magdalene…in any of your lifetimes," he countered. "Whenever they came close enough to reaching that goal… Eran followed a protocol, one that you mutually established. He would initiate the end of your life…to protect you from eternal death."

I released my breath in a rush then, the realization hitting with such power it felt as if someone had knocked the air out of me. When I inhaled, it was raspy and inefficient.

"I understand now…why Eran is so serious about his responsibilities as my guardian…why he preserves his guilt when he is unable to protect me. I can't imagine the pain he's endured having to…do what he's done…How unfair to him." As the realization continued, I felt anger, deep and driven, well up in me. I had to actively contain it. "My parents died protecting me…Eran has had to endure the anguish of causing me pain…Everyone near me is in danger by the Fallen Ones. How do I end this?" By this point, I was so determined that my question came out as a demand and remained that way when I insisted, "Tell me how to end it."

"It is the same with Fallen Ones," Mr. Hamilton revealed. "They suffer eternal death when they die at the hands of a messenger."

"It's why we wish to train you," Ms. Beedinwigg added earnestly.

I suddenly felt focused, determined. "We're wasting time. When can we begin?" I asked.

Smiles immediately rose up on the faces of Mr. Hamilton and Ms. Beedinwigg but it was she who said, "Follow me."

She led us out of the library, towards the back of the house and down a long hallway, stopping abruptly in the middle of it to place her hand on the wall and push. The wall spun on a pivot so that part of the hidden door swung out into the hallway. The other half opened to reveal a staircase winding down to another concealed level.

"A hideaway," Ms. Beedinwigg explained. "Watch your step. The ground is saturated so, despite our efforts, water seepage makes the stairs a bit risky."

She wasn't understating that warning. All of us were saved at least once by a firm grip to the railing as we descended almost two stories underground.

When we'd reached the bottom, she flicked a set of switches and the room was illuminated.

"This was a hideaway?" I asked. "It looks like an entire town could fit down here."

"We've expanded it some," she replied indifferently, moving into the room.

I followed, slowly, astonished at what I was seeing.

The room was vast, built in sections with each seeming to be dedicated to one purpose of study whether it were agility, endurance, reflex, or skill. I couldn't count the number of contraptions, pulleys and levers, platforms, and sandbags, all designed to create the optimal training ground.

"When were you able to build this?" I asked, still in awe. "I mean…you've only been in town for a week…"

"She is attentive," Mr. Hamilton pointed out.

"I told you…" Ms. Beedinwigg gave him a look of satisfaction.

I realized then while Ms. Beedinwigg had been posing as my teacher, she'd also been evaluating me and relaying her assessments back to Mr. Hamilton. I had never been one to care what others said about me, yet I was left wondering what had been relayed. From their brief discussion it seemed to be positive.

"In answer to your question, we completed it last night," Mr. Hamilton replied proudly. "Just before I sent Alfred to deliver your invitation. You may have noticed the new shrubbery around the house? It was meant to hide the construction damage."

"Interesting…You didn't waste any time…" Campion observed.

"We don't have time to waste," said Ms. Beedinwigg, her tension not going unnoticed. "Now, I'd like you to train every night. Is that possible?"

"Absolutely. What do I learn tonight?" I started into the room.

"Starting tomorrow," she said. Noticing that I began to protest, she cut me off. "When you're no longer angry. Anger is a disruption in training. We need you calm and alert."

"We do, however," said Mr. Hamilton, "have an assignment. We'd like you to go back and review each of your lifetimes."

I felt my forehead crease in confusion. "I'd be very impressed with myself if I could do that…"

"You can," said Ms. Beedinwigg undaunted. "When you move your finger across the scroll over the name of the person you wish to locate on the other side, you are immediately transported to them, correct?"

"Yes," I confirmed.

"Try doing the same thing over the scroll imprinted with your names. It will take you through that lifetime, specifically to each key point in it."

Again, I was taken aback. "That works? How-How do you know that?"

Ms. Beedinwigg laughed as if I'd made a ridiculous understatement. "My family recorded everything…which we will begin sharing with you when you return tomorrow evening."

She headed back towards the stairs but I had to inform her of something first and this was as good a time as any.

"You should know that Marco, his security team, and several students and faculty at our school are Fallen Ones."

She looked back, appearing unflappable. "I already do. They are the reason for the hasty invitation to tonight's dinner."

My respect for Ms. Beedinwigg immediately doubled.

By the time we reached the foyer, I knew what I would be doing tonight. To keep my mind off Eran's dangerous pursuits, tonight I would test her theory and visit one of my past lives.

9. MUEHLHAUSEN, GERMANY

We arrived home to find the windows dark. It was late and we both knew without having to say it that our housemates had gone to sleep.

Campion followed me up the stairs, alert and responsive to the sounds inside the house. A moment later, I heard my French doors open and Campion step on to the balcony, as he did most nights while guarding me.

"Enjoy your assignment." Campion's voice came through the dark as I slipped into my bed.

My mind was racing from all that I'd learned tonight so getting on with my assignment might take some time, I realized.

"Campion? I'm having a tough time sleeping. Would you mind?"

He turned to face me and no sooner did I finish my sentence did sleep overtake me.

The Hall of Records was just as quiet as when I'd last visited it, but I was not alone. One other person floated several stories above me, reviewing a scroll, his admiral blue robe flowing around his ankles. I left him to his reading.

My scroll was in the B section, under Billings, Montana, as scrolls were stored by last place of death.

I had to climb several stories to reach it but in the afterlife this wasn't difficult. It lay neatly curled in its tube, opening only when I withdrew it and allowed it to unravel.

I spoke my name aloud and the scroll slipped through my fingers until my name landed between my thumbs. Giddiness overcame me then. It felt as if all my internal organs were springing up and down. Calm down, I told myself. This could be just as unpleasant as it is exciting. If Ms. Beedinwigg was even correct...

With that in mind, I reviewed the list of my past lifetimes. I figured the beginning was as good a place as any to start and took my right index finger to move it across the words:

Previously   Friedricha   Schaffhausen   –   Died Muehlhausen, Germany June, 5, 1525

This time the hall did not disintegrate and fall away. I was not carried above other people's heavens or versions of their afterlife.

I was yanked, much the same way I returned to earth each morning, as if I were on the end of a rubber band and that band had been pulled taut and released.

Then I was cold and hungry and my back felt as if it were lying on a bed of nails. I had no control over any of this and certainly not over my physical body. Yet, I could hear the wails coming from my mouth, rattling my eardrums, and the feeling of absolute despair.

It took me a moment to comprehend that I was encapsulated inside the body of a toddler, left in the middle of a barren field. Rain clouds gathered overhead and the wind howled through the tall grass, bitingly crossing my skin. Tears began falling down my face, which I tried to suppress, unsuccessfully.

"Here! Over here!" a voice cried out. Though the words were in German, I understood them as clear as if they'd been in English.

The crunching of the dry grass stopped suddenly and I opened my eyes to find a woman kneeling over me. A man appeared next to her, pulling his hat down against the wind. My immediate reaction was one of calm reassurance. Somehow, I knew these faces. An intuition deep inside me confirmed that I had chosen them as my parents before I had fallen.

"Who could have left this poor thing out here in the cold?" she asked, her hand over her chest in astonishment.

"I'll carry her," the man stated, picking me up and supporting me against him.

I was yanked yet again, pulling me down a tunnel, away from the man and woman. When it stopped, the field was gone. It was night and I was sneaking out the door of a small house, glancing back at the face of the man and woman I'd just seen as they slept in front of the hearth. They were older now with sprouts of gray hairs and wrinkles. I found myself inundated with love for them and for the other girls and boys sleeping around the fire. Vaguely, it registered in me that this was my family.

Why am I running away? I desperately wondered. Stay, I tried to tell myself. Stay…

My thoughts and desires did nothing to stop my body from moving out into the night and drawing the hood over my head against the chill in the air.

The gravel crunched beneath my feet and then quieted when I met the dirt road leading to a city illuminated in the distance.

"Stop," a voice commanded. Despite the German translation, it was a voice I knew, one that I would know anywhere, even in another lifetime.

My body turned to find Eran moving swiftly towards me. I felt a swell of fear and I knew that this body – my body in this lifetime – did not recognize Eran.

My hand reached inside the edge of my cloak to firmly grip the handle of my sword and my arm withdrew it just as Eran reached me.

I watched, helpless, as this body of mine fought feverishly against him, advancing on him as I would my worst enemy. He met my attacks with equal grace, thankfully, his sword connecting with mine using the same force and vigor.

Then he slipped, a puddle of mud causing his foot to twist beneath him, and my weapon came dangerously close to his neck.

He jolted back, swung around in to a crouch, and attacked.

My back hit a tree and Eran's hands came around my own, squeezing until my sword fell. Using his free hand, he shoved back the hood of my cloak.

The surprise washing across his face was evident.

"You're-You're a girl," he said in German, though I still understood him.

I noticed then, the intrigued excitement building in my body, the burning sensation coursing through my torso. Apparently, I had an instant attraction to him, even then, at our very first meeting.

"I thought," he backed away, releasing my hands, and laughing to himself. "I thought you were a boy up to no good." He evaluated me from afar. "But...you are certainly no boy."

"No," my voice declared in German. "I am not." I pulled my cloak tighter around me. "What were you doing attacking me? I could have killed you, you know."

Eran broke in to laughter, the force of it causing him to bend over and brace himself against his knees. "I strongly disagree."

"I truly don't care," I retorted, heading back into the road.

He followed, coming up beside me as if I'd invited him on a stroll. I hadn't and as a result I felt myself being torn. Part of me wanted to send him away and part of me wanted him to walk just a little closer. "What are you doing out this late at night? A girl like you shouldn't be alone."

I chuckled confidently. "I can take care of myself."

"Hmm, yes...yes...I could see that..." he muttered and yet continued to walk with me in silence for a few paces. "Just in case..." He leaned forward so that he came into my view. "I'm going to escort you."

"I don't need an escort."

"May I walk with you then? You might find me to be of some assistance..."

I felt a mixture of annoyance and thrill but didn't show either in my response. "Do as you wish."

"Thank you," he replied in mock appreciation. "So...where are we going?"

"To deliver messages," I replied hastily. I could feel in myself that the rush of words was meant to cloak the fact that I actually enjoyed him coming along but didn't want him to know it.

I sensed him staring at me. "It's settled then...you'll deliver your messages and I'll guard you along the way. And I won't even charge you for acting as your guardian."

My response was a haughty snicker.

I never heard his reply. The yank returned and I was shot into another part of my life.

Makeshift tents surrounded us now. Hundreds of them, I guessed, as a mist obscured the entirety of them. We stood beneath a section of contorted, dead trees, watching over the camp as the sun rose on the horizon.

Eran was facing me, inches away. "Why are you smiling?" he asked tenderly in German.

I found that my cheeks were lifted and giggled quietly so that the camp didn't wake. "I didn't know I was…"

"You enjoy my company, don't you?" He didn't seem to notice he was being conceited.

I snickered, mockingly. "That…is arrogant of you."

"Maybe, but it is true. Isn't it?"

My head turned away, appearing disinterested, not wanting him to know the truth. When I looked back his eyes had softened, filling with passion. "I enjoy your company…" he admitted and I felt my stomach tighten in exhilaration. From the reaction in my body, I knew that I'd waited to hear those words for so long and when they came I was both comforted and thrilled. His face stiffened then. "But there is something I must tell you. It may scare you a bit. But…it's important that you know…"

I was completely at ease. Very little ever scared me.

"I have something to tell you too…" I confessed. Then I was the one who grew nervous, jittery about how Eran might respond to the secret I'd been keeping from him.

He dipped his head at the unexpectedness of my statement. "All right. You go first."

I drew in a breath but then found it locked in my throat. The hair on the back of my neck came alive and the rest of my body began to shake.

"Friedricha?" he asked, restrained, and in the back of my mind, opposing the pain I was now in, I registered that he was referring to me by my given name in this lifetime.

Unable to answer, I closed my eyes against the panic rising in me and when I opened them the Kohler twins were standing before us. A third one with the same bright white hair and similar facial features stood beside them. He was smaller with more defined muscles, but held the same sneer. In the back of my mind, I recognized there had once been three of them.

"Friedricha," the larger boy acknowledged me scornfully.

My body, clearly reacting to the Fallen Ones, suddenly began to refocus. The pulsating sound of their beating hearts reached my ears. Unwashed, their stink filled my nose. My eyes moved rapidly to account for their weaponry and those items around them that they could use as weapons.

Calm now, I felt my core relax until all my muscles were pliable again and my racing heart had calmed. Then my limbs loosened and I was able to slip off the cloak I wore.

Then, as if it were merely a reflex, I felt something emerging from my back, directly between my shoulder blades. My shoulders arched forward slightly in habit, allowing them room. While my tunic had torn apart in the back, I noticed the front remained, fluttering lightly in the breeze. Purely by thought, I flapped my appendages, feeling the urge to stretch them wide, and they expanded out nearly the length of my own height and then settled into a composed position and ready for use.

"This…" I said to Eran, "is what I was going to tell you."

He didn't seem the least bit taken aback.

"Funny," he replied casually. "I was going to tell you the same thing…"

Then I watched as stark white wings appeared from behind him. While he had been composed when I exposed my secret, I could feel my astonishment taking hold as he revealed his secret.

"I never knew…" I heard myself say.

Eran responded without words. His expression, always confident, changed into an arrogant smirk.

The sight of it took my breath away.

"Kohlers," Eran turned his attention to the twins. "It's a bold move for you to return here. Your names and faces are on everyone's mind. They're intent on justice."

"And as you can see," I said, "there are hundreds of them."

"They are peasants..." the boy replied with disdain. "They won't be able to touch us...and they surely won't be able to help you."

Eran chuckled arrogantly. "We won't need their help."

The Kohler twins now had their wings out and had lifted off the ground. Eran and I met them in midair, taking a few tree branches with us. Amidst the snap of wood and hideous animalistic grunts by the twins, I was able to position myself against the girl while Eran took on the two boys.

What I noticed instantly was the lightning fast speed I had in responding to her movements. It made my body on earth feel sluggish, restrained in comparison. I deflected or avoided each of her advances as if I already knew where she would be moving. Regardless, the girl was quick. Only her endurance failed her. With her wings working hard, her breathing became labored within minutes.

It gave me time to look for Eran. He was defending himself against the boys, and doing it well, but I didn't know the limits of his endurance.

Our fight took us farther into the fields, away from camp. I caught sight of Eran and realized that his fight had done the same. The girl and I were tumbling against the ground now, spraying dirt and dried grass but I felt no pain. The adrenaline rushing through me denied it.

Deep inside this body, as I watched it fight so efficiently against our enemy, I could sense that I was searching for her ultimate weakness, one that would incapacitate her.

We broke free, each dropping to the earth, crouching, ready for the next advance. Her eyes flickered, noticing something behind me. Immediately after, her wings pumped once and she was lifted directly into the sky where she spun and soared away at full speed. Another joined her in the air, though it struggled as it was now missing a wing, and they fled over the hillside.

I turned back to find Eran standing over the smaller boy where the boy's head was twisted at an improper angle and his wings were sinking back into his body.

Eran was staring over his shoulder at me but then quickly rotated on his heel and sprinted in my direction, his expression turning to fear.

Only then did I notice the blood streaming down my forehead, drenching my hair. I had been wounded, I realized in a state of shock. I lifted my arms to meet Eran but he never reached me.

I was yanked through another tunnel and entered my body at the end of my life. Still whirling from my previous encounter, it took some time before I became aware that I no longer felt the energy of my youth. It had been replaced with fatigue as I had to put effort in to the simplest actions, such as breathing and keeping my eyes open. The bed I laid on was uneven, awkward, but that didn't bother me. I was surrounded by family and friends, with one being most familiar to me.

Eran leaned over me, his dark hair now gray, his handsome face no more lessened by the wrinkles he'd acquired. "How are you feeling?" he asked, again in German.

Unable to answer him, the weight of my body pressing me down, I simply smiled.

"Are you sure you have the strength to finish?"

I found the power to smile again.

He stared down at me, shaking his head in wonder, his affectionate eyes encapsulating me. "I don't understand why you put this on yourself…"

Alert to the fact that I was about to try and argue, he diverted it by waving on a woman behind him.

She wished to send a message to her brother who had died during the wars. The man behind her had a message for his mother. The family behind him longed to tell their grandfather about their prosperity. The line leading out the door slowly diminished until the last customer had given me her message for delivery.

Eran returned, leaning over me with a wet sponge, dabbing my brow, cooling my fever.

He wiped back tears and cleared his throat, and I craved for the strength to hold and comfort him.

"I-I have a confession to make. It's a secret I kept not knowing how...how you would react." He paused to swallow hard before continuing. "The night we met...on that road outside your family's house...You were not a stranger to me."

I felt my eyes widen.

"Don't mistake me...I truly didn't know it was you beneath your cloak then. That was...a pleasant surprise...because...we had never been introduced. I knew of you from afar. I had heard of you practicing, training, before you came here...before you fell. I was amazed by you back then...enamored..." he chuckled at himself, "like a school boy. But here, after spending a lifetime by your side...you are so much more than I imagined." His tone became desperate, vehement. "You are all I care about. Nothing else matters."

The urge to tell him that I felt the very same way was strong but I failed in trying. I knew my time was close.

As if sensing this, he leaned in, gently placing his mouth next to my ear. "I'll see you soon," he whispered and released an aching, quivering sigh. "But it won't be soon enough."

The last thing I felt was his tears fall against my cheek and I was yanked away.

A moment later, I was again standing in the Hall of Records, still holding my scroll between my hands. Glancing down at the fluid paper fluttering in my hands, it all seemed trivial when compared to what I had just experienced. Unable to move, I stared at the pockets along the wall without actually seeing them, Eran's words repeating in my mind.

Those words didn't fade even as I replaced my scroll in its pocket. I climbed down and decided to wait on a bench in the hall until I felt the familiar pull back to my bed in New Orleans.

It came but not before I acknowledged that the visits through my past lives would likely prove to be more difficult than I'd anticipated.

10. LONDON, ENGLAND

"Thank you for telling me," Eran was saying. His voice was distant, coming from across my balcony.

I opened my eyes to find him standing with Campion beneath the morning sun, and I instantly felt cheerful. He'd come back again.

"I appreciate you keeping me informed," said Eran.

"Yes, sir," Campion responded.

I watched their interaction, realizing that Campion must have told him about our dinner meeting.

Eran clapped Campion on the shoulder and they entered the room. Seeing me awake, he told Campion to meet us downstairs and Eran approached me, his demeanor content.

"Welcome back," he said, taking a seat on the edge of my bed since this had become his tradition. He watched me and then tilted his head. "Do you have something on your mind?"

"No...No. I think Campion has probably said it all." I couldn't imagine him leaving out any important details. "Do you have anything to tell me?" I hinted about his ventures out during the night. "Any ideas who came after us in the cemetery?"

His face fell and he became visibly uncomfortable. "Nothing is confirmed yet. I'm going out again tonight."

"All right," I replied, staring in to the face of the man who I'd seen tearing up at my death bed a few minutes earlier. He was now relaxed, at peace. It all felt so surreal.

"Are you sure you have nothing to tell me?"

"Nope," I replied. I wanted to keep that remembrance to myself.

"All right," he said unsure. "By the way, you'll have a busy day in The Square. It's sunny outside." He nodded towards the now closed French doors.

"Then we'd better get started," I said, swinging my legs off the bed.

"Yes, we'd better," he agreed lightheartedly with a chuckle. It was a nice contrast to our last interaction together.

Eran was correct. I was kept busy at The Square. Not only did I need to relay return messages to those I'd delivered the night before but I took new messages for delivery with the agreement that the customers would return the following weekend when I returned to The Square.

Occasionally, I would search for Eran in the crowd and find him perusing the other vendors' tables or reading the newspaper in the shade. I knew, however, that these were just acts. He would never divert his attention from the task of keeping me safe. I knew this now more than ever.

I found myself thinking about my time in Germany and then forward to my first session with Ms. Beedinwigg tonight, wondering how she would train me for protection against the Fallen Ones. Though I couldn't comprehend how she would do it, I trusted Ms. Beedinwigg that she knew what she was doing. I had to…for everyone's sake.

Eran and I rode home together at sunset and I began to realize that I wasn't irritable about his aloofness towards me. I understood now. My desire to be close to him hadn't faded and we sat just as close at the dinner table as we usually did; but I noticed the feeling of rejection dissipating by knowing why he chose to be so aloof towards me.

Before he left for the night, I whispered to him, "See you in the morning."

He was pleasantly impressed with the change in me. "Yes, you will."

I watched him ascend into the night and then Campion and I took my bike to Mr. Hamilton's residence across the city. The house was dark with the exception of the porch light that cast a hazy orange glow across the doorway and columns.

Alfred met us at the door, just as before, wearing another proper butler uniform and reserved expression.

"Good evening, Alfred," I said, entering the house, noticing how it was so quiet. If it weren't for the furniture and artwork, I would have second guessed that anyone still lived there.

"Ms. Tanner," Alfred replied once the door was closed and we were standing in the large foyer. "Ms. Beedinwigg awaits you below."

He escorted us to the hallway where Ms. Beedinwigg had exposed the hidden staircase and pushed the same space on the wall. The wall swung open and we descended the stairs, finding that the lights were on and Ms. Beedinwigg was in the process of checking her equipment.

"Ms. Beedinwigg," I called out, letting her know we'd arrived as Campion took a seat on a folding chair against the wall.

"Welcome," she said complacently without looking up. She then strolled across the room towards us, her long dress almost catching on the edge of the machines as she approached.

Once reaching me, she stopped and surveyed what I was wearing. "Your biker boots may be a problem."

"These are all I wear," I said appalled at the idea of changing them.

"Then you'll have to make due," she stated. "I need to get myself ready."

I'd expected her to climb the staircase and return a few minutes later but she never took a single step. She proceeded to strip off her clothes, revealing a skintight leather suit beneath it, and slip the glasses over her head to place them on the table next to her dress. Lastly, she unwound her bun, allowing her auburn hair to fall down her back and over her shoulders.

Standing before me now, I saw her for what she was…a warrior.

I then glanced back at Campion who gave me a nod of approval.

"So," she said appearing not to notice my exchange with Campion, "are you ready to learn to fight?"

My eyebrows rose. "Never been more so."

She smiled briefly, turned and entered the practice room. "What do you know about the Fallen Ones?"

I followed her while answering. "They look like us but they each have unique superhuman abilities."

"And?" she persisted.

"And these abilities give them unique defenses. What kills one doesn't necessarily kill the other."

"Good." She seemed pleased. "What else?"

"They're strategic. They don't act on impulse."

"Correct. Most have been here for hundreds of years. They have all the time in the world."

She was leading me through one of the aisles of equipment, though she was no longer inspecting them. "What else can you tell me?"

I shrugged. "They don't know what our defenses are either."

"That's right," said Ms. Beedinwigg, spinning to face me. "And we'll be working that to our advantage. Now…did you visit your past lives last night?"

"One of them," I said following her.

"Visit them all," she instructed. "Each lifetime you will learn how to kill a Fallen One or, at the very least, maim them. You will also learn how they kill. Learn their ways, what makes them weak, vulnerable, and use that knowledge in battle."

"I will," I promised.

"Now…I know from Mr. Warden's records of you at school that you have no defensive training so we will start with the basics," she informed me. "Strength, flexibility, cardiorespiratory…balance."

We had reached the far corner of the room where a piece of equipment had been created, running the length of the wall. She ushered me towards it and I stepped up to the opening, noticing the pulleys, levers, and platforms crisscrossing my route.

"I'll need to assess your abilities. Make it through as best you can. I'll be waiting for you on the other side with my stopwatch. It may be a little challenging in the beginning," she warned. Then, without any real warning, she shouted, "Go!"

Her forewarning turned out to be an understatement.

I raced into the contraption as fast as my body could take me, surprising even myself at my dexterity, using overhead bars to pull myself above ground obstacles. It turned out the course grew more challenging the farther in I reached, becoming an obstacle course with rapid triggers. Each time I landed, my foot activated a sideswiping board; every beam I used to balance myself set off a tripping mechanism aimed at my feet. I couldn't touch anything without causing a reaction. At the end, panting and dizzy, I found that she and Campion were frowning.

"You'll improve. Muscle memory," she explained, "will help your muscles to react spontaneously, in reflex when needed."

She then led me to a circular board large enough for two people to stand on. Because a ball was anchored in the center at the bottom of the board it tilted to the side, resting one end on the ground.

"I'm going to show you combat techniques now and I want you to use them to defend yourself on the board, so you'll need to commit them to memory."

After a brief overview, she stepped on the board and pointed to the opposite edge. The moment both my feet were planted on it, it began to wobble but this didn't seem to affect her. On the other hand, as she threw her punches and kicks, I ended up on the ground more often than on the board.

By the end of the session, I was bruised and exhausted.

"Rest up," she said, escorting us to the front door. "I'll see you tomorrow in class and we begin again in the evening."

That's right, I thought miserable at the realization. I had school tomorrow and I wasn't sure how my body was going to get through it.

"And Maggie..." she added. "Keep visiting your past lives. It may be tough at times but you'll appreciate the knowledge they can give you."

"Right...London tonight," I muttered to myself.

"The Black Plaque," she said, again amazing me at how much she knew of my past. "That will be particularly grueling."

"Looking forward to it," I replied sarcastically upbeat.

She gave me a sympathetic smile and then watched as we reached my bike and took off for our house.

That night, I didn't need Campion's help getting to sleep. It dominated me the moment I pulled the covers up and within seconds I found myself in the Hall of Records. Without wasting any time, I pulled my scroll from its pocket and found the next name in my span of lifetimes. Moving my finger over the name Anna Willowsby yanked me in the same method as the night before, into the body I used during my lifetime in London, England.

I found myself walking a long hallway lined with doors beside a man in an unkempt white coat. His hair and face were dirty and his eyes were tired, keeping watch on the nurses racing along the hallway passed us.

I sensed but, again did not have the motor control to confirm it, that Campion and Eran walked behind me.

"Our nuns have fallen ill," the man was saying to me. "We are unable to care for the dying, much less those who are arriving each day. There appears to be no end to this...this disease."

I placed my hand on the man's shoulder, hoping he would find some consolation from it.

He choked back a sob, recovered, and continued. "Relatives are abandoning their loved ones. Lawyers refuse to visit the sick and draw their wills. Mortuaries, monasteries, hospitals, ours included, are overwhelmed..." He paused and, eyes filled with tears, turned to me. "You are the messenger for the dead, correct?"

"Yes," I replied meekly.

He slumped forward, shaking his head, helpless and desperate. "Life after death...I've always considered to be fictitious, a fabrication the ill cling to when death arrives. It is in direct conflict with all that I believe...all that I've learned. Yet, I stand here, having called for you, to ask for your help." He stifled a sob. "If you can truthfully speak to the dead...ask them..." he pleaded, "what on this earth is killing us..."

He opened the door that we stood before to find the bodies of the dead lining the vast room beyond, so many that some were without sheets. On the ones closest to us, I caught sight of the black spots and swellings that had become known as key symptoms of this plague.

Noises came from Eran and Campion behind me, neither of which was comforting.

The doctor continued, his voice breaking, "Ask the dead so that we may save ourselves from extinction."

Terror rose in me, my heart thudded in my chest, and my body trembled uncontrollably. I pushed these reactions back but I couldn't fight the weeping. My eyes scanned the bodies again and I screamed "Fleas!" Yet, no one heard me, my mouth did not move, and no sound emerged. I realized that back then, when I occupied this body that I was seeing through now that no one knew it was the flea-infested rats transmitting the plague, myself included.

"I will, doctor," I heard myself mutter, swallowing back my tears. "And I will bring you the answer."

Still despondent, yet with a small glimmer of hope in his eyes, he closed the door.

Suddenly, I was yanked away and deposited again in my body sometime in the recent future.

Night was arriving quickly now. The shadows were creeping longer, like gnarled fingers reaching for each other and intertwining across the city. Dampness clung throughout the narrow cobblestone streets, aided by a thick fog that had begun to roll in from the River Thames. Along the streets, windows were now lit with flickering yellow candles warding off the darkness and the cold. In the distance, harsh coughs mingled with the howls of loved ones lost to the mysterious condition overtaking London.

As I turned the corner, my feet scuffed across the stones making a noise that I knew was too loud. I kept the flap of my cloak tightly wound to me, doing my best to minimize my appearance. I was just five feet tall but even at that height I was too conspicuous. Ducking lower, I kept moving. My eyes scanned the buildings ahead of me, and as best I could, behind and to the sides. I hadn't seen them yet but there were still a few streets to go before I reached my destination.

A howl rose above the rooftops and I stopped. It was a sound familiar to me and it caused the hair at the back of my neck to stand up. My hands began to shake and small beads of perspiration rose up from my brow.

It was close. Very close.

I began to run, paying special attention to quieting my footsteps as I made my way through the labyrinth of London's corridors.

The street that would take me to safety was only a few yards away and then my skin prickled worse on the back of my neck, the hair there standing straight out now.

Glancing up I found it perched on the roof of the building ahead. What appeared to be claws dug into the edge, its body cocooned in thick, black wings. Its head was tilted down so that it could watch me better.

I didn't stop this time. My pace became a sprint and suddenly the gas lamps dimly lighting each side of the street blended in to one and the moist air on my exposed face collected and fell like raindrops down my cheeks.

The thing gave a brief shudder – a sign of excitement at the prospect of murder – and unraveled its broad wings. With a single pump, the wings lifted it into the night sky. It hovered for only a moment and then dove towards the earth, towards me. It made no sound other than the wind whistling over its fluttering wings.

We were now on a collision course unless one turned and fled the other direction. This, I knew, would not happen.

Fleeing, at this point, was not an option. I leaned forward, the balls of my feet barely touching the ground as I increased my speed.

I looked at my attacker, watching as a wicked smile of stained, jagged teeth stretched beneath its gleaming, eager eyes. My own eyes were now narrowed, mustering every conceivable prowess I had in me. I would need it.

The collision never came.

From a side street emerged a movement so blindingly fast it was indistinguishable. The winged being and my defender slammed into a building wall, becoming a mesh of entangled limbs, crumbling brick dislodging from the force.

"Eran," I screamed, though it came out a whisper.

"Stay…back…Magdalene," he struggled to warn me.

Without thought, I tore the cloak from my shoulders and joined the fight.

My wings had already surfaced and were being used to stabilize my assault. I attacked from the side, again noticing how this body's swift and powerful capability was far beyond anything I'd experienced on earth.

A grunt escaped from it on impact and I felt somewhat satisfied.

I prepared for another strike only to realize that Eran was maneuvering it away from me.

I sighed in frustration. This was as much my fight as it was his.

Their bodies were now tumbling along the side of the wall, leaving indents in the brick structure. I trailed them looking for an angle in the blending of bodies and limbs.

Eran struck it from all angles, pummeling it with such speed that I couldn't deny the admiration I felt. His attack was so fluid that I never saw his final maneuver coming.

They had nearly reached the end of the building when it released a dazed groan.

Eran took that moment to spring off the wall to a lamppost behind him, breaking off the encasing, shards of glass shattering to the street below.

He was suddenly on the beast again, pressing it against the wall.

His fingers, wrapped around the burning metal fixture, shoved it into its heart and penetrating so deep Eran's arm was lost inside it.

Instantly it was engulfed in fire, falling to the street below. It landed with a thud, bent forward, flames licking the sky until its body turned to dust seconds later.

Eran, barely panting, turned to me. "Are you hurt?" He flapped once to land beside me where his wings retracted.

"I'm fine," I nodded woodenly, lowering myself to the ground.

My wings sank into my back then. I noticed they felt like soft, uneven limbs, as if they were simply my arms withdrawing into my body, while the area where they had emerged tingled slightly.

"What are you doing here?"

"You don't sound happy to see me," he feigned offense.

"Of-Of course I am," I said, not wanting him to even consider it. "It's just that I haven't seen you in so long."

"Since you fell," he agreed.

"That's right. So I'm wondering why you are here now."

"You were in danger."

I felt like we were doing a verbal dance around the actual truth.

Sighing, I said, "I mean that you came to my rescue as if you were my guardian. I'm slightly confused."

He smirked lightly. "I can see that."

"Eran…" I started to grow angry.

"William," he corrected. "My name is William this time."

I rolled my eyes. "All right, William…are you going to tell me why you are here?"

"I have the instinct that you won't like what I'm going to say."

"Tell me anyways," I demanded.

He moaned and ran his fingers through his now untidy hair. How could he look so handsome after such a virulent fight?

"I came to your rescue because I am now your designated guardian," he announced slowly as if he was hesitant to speak the words.

"Designated guardian? I've never had one before and I certainly don't need one now," I said, picking up my cloak and started down the street towards home.

He followed my quick pace effortlessly. "Have you considered that I might actually be of some assistance?" he replied plainly.

I ignored that suggestion. "Who appointed you as my guardian?" I spun around, borderline incensed.

"I volunteered," he answered calmly, watching me closely.

My shoulders slumped and I shook my head, bewildered. "But why? I can take care of myself."

"If you're asking me to quit I won't," he countered. "It's not in my nature." That was a commendable trait to have in a guardian, I knew. In fact, he would be a fine guardian. He was alert, skillful in combat, understood our enemies. More so, he was a cerebral fighter. He thought through his actions and then executed them in the precise, rapid sequence in which he'd planned.

The truth was I rejected his offer as my guardian knowing that our relationship as such would prevent us from ever being more…and I wanted more, much more.

He stepped forward, closing the gap between us, causing the excitement in me to turn from anger to anticipation. "I can see that you can take care of yourself.

I've known you for some time now. But in the case that I am present and your enemy is present…I might be of some help," he offered.

"Listen," I said, avoiding his striking blue-green eyes or I'd be unable to finish my thought. "I could have defended myself back there…I was ready to defend myself. Now I don't mean to dismiss your position as my guardian but if I am attacked or if I have the opportunity to attack I won't be compelled to wait for you."

He leaned back, a smile lying beneath the surface. "Now what makes you think I'll be late?"

"I don't know. Maybe you will, maybe you won't. I simply want to set the ground rules now. And while we are on the topic," I continued without allowing him to respond. I needed him to understand how I envisioned our new relationship to be. "I will not rely on you to protect me, I will not reject a fight, I will not cower from my enemies, and I will not flee. I will use the abilities I know…combat abilities…if the need should arise."

"I would expect nothing less. Any more ground rules I should be aware of?" He seemed to be taking this lightheartedly, which frustrated me.

"I want to make it very clear…"

"You don't require a guardian," he finished my sentence.

"That's correct. I do not."

"I understand."

"Good."

We stood facing each other, both uncertain on what to do next.

"I'm glad we've made that clear," he implied.

"Yes," I responded firmly.

From inside this body, I stood in awe. I had just witnessed the very moment that Eran had become my guardian.

Without warning, I was again yanked away and deposited into my body later in this life. I knew this because I was now inside a carriage racing down a rutted path, aggressively jostling me from side to side. I nearly slipped off my seat and Eran responded instantly with a helping hand and a humorous smile. Campion sat beside him, appearing as if he were actually enjoying the ride.

As we seemed to turn down a smoother path, I peered out the curtained window to find that we had just reached the outskirts of an estate. The grounds were impeccably manicured and the manor house ahead was impressively designed. Apparently it had just rained as the air smelled damp and everything I saw seemed to shine.

The carriage pulled up to the main entrance and stopped at the feet of a young man. He opened the door and we stepped down to follow him inside.

The manor was well appointed with paintings of the family lineage mounted down the hallways, stained glass windows detailing family victories, and light shades covered in jewels.

We reached a study where a man stood, smoking a pipe and gazing into the flames at the hearth where he stood. His mood appeared somber as if something was troubling him.

"Mr. Snowdon…your guests have arrived," said the young man before closing the door behind us.

"Come…Come in," the man welcomed, motioning for us to enter the room and to take a seat on one of the luxurious chairs where he also then sat. Campion remained near the door while Eran sat beside me. I had the sense that he was staying close as a measure of protection though we all seemed to be at ease with our host.

"Have you been well," asked the man.

"As good as can be expected," I replied. "And you?"

"Winter is approaching but the disease appears to be lulling." He turned his eyes towards the hearth, his expression pensive. "This is good."

Eran and I nodded our agreement.

"A doctor in the city has concluded it was initially transmitted by rats…until it spread to the people."

Eran glanced at me, knowingly, before inferring, "That is the conclusion we've all come to."

"Catherine didn't fall ill from rats," he declared. "It was the chambermaid who brought it back from the city." It was easy to detect the blame in his tone and I thought a change of subject may help redirect his thoughts.

"How is your daughter feeling?" I asked gently.

"The cloths we wear over our faces frighten her." He swallowed. "I'm-I'm afraid…that Catherine's time is near."

"I'm terribly sorry."

"Mrs. Snowdon…She's not accepting this well. With Beverly having already been taken from us…"

My chest swelled then at the pity I felt for them. It wasn't fair for any family to endure what they had.

Mr. Snowdon appeared to overcome the undisclosed thoughts afflicting him and lifted his eyes back to us. "Thank you for coming."

"Certainly…of course…"

"I understand you've been making other house calls…delivering messages for my neighbors as well," he surmised.

"Yes, we have."

"I'm sure they appreciate your help," he said weakly.

"I do hope so. Did you want to send another message to Beverly?" I proposed.

"No…" He turned his head back to the fire, his eyes again glossing over in a daze. "No, I called you here for another reason."

Out of the corner of my eye I saw Eran bristle.

Then the hair on the back of my neck stood up, pulling vigorously at my skin. "William…" my voice said, addressing him by his name in this lifetime, sounding distracted and in terror.

He was already on his feet, his wings were extended, and Mr. Snowdon was bowing back over the arm of his chair in fear of Eran.

My own fear had rapidly turned to panic but was now intentionally being submersed by a wave of calm. I had closed my eyes against it, drawing in a deep breath, allowing my body to relax. Instantly, my senses came alive. I smelled the alcohol used for sterilization drift through the room. I felt a cool breeze making its way into the house from a crack in the wall. Most of all, I heard the wings of those coming for us beating the air, fast and rhythmic, and rapidly approaching. When I reopened my eyes, I found Campion now hovering above us, his wings also extended, facing the windows in preparation.

"They're here," my voice stated with absolute composure.

Then the windows exploded inward, spraying shards of glass at us, shredding the drapery and destroying the wall tapestries.

Only Mr. Snowdon ducked.

The rest of us faced our enemies.

The three attackers entered the room and lingered, wings outstretched, each one teaming up with Eran, Campion, and myself.

Although they were familiar to me, it was Eran who addressed them.

"Abaddon," he said, almost cordially, to the one directly in front of him.

The man responded with a brush of his long, oily hair from his shoulder, his scowl never wavering and his narrowed eyes never widening.

"I see you've convinced Sarai to follow you," said Eran nodding towards the Indian girl with flowing hair the color of coffee and exquisitely smooth swarthy skin. "Did you inform your daughter that she'd be living an eternity of retribution?"

Sarai opened her mouth to speak but Eran didn't allow for it. "Elam, however, I'm not surprised by." He glanced towards the genteel, older man who was facing Campion. "You always were a follower."

"I'm sorry," Mr Snowdon unexpectedly screamed in dread. "They-They promised to help save my daughter." His repentance complete, he returned to cringing in the outer corner of the stone hearth.

Without turning away, Eran informed him, "The only help they can offer your daughter, Mr. Snowdon, is to kill her and condemn her to the same fate as they face…incarceration in the worst kind of prison or absolute and eternal death. By agreeing to this deception you have affectively ensured your daughter never visits heaven again."

"No…no," he demanded but a fleeting look at Abaddon told him the truth.

The comprehension spreading across Mr. Snowdon's face was clear just before he released a horrified whimper and ran from the room.

Someone moved then although I couldn't tell you who and the room became a battleground. My own actions, unrestrained by the limitations of being a human, again were so fast I nearly became a blur. In this body, with its powerful wings and extraordinary abilities, it was hard to see how I could be defeated.

These Fallen Ones, however, helped me understand my susceptibility.

Sarai and I met in midair, colliding with such force that we spun several times before I ended up against the opposite wall.

She grinned wickedly, as if she'd gotten the best of me. That, I was not going to allow happen.

I shoved back from the wall and across the room, barely missing Eran who was expertly inflicting his own harm on Abaddon.

I had Sarai by the shoulders, her wings positioned outward in an attempt to slow her backward thrust. It didn't help and she collided with the fireplace mantle, crumbling it in to pieces.

Her body shook violently as if it had gone into a spasm and I could hear popping coming from inside her. Her body straightened and I realized that she had just repaired the bones she'd broken against the mantle. She rolled her shoulders then, opened her eyes, and smirked at me from beneath her lashes.

"My turn," she seethed.

Suddenly I was spinning backwards, hitting the ceiling and then the floor. They came in rotating thumps as she flip flopped me back across the room. Again, I ended up against the wall but this time my right arm dangled awkwardly at my side. I lifted it directly outward, smiled tauntingly at Sarai, and snapped it back in place without feeling any pain whatsoever.

"That felt good," I told her. "But this will feel better."

I drew back the same arm, closed my hand in to a fist, and flew forward, propelling my entire being towards her. I connected with her face a second later and watched her slide back through the air, limbs outstretched.

Elam caught her from the side, scooped her up, and fled out the window. Campion followed closely behind until they had disappeared from the room.

What happened next I never saw coming.

My body stiffened, refusing to move. It was as if I'd been placed in cement. As I was realizing this something moved passed me, inches away, and was gone. It twisted at the corner of the room and ducked out the nearest broken window and into the night. Eran stayed close behind it, repeatedly reaching for its feet and narrowly missing it until it was no longer in sight.

Eran floated at the broken window, ensuring that none would return, and then spun around.

His eyes searched for me, landing seconds later at my torso. What I saw in him next shook me to my core.

Terror crossed his face only to swiftly be replaced with rage.

He released a roar that vibrated the room, rattling the fireplace pokers and knocking books against one another.

Then he was at my side, gentle and consoling.

I couldn't understand his sudden change in behavior until I was overtaken by an incredible, pulsating pain.

It came from my abdomen but, being unable to control my head movement, I had no ability to look down in search of the cause. Instead, I heard Eran talking to me.

"Look at me, Magdalene. Look at me," he commanded.

I did and found his eyes wide, apprehensive.

"You'll be fine," he said, anxiously. "We'll get you to a doctor…the one in the city…the one you informed about the rats…"

Campion came up behind him with the same dreaded expression. "There isn't enough time."

"There is," Eran snarled.

I wanted to believe Eran but the pain told me that Campion was correct.

"Lay me down," I murmured, unable to raise my voice, the pain sapping my energy.

My wings retracted and he carried me to the middle of the room that was now in shambles, using one hand to flip a couch right-side up.

"Mr. Snowdon will be shocked at our redecorating," I commented, hoping to conjure a smile.

Eran simply stared at my torso. I knew he was using his innate ability, one that he had brought with him to earth, to view inside me and assess the damage Abaddon had done. Judging from his expression, it was significant. I could already feel the warmth of my blood covering me, running down my legs.

"He froze my movement," I whispered, referring to one of the traits Abaddon had brought with him to earth. "He got to me, Eran."

Eran nodded, frantically moving his eyes along my body in search of an answer to heal me. "I know…I know…"

"You understand what that means," I stated as tenderly as I could.

He hadn't considered it. He had been focused on my wound, on the pain I was enduring. He hadn't yet considered the consequences of what had just happened.

Campion gasped. "Eternal death."

I gave Eran a wavering smile, gathered my strength and reached for his hand. He took and squeezed it, holding it against his chest in agony.

"No," he said fiercely. "No, I won't allow it."

"It's not up to you," I said gently.

In return, Eran trembled, refusing to believe what was happening. He was always in control, could foresee nearly any outcome. This…my impending eternal death…he could not accept.

"I can do something," he assured. "There must be something…"

Then our eyes met and we came to the same conclusion at once but it was Campion who voiced it.

"You can take her life so she can avoid eternal death at the hands of a Fallen One…" he reflected. "It's the only way to save her existence…"

"I'm sor-sorry," I gasped. The abject horror lingering in Eran's face impacted me far worse than the pain Abaddon had inflicted. There was nothing in the world more sickening.

He released a ragged breath and for the first time since I'd known Eran I saw absolute fear in him. "I just never thought it would come...that I would ever need..." his voice trailed off.

"I'll understand if you're..." I cringed against the throbbing, "...if you're unable-"

His face tightened then and I saw the confident, motivated Eran that I knew so well return. "Campion, your sword," he ordered.

The weapon landed firmly in Eran's hand a second later.

Our gaze never broke as he took the handle and raised the sword above my chest, the tip of the blade pointing down.

I wheezed against the blood now filling my lungs, unable to speak my thoughts. Neither was Eran capable of speech. Knowing this, our eyes conveyed our thoughts.

Both shaking, flooded with emotion, we said the very same silent words, "I love you..."

The blade then drove down into my chest, disappearing from my sight. I never felt it enter my body. I was limited only to the pain of witnessing the absolute despair Eran endured taking my life.

Then I was wrenched away, flung down the tunnel, and out of my past life.

11. ELSIC

I awoke the next day more tired than when I had gone to sleep, something I attributed to the devastation of watching Eran slay me.

Lying in bed, I realized that while these visits to my past lives had given me a better understanding of what to expect from the Fallen Ones, I was also learning more than I ever thought possible about Eran. I couldn't calculate all that he had sacrificed for me. It was immeasurable. More than simply being caught here, without access to the familiarity or comforts of the afterlife, Eran had given up his innocence to protect me. Last night, when he had plunged the sword into my chest, told me so.

Beneath the covers, I still quivered at the realization.

"Chilly?" Eran's voice came to me from across the room. It was coddling and comforting in comparison to the horror of just a few minutes earlier.

He was already drawing another blanket from the closet, his expression blank, having no idea what I'd just experienced.

As he reached the bed, he paused. "No...you're not chilly," he stated apprehensive.

I sat up and sighed heavily.

"Do you want to talk about it?" he asked sincerely, sitting at the edge of the bed.

I shook my head. Talking about it would mean reliving it in my mind and I was already working on blocking those images. "School today..." I muttered. "We need to get ready."

He evaluated me without moving, knowing something was wrong and that I was keeping it from him. Yet, I reasoned that there was no sense in recounting the horrific memory to him.

He'd already lived it.

I stood up to begin my morning routine, Eran's eyes following me around my room until I left to start the shower.

When I returned, he was gone making the room feel vacant. The floorboards squeaked across the hall and I knew he was also getting ready for school.

Without much thought to it, I left my room and pushed open his door. He turned in the middle of the room and I was momentarily distracted. His windblown hair had been brushed now and his clothes were changed. Wearing a tight white t-shirt and blue jeans he looked like a young James Dean, just as wild and unpredictable.

I crossed the floor and lifted my arms around him, pulling myself into him. He welcomed me, the firmness of his body pressing against mine.

I laid my head on his chest and breathed in his fresh, earthy scent. "How can I repay you for all you do for me?"

"Repay me?" he asked bewildered. "Where is this coming from?"

I shrugged against his body, having no answer for him.

Inhaling deeply, he laid his chin lightly on my head. "You feel guilty but I'm not sure why. Everything I've done...ever...has been by my decision, by my judgment

139

alone. Don't take on the burden of my choices, Magdalene. They aren't for you to resolve."

He pulled me away from him, grasping me by the shoulders and ducking to view my downturned face.

"I regret nothing, Magdalene. Nothing. Because all of it...every decision I've made has led me to you and kept me with you...and that is all that matters to me." He paused. "Please look up."

I followed his request, slowly, and noticed he was just as handsome puzzled.

"I don't think you're taking in to account what you've done for me..."

I frowned. "Run you ragged...test your resolve...leave you frustrated..."

"Yes, all those," he said joking, his mouth tilting in a half-smile. "You give me life, Magdalene. Every moment I am with you I feel alive. Without you there is no color, no humor, absolutely no joy in existing. Life...is what you give me. Staying...is what you do for me."

He groaned and pulled me towards him and before I knew it his lips were on mine. It was a hard, passionate kiss and the thrill of it drew me out of my daze. I leaned in, wanting more. Sensing this, his arms fell from my shoulders and slipped around my waist as his kiss deepened.

After what seemed far too short of a time, he drew back and reviewed me as if I were a sculpture. "Yes, I believe that did the trick to shake you out of your mood..."

"Eran," I hissed. "Don't tell me that you didn't enjoy it too..."

"Oh no...I never said that," he replied with his traditional smirk. "I enjoyed that very much."

I scowled playfully at him and then spun around and headed back to my room to finish getting ready. I began to smile then, a complete reversal. Somehow, Eran always knew what to say and do to make me feel better. It must be, I deduced, because of all we'd gone through, the wonderful and the horrible.

We met again downstairs in the kitchen where Felix was impressing Campion with his escargot omelets, while Rufus looked on successfully subduing his disgust. Ezra sat behind her newspaper, sipping coffee, and ignoring the scene at the stove.

"You should try these," Campion suggested, taking a forkful of egg and snails.

His wide, encouraging eyes could not convince us though.

"I think we're going to treat ourselves to coffee and beignets before school," Eran informed them. "Café du Monde?" he said to me.

"Great idea," I replied and then caught sight of Felix's disappointment. "Although since we'll be missing out on the omelet...maybe you could save us one in the refrigerator?"

I was already certain it would end up down the sink disposal but the request seemed to appease Felix, who turned back towards the stove to cheerfully start another omelet. Eran and I headed out the back door but not before Eran winked his approval at my approach.

The ride through morning traffic was slow and we had only a few minutes before class started – biochemistry with Ms. Beedinwigg - but that wasn't what concerned me. As we moved through the streets my hair stood on end and then rested down repeatedly, similar to a static-laden brush nearing and pulling away from the hair on one's arm, except mine came with searing pain. The reaction, I knew, was towards the hidden Fallen Ones now entering the city.

I tried to hide the fact that I was feeling this way but the moment the bike stopped Eran turned to me. "More of them have arrived, haven't they?"

"Yes," I replied, getting off the bike while diligently scanning our surroundings.

"I could feel your responses as we passed them," said Eran also surveying the area.

I sighed, aggravated. "I'm still working on controlling my reaction."

"You'll get there," he reassured me. "How about we pick up those coffee and beignets and get to school?"

As we stepped into line, I noted that he seemed more relaxed now that he'd planted his army around us for additional protection. One thing hadn't changed though. He still refused to show any romantic interest in me while in public. This was incredibly dispiriting but I knew it would not change for fear that if the Fallen Ones knew of our feelings for each other they may decide to come after me simply to hurt Eran. Eran had been through more than enough. For this reason alone I fought back the urge to take Eran's hand and kept some distance from him until we'd eaten and were back on the bike. At that point, I was allowed to touch him or I'd fall off the bike while turning the corners. I was very thankful for the corners.

We reached school and made it into our seats just as the bell rang.

Ms. Beedinwigg was already at the front of the class, dressed in her usual drab dress and combat boots. Her hair was recoiled in a bun and her glasses again hung around her neck. This, I realized, was her camouflage. No one would ever suspect that she was an expert in combat.

She didn't address Eran or I throughout the class, instead concentrating on her lesson of lipids interaction with the body. There was absolutely no sign that she was part of a family hired to train me in defense.

Bridgette and Ashley, however, paid plenty of attention to us.

While Ashley stared emotionless and with trivial interest, Bridgette held a concentrated stare as if she were working out something in her mind.

Throughout the next hour, Bridgette glanced continually in our direction, irritating me more each time.

If Eran noticed, he didn't act on it. He kept his focus on Ms. Beedinwigg, never bothering with notes as he already knew it all.

It wasn't until after class did I learn what it was that bothered her.

At the bell, Ashley stood, slipped her laptop into its bag, and headed for the door. Bridgette, however, crossed the room towards Eran and me.

"Eran," she called out, smiling like a hunter who's just caught its prey. "Have you thought any more about participating in the prom?"

"No," he said flatly. His head was bowed down as he collected his book and notepad but I had the feeling he was avoiding her.

I didn't bother hiding my grin.

"Well, I'm holding on to hope," she joked, playfully tapping her finger against his shoulder.

"You may be holding on a long time," he replied plainly. "Magdalene, I'll be at the door."

"I'm right behind you," I said, unable to restrain my grin at this point even if I'd wanted to.

Then I turned and saw Bridgette's face.

She was my least favorite person out of a student body that hated me. I couldn't detect a single redeeming quality in her. Now, she was openly flirting with the love of my life. Yet still, after that single glance, I found sympathy for her.

The expression she held while watching Eran stroll away could be described in one word: dejected.

The hunter had turned into a child having been told no.

Then, as quickly as it had developed, my compassion for her dissolved.

As Eran reached the hall, and beyond earshot, she seized my arm.

Stunned, I tilted my head towards her. "Bridgette, release me," I said calmly.

"I see you leave with him every day…and then you ride up on your Toshiba-"

"Harley," I corrected her.

"Whatever…You show up with him each morning. You sit together at lunch. He walks you to your classes. What's going on? Are you two dating or not?"

It wasn't any of Bridgette's business, really. She had no right to know about us. Yet, every part of me wanted to tell the truth…that Eran and I had loved each other for centuries, a love that started in mutual respect and friendship and grown into an unconditional, absolute, and profound devotion to one another.

While that was my desire, I had to refrain. Telling her that we were in love would jeopardize our lives since Bridgette would never keep that kind of gossip to herself. The entire school would know by lunchtime and so would the Fallen Ones.

Bridgette waited impatiently for her answer so I gave her one.

"He's not interested in you," I said not really caring if she were offended or not. "You're only making a fool of yourself at this point…Look at the way he just behaved towards you and you'll see it."

Bridgette's face changed then as her memory rewound to the moments before. It became clear to her that she had been disrespected and her entire being seemed to darken.

I left her standing at my desk and met Eran at the door but not before peeking over my shoulder at her. She had her eyes on us, narrowed and brewing, and this time she didn't try to hide behind an artificial smile.

Now, she was a scorned woman.

Eran didn't ask about the discussion on the way to my next class. It seemed he already knew what had transpired without me needing to tell him. Personally, I was happy to ignore it too. Bridgette wasn't my preferred topic. Instead, I started the conversation on a more pleasant note and mentioned that my sculpting class had received their clay and today we would begin carving a chunk of it.

My anticipation and his enthusiasm for me lasted until we reached my classroom door. There, he gazed at me briefly and then started down the hall towards his class.

Neither one of us knew that my excitement would be short-lived.

Once inside, I chose my sculpting tools from a bin and took a seat on a tall stool in front of an even taller miniature desk. The clay was passed out by Ms. Johnson who explained the assignment as she circled the room.

"Art is self-expression. We must embrace that creativity, not deny it. Therefore, I'm giving you carte blanche authority over this clay. Create what you wish. Take a moment to envision what this block of clay will become. It has a purpose...It wants to be something. Listen to it. Allow it to tell you. Visualize it and then begin."

Following her instructions, I closed my eyes and the vision came to me. From that moment on, I could not recall a single thought or movement until she was standing over me. For an indeterminable amount of time nothing disrupted me. No voices, no scuffing of the stools against the concrete floor, no shuffling of notepads, absolutely nothing penetrated my awareness.

Then Ms. Johnson cleared her throat, shaking me from my trance.

"What are you doing, Ms. Tanner?" she demanded.

I blinked several times, trying to regain my consciousness.

"Do I need to ask it again?" she said, in a self-aggrandizing way.

"I-I don't know what you mean," I replied.

"That is what I mean." She pointed past my shoulder to the chunk of clay I'd been working on, although it was no longer a chunk.

What had started out as a large, gray brick was now an immaculately detailed rendering of what looked to be a Fallen One. It was perched on the board where the clay had sat, its feet positioned at the edge where its overgrown fingernails hung. Its mouth was open as if it were screaming exposing long and jagged teeth. Its wings were out, extending past the foot long board, and so defined that I'd carved its feathers in detail.

I recognized it instantly as my winged attacker during my time in London.

Taking a sweeping look at the others students' clay, I found that none of them had come close to what I'd done. Most were lopsided chairs, nondescript head busts, or warped logs meant to be something more.

All in all, what I'd accomplished, in a seemingly very short time, was remarkable. Ms. Johnson, however, did not feel the same way.

"Its hideous…Get it out of my class," she ordered before turning to the rest of the students. "I said make this clay your own…I did not say to take your under-indulged, juvenile, dungeons and dragons fantasy out on this innocent clay."

I should have been fuming at the way Ms. Johnson scolded me for, by all reasons that I could determine, an exemplary job. Yet, as I picked up the sculpture and left the class that was the last thing on my mind. I was immersed in trying to understand how I could have created this detailed and proportional replica of my enemy without any previous sculpting experience and without any recollection of actually doing so.

I was so deep in contemplation that it wasn't until I was halfway down the hall did I notice I wasn't alone.

The hair on the back of my neck tickled and gradually lifted to pull aggressively at the back of my neck.

Turning, I found Marco approaching me in the empty hallway, wearing his polo and khakis security uniform.

"Ms. Tanner," he said, mockingly. "Do you have a reason to be out of class?"

Focus, I told myself. Focus on something other than your reaction, control it or risk being unprepared if he tries anything.

Suddenly, like a curtain being drawn open, I noticed the world around me. I heard a teacher's voice through the walls as clearly as if I were standing in the very same room. She was lecturing on the Civil War. I smelled the mint bubblegum left on the door of a locker down the hall. I heard the static of the electronic signs mounted along the walls. Lastly, I noticed that the hair on the back of my neck was settling down enough to respond.

"Don't patronize me, Marco," I snapped. "Eran told me about you."

"He did?" said Marco, stepping closer. Too close. "So you know of our history together?"

"We have no history."

"Then he didn't tell you everything."

"I'm not going to play this game with you, Marco."

He moaned seductively. "I've missed the way you speak my name."

Instinctually, my lip curled up, repulsed.

"I can see that you haven't..." he pouted.

"No," Eran's voice, declarative and unyielding, came up behind me. "She hasn't."

I turned to find him marching up the hallway, drawing in my breath at the sight of him.

"You're testing my patience, Marco," Eran said irritably, stopping beside me and a small step ahead, blocking Marco from me.

Holding his ground, Marco refused to take a step back.

147

"What do you want with Magdalene?"

Marco shrugged. "Just catching up with an old flame…"

Unaffected at the jibe, Eran stepped forward, closing the gap between him and Marco. Their chests were nearly touching now. "Consider yourself caught up," said Eran, blatantly hinting for Marco to leave.

Marco appeared unflustered. "It doesn't seem like you've acknowledged it so I'm going to explain it to you…I'm the authority here. You're the student," said Marco, his tone foreboding.

Eran responded through tight lips, his anger heating up. "You have no authority."

"On the contrary…" said Marco sneering, "I could assign you to detention. That would leave dear Maggie exposed…vulnerable."

Eran chuckled contemptuously then. "You don't seriously think I would ever leave her alone?" His shoulders shook with quiet, ridiculing laughter. "You don't think I've left my army in the afterlife? Marco, they are all here…prepared to intervene if it becomes necessary…Eager for it, in fact."

Only then did Marco step back, fear floating across his face. Yet, he was still compelled to counter. "That may be the case but more of us are arriving each day. Attendance here has never been higher. Soon you will be outnumbered."

Eran smirked, radiating confidence. "I look forward to that."

Marco scoffed. "You have no idea what you're up against, what is headed your way. Revenge will be so rewarding…" He continued backing down the hallway until he was a safe distance and he could flee unharmed. "They'll be here sooner than you think."

After Marco disappeared around a corner, Eran turned to me, drawing in a deep breath. "I felt your radar go off," he explained.

"I figured," I said, now smiling. ""How did you get out of class?"

"Excused myself for the bathroom. And you?"

"Oh…me?" I scoffed, now slightly perturbed by Ms. Johnson. "I made my first sculpture…which I'm fairly proud of despite what it depicts." I lifted it to show Eran, noticing I'd squeezed the moist clay arm where I held it into an odd shape during my moment of panic.

Eran's face suddenly contorted, erasing any sign of encouragement and replacing it with concern.

"It's a Fallen One…" I explained, not understanding how he failed to distinguish it. "I mean, except for the teeth and fingernails."

"Those aren't fingernails," Eran said, tensely. "Those are claws."

"Sure, if you want to put a fine point on it…"

"No, Magdalene, they truly are claws."

I studied him. "What are you not telling me?"

"You've sculpted an Elsic, Magdalene."

"I'm sorry…A what?"

"An Elsic," said Eran, glancing around to ensure we were still alone before continuing his explanation. "Over the time Fallen Ones spend incarcerated, many of whom have been imprisoned for centuries, they change…they morph. Living underground, off each other, and only in the presence of pure evil they become darker, if you can imagine that. Their evil transforms them…They can no longer pass as humans, by appearance or by behavior. They're far too…" he paused to search for the best description, "sinister. It isn't simply their bodies or motives that transforms…It is their soul. They become so malevolent that those who die at the hands of an Elsic are sent to eternal death."

"Eternal death?" I asked. "I thought only Fallen Ones had that ability and that their ability only applied to me. You're saying these creatures...these Elsics have this ability too?"

"Yes, but with the Elsics, their ability applies to everyone, mortal or otherwise. As Fallen Ones, this power only applies to messengers...to you specifically. Yet, as they transform, their power develops, it increases to include all living things." He paused and then asked curiously, "How...How were you ever able to create their likeness when you haven't seen one?"

"I have seen one...in my past life...in London."

"You've been visiting your past lives?" he asked, suddenly alarmed.

"Segments of them, the more important times in those lives. That's how...That's how I saw the Elsic. I watched you kill one on a London street."

His gaze dropped as he nodded reflectively. "Yes, that one escaped from the prison. I remember it well." He drew in a breath and brought his eyes back to me. While mine were wide, his were pensive.

"Eran, is there a problem with me reviewing my past lives?"

Eran's face contorted into a multitude of emotions from trepidation to sorrow to compliance. I got the distinct feeling his mind was running through the memories of those lives. "If you wish to watch your past lives it is your choice but prepare yourself, Magdalene. Your journeys have been...challenging to say the least. Not all of your experiences are pleasant."

I snickered at his understatement. "Yes, I've already figured that out." I paused for a second, considering whether to ask my next question until I realized that what I'd learned of myself during my past lives was too important to dismiss.

"There is one thing that I can't seem to figure out though," I said. "Every time I've died...so far at least...I-I never came back. I never fell back to earth after I took my last breath. It doesn't make any sense...leaving you here...on earth...alone."

"Fair question," he stated plainly, though he didn't appear overly eager to answer it. His lips turned down briefly as he glanced down the hall without really looking at anything in particular. "It was decided long ago that should a messenger die at the hands of their own guardian they would be unable to return to earth immediately. This is a precautionary measure as it was assumed that should a guardian take the life of the one they are guarding it is because the messenger is at risk of dying at the hands of a Fallen One. It is a last resort, of course, but should it happen as it has with us..." his voice trailed off and he cleared his throat, clearly uncomfortable with the memories of these instances, and then continued. "Should it happen, should a guardian take the life of those being guarded, it is deemed that to return to earth immediately would be unsafe and thus you are barred from ever doing so."

"Who decided this?" I asked, stunned at the shortsightedness.

"You," he replied and then wavered. "Well, I brought it up and it took some convincing to get you to agree."

My mouth fell open. "I can't," I muttered. "I can't believe I would ever agree to that...that restriction."

"It is for your own good."

"Is that what you told me when you were convincing me?" I asked, irritated.

"Yes," he replied without regret. "It really is for your own good, Magdalene."

"Regardless..." I said, appalled at myself. Mentally shaking off this unwelcomed news, I needed to clarify these parameters. "So...if I die at the hands of a Fallen

One I suffer eternal death. If I die by the hands of my guardian…you…then I suffer timeless bliss."

"Correct."

"And every life up until this one, I have died by your hands…by your actions?"

He nodded slowly, uneasy. "All but the first one when you died of age. Have you…have you been through your life in America? In Pennsylvania?"

"Not yet. I've been working my way up the list. I still have my life in Paris and then in Gettysburg." I watched him closely. "Why? What happens in Pennsylvania?"

He opened his mouth to answer and then closed it. After a moment of thought, he spoke cautiously. "I think you'll need to watch it for yourself." He said nothing more, the concern etched in to his expression telling me that he preferred not to recall it.

I was certain that if he had the choice he would prevent me from seeing it and whatever tragedy he refused to recount for me. Always, his primary instinct was to protect me. My instinct was to learn and I'd already decided that I would finish reviewing the list entirely, including a visit to Pennsylvania where I would learn about the tragedy too horrible for Eran to describe.

12. TRAINING GROUND

For the remainder of the day, as Eran walked with me between classes and sat with me at lunch, he didn't bring up the subject of me visiting my past lives again. Still, I had a lingering feeling that he was anxious about it. Instead our discussions were limited to class assignments and our hesitancy at tasting Felix's salmon meatloaf pie at dinner.

Our drive home was even slower, as if Eran was reluctant to get me any closer to my room where I'd eventually fall asleep and return to reviewing my past lives.

After Felix's unappetizing but nutritious dinner, Eran and I stood at the back porch as was typical when he was preparing to leave for his nightly mission.

"Where are you going this time?" I asked as he removed his shirt to make way for the emergence of his wings.

His muscles rippled seductively in the shadows, causing my breath to catch in my throat. No matter how often I watched this scene unfold before me, I never tired of it.

"I try to keep the details of my missions to myself," Eran said, handing his shirt to me. "I don't want to worry you."

"I worry anyways."

"Yes, Campion has mentioned it," he said, his wings expanding now behind him. They shuttered, as if to shake the stiffness from them, and settled down against his back.

"The little spy…" I grumbled.

Eran laughed lightly and then pulled me close, wrapping his arms around my shoulders. "He's only keeping me informed."

"I know…" I said my voice muffled with my head tucked in the crux of his shoulder. I tightened my hold, enjoying the feel of his solid body against mine. "Wherever you go tonight, just be safe."

He pulled away to kiss me, quick but deep. Then his wings pumped and he was drawn backwards still facing me.

"I will be safe, my dear Magdalene," he said, expertly hovering a foot above the ground with his gorgeous, trademark smirk.

"Showoff," I muttered with a smile.

Hearing it, he winked. "Always."

He spun around then and lifted up into the darkness.

I watched until he could no longer be seen and then went inside to tell Campion it was time for my next training.

The truth was my session at Ms. Beedinwigg's home might prove to be just as dangerous, considering the training she made me endure last time. Secretly, I didn't mind. As much as it was tiring, it was also exciting to test myself against her contraptions.

I'd now seen how the Fallen Ones fight. There were no inhibitions, no boundaries, and only the dedication to kill. With their skills, developed over centuries at battle, they were formidable enemies. I needed all the training I could get.

We arrived on time and again were escorted by Alfred to the training area below ground.

"Maggie...Campion," she greeted and then launched right into another lesson.

She instructed me to sprint through the same contraption as last time and was as pleased as I was when I reached the other side with less bumps and scratches. My timing also improved, surprising me when the stopwatch confirmed it.

Leading me to the next contraption a few feet from the last one, she timed me, recording it on a clipboard, as I sprinted through this one as well. While the last test required me to stay on my feet, this one forced me to stay off them. I rolled, jumped, and slid along thin beams or risked being crushed by the levers. She seemed pleased with the results.

The remaining time was spent practicing on the balance board and avoiding her punches and kicks.

All in all, it was just as exhausting as the first session and I couldn't wait to climb into bed. It always seemed that while my body stayed on earth throughout the night it recovered from the day, healing injuries or illness, repairing muscles and any aches – something I couldn't appreciate more.

I awoke in the Hall of Records, as usual. Although unlike most other nights, I was not alone.

Sitting up, I stretched, though it was unnecessary here, and looked around.

I jolted after finding Gershom standing on the opposite side of the bench, facing the scrolls. It looked as if he was inspecting them.

"Nice to see that you're up," he commented casually without bothering to turn around.

He must have heard my movement, I reasoned. "Thanks…What are you doing here?"

"Oh, I figured I would say hello…visit the Hall of Records. I've never been here before, you know…"

"Really? I'm here every night…"

"Maggie, of course I know that," he said, turning then to float over the bench and take a seat next to me. "That's why I came. You haven't been back to see me. I was getting worried. Are the Fallen Ones still arriving?"

I sighed, rubbing my eyes. "That's right. I did tell you about the Fallen Ones and that upcoming battle."

"Yes, you did and I've been considering a return to earth…falling to help keep you safe." I knew he was being sincere despite the absolute agony Campion had warned of when falling.

"Gershom…" I said, astounded at the significance of his offer. "That is completely unnecessary. We don't…We're still waiting to see if the threat is even valid."

"So Eran's nightly missions haven't turned up anything?" he asked, pensively.

"If he's found anything he's keeping it to himself." I sighed. "He doesn't want to worry me," I explained.

Gershom laughed through his nose. "That sounds like Eran…"

"It does," I agreed spending a moment to reflect on how protective Eran is of me in every possible way.

"So with Eran on nightly missions," said Gershom, "what are you doing to keep yourself so busy? Why haven't you been back to see me?" His brow lifted as he silently evaluated me.

"You won't believe this…" I said with a chuckle. "I've been visiting my past lives."

Gershom's head snapped back in genuine surprise. "Well now, tell me what you've learned.

I then went on to explain each life I'd visited, how Ms. Beedinwigg and Mr. Hamilton had found me on earth and introduced the concept to me, and finally how I was now in the midst of being trained to defeat the Fallen Ones in a secret underground combat facility.

Gershom listened intently, laughing at times or shaking his head in amazement. In the end, he agreed, "You have been busy."

I nodded. "Next past life to visit is Paris, France."

"Then you'll be running across Achan," Gershom said, shivering from the memory of him.

"That's what I suspect…"

"So…" he leaned back, stretching his legs out in front of him, "now that you're training on earth are you training here too?"

He asked the question as if it were a logical one.

"Gershom, how would I ever be able to train here? The facility is back there, beneath Mr. Hamilton's house." I rolled my eyes at him.

His brow creased in confusion and then his legs sprang back towards the bench. He was suddenly standing with his hands on his hips. "Do you mean to tell me that you've never been to your home in the afterlife? You've never seen what you've created?"

I was now the one confused. "I have a home…here?"

Gershom laughed at me though I wasn't offended. I agreed with him. I should have considered it.

"Where did you think you spent time in between phases on earth?"

"Well, in Eran's heaven, his piece of the afterlife…his cabin. I figured it was both of ours…"

"The cabin he recreated here from your time together on earth in the Pennsylvania Appalachian Mountains." Gershom summed it up nicely.

"Yes, that one."

Gershom chuckled again. "You've never been to your own?"

"Nope…" I replied feeling very foolish now.

"Well, would you like to go?" he offered.

My chest tightened at the thought of it. "You've been there?"

"Absolutely."

"Why?" I asked, my voice sounding ridiculing though I didn't intend it.

He shrugged. "I was…curious…Do you want to go or not?"

"Yes," I said so enthusiastic that my voice echoed down the length of the hall.

"Well, come on," he said, waving his fingers at me in a gesture to follow him.

When I was standing, he took hold of my hand and we lifted into the air. Unlike me, who was unable to fly for a reason unknown to me, Gershom had this wonderful ability and he did it well.

We soared through the hall at speed that would have left acute wind burn on my exposed skin if we'd been on earth. Here, however, it felt like a soft, warm breeze.

After reaching the end of the hall's arched entrance, we lifted into the sky, passing others who were also flying to other various destinations.

As we drifted higher, the cities and wilderness below us faded in to patches of color. Unlike on earth, the air remained pleasantly warm without a single cloud for as far as I could see.

We glided at the higher level for several hours, while he asked questions about my housemates, Eran, school, and the Fallen Ones. Then he told me to hold on and maneuvered his body to slant downward in a descending motion.

As the ground grew closer again, I noticed he was headed towards a large green patch of land. As I squinted for a better view, I could see the irregular peaks of tree tops and the asymmetrical outline of lakes and rivers. My thought was that I had created a forest, much like Eran, but just before we landed I learned I was wrong.

Gershom pivoted so that he dropped straight down, slowly, until our feet had touched the earth. His wings curled back behind him and settled against his shoulders.

"Welcome home," he said, glancing around.

"It's…It's a jungle," I stated rather disappointed.

Perspiration had already begun dripping down my temples.

I realized then that I had been planning to find a picturesque country estate or a sandy beach in the middle of a vast ocean. Instead, I stood at the base of what appeared to be ruins from a long deceased culture.

Steps and ledges had been carved into the wall to our left, hidden mostly by thick mossy vines curling up and through the rock. Directly in front of us was a cliff nearly three stories high and at the top was a mass of trees dripping with slime. To our right and behind us was the continuation of a decrepit jungle of thick trees and drooping foliage. At our feet, in the basin where we stood, was an amphitheater surrounded by long, circular benches carved from rock and a stage long since covered in decaying creepers.

"Nice…" I muttered.

"It's actually quite effective," he replied. "Just watch."

Gershom then sprinted towards the chiseled wall to our left, sprang from it, and landed on the cliff above. What impressed me wasn't his ability to leap so far…It was his agility in avoiding the vines snapping at him along the way.

"Do you see what you've created?" he called from the ledge above.

"Yes," I shouted back. "An elaborate vine snapping game."

Even from my spot below I could see his eyes rolling up. "You've created your very own obstacle course."

Of course, I knew this already. I was simply joking with Gershom, who didn't have a single ounce of humor in him. The fact that I had devised a testing ground dawned on me the moment Gershom was snapped with the first vine.

Still, Gershom drove home his point. "This is what helps you stay fit, adept at fighting, when you return here between lifetimes."

A smile, unintentionally, rose up then as I allowed myself to acknowledge the pride I felt.

"This isn't all of it, of course," he implied, floating down to stand beside me.

"It's not?" I asked, glancing around. "Where's the rest?"

Gershom grinned and took my hand again.

We ascended over my jungle and I could see that it was far more expansive than the basin where we'd landed. That, however, wasn't what Gershom was referring to.

As soon as we'd risen, we had begun our descent, landing in a cluster of high rises that resembled New York City. It was much cooler here with steam emitting from vents running down the middle of the street. Where we now stood was lined by buildings so tall they blocked out the light and shaded the street with a hazy darkness. The putrid smell of garbage was nearly stifling, though I saw none in sight. The steps leading to the apartment buildings were vacant even though some windows were lit behind the drawn drapery. That was the only sign of life.

Other than Gershom and myself, there was no one else on the street.

"I figured," said Gershom, "that you created this one so it would seem familiar to you if the Fallen Ones ever attacked you in the street."

"They already have…" I said reflecting on the incident in London. "But this…" I shrugged, "this doesn't seem so bad."

And then I stepped forward.

The moment my foot touched the ground again, winged beings assembled on the rooftops, silhouetted against the sky's dim light. They screeched in unison, and I unintentionally shuddered, recalling their sound so vividly.

They lifted into the air and circled, just as a flock of vultures would, above the rooftops. In the next moment, one of them pointed directly downward and the rest followed, forming a vertical line that pointed directly for me and Gershom.

"Ummm…Maggie?" he asked, uncertain.

"Yeah?" My eyes were locked on the line rapidly approaching us.

"Are we in trouble here?" he asked, his head also tilted towards the sky.

"How should I know? I don't remember anything…"

He sighed but didn't move.

Apparently he'd come to the same conclusion as me. If he'd wanted to flee it would have been too late by that point anyways.

The one in front came into clear sight then, arms extended, eyes wide, mouth open, releasing a bone-chilling screech.

It never stopped. It never hesitated. But, it never reached us either.

The moment before it came in contact with me, its claws reaching for my shoulders, it exploded in to dust. The next one did the same and the remaining ones followed suit.

In the end, we turned to each other and burst in to laughter. Whether it was from enjoying the test I'd created so long ago or the pure adulation of surviving an attack of

Fallen Ones without a single movement, I couldn't be certain. It may have been both.

"I may have to try fighting them at some point," I mentioned when I'd caught my breath.

"You may…" he drew in a breath, trying to contain himself. "You may have to."

He noticed my expression then and asked, "What are you thinking?"

My shoulders shook one last time from a final laugh. "I just realized that it was no wonder I had been upset with Eran for interfering with the Elsic in London…I had trained for that fight."

He tilted his head, speculatively. "I'd say you've trained for a lot more than just that one."

"Yes," I said, now contemplative. "But I don't remember any of it and that concerns me."

"Then let me help," Gershom insisted. "Beedinwigg and Hamilton will be your trainers on earth. I'll be your trainer here."

My eyes widened. "That…I would really appreciate."

"All right as your now newly appointed trainer in the afterlife, I'm going to show you the rest of your heaven. But first, I'm taking you to your home base." He had suddenly taken on such an authoritative, commanding presence I didn't see a hint of the amicable Gershom I knew so well. I had to admit it, though. I did like the change.

He took hold of my hand and lifted me again into the sky, over the rooftops and across the city. The buildings stopped abruptly and we entered a mountain range spotted with foliage. We coasted towards the highest peak and the closer we came the more I recognized it as a narrow, oblong-shaped piece of land, where groupings of tropical trees stood. At the edge of a slanted cliff a rather primitive encampment had been constructed. Behind it, for the remainder of the flattened peak, tropical trees stood in a massive grouping. This stood out to me. Nowhere had I ever come across a level mountain peak and certainly not one with robust, healthy tropic trees growing from it.

Gershom took us directly for the encampment where our feet settled down into soft, forgiving sand. The air was warm here, unlike the other two areas of what was supposed to be my paradise. However, this place didn't look any closer to that purpose either.

Then we watched as water seemed to spring from tiny pores in the mountain range around us, filling the caverns and narrow corridors until nothing could be seen where rock had once been. The mountain range was now covered with clear blue water, lapping gently at the beach where we now stood.

I looked to Gershom with my jaw dropped.

"I know," he said, obviously also impressed.

My feet took me forward without my really telling them to and I entered the warm water. I could see my feet clearly as the sand softly settled down after my disturbance of it. Peering across the ocean before me, I grasped that it was the same blue-green as Eran's eyes.

That couldn't be a coincidence.

Certain there were more clues to his existence here I spun around and moved towards the makeshift hut against the trees. Two hammocks swung in the light breeze, suspended in midair and attached to nothing at all. A small campfire burned on the sand outside the hut where fish was being cooked on rotating skewers. I breathed in deeply, enjoying the delicious smell. Coconut shells were left in the sand, empty until I approached. When I was a foot away, they quickly filled up as if an invisible pitcher were filling them until an opaque white liquid had met the rim. I could only guess it was coconut milk.

The hut didn't have a door, simply an opening cut through the palm leaves that lay over each other to form the hut's walls and roof.

After stepping inside, I quickly noted that it looked as if I'd just left.

To the right, a book lay open on the small table next to a rocking chair. They were set next to windows that had been rolled up for a view of the ocean now outside. The aroma of cinnamon tea came from a pot steaming on the stove, which mixed with the scent of grilled fish from outside. A small table and two chairs built from driftwood were placed to the left with a bowl of mangos and bananas set invitingly in the center. I took a banana, surprised when it peeled itself. I bit in, savoring the smooth texture and simple sweetness.

Then I saw it.

On a wooden beam, holding up the left corner of the hut's walls and roof, initials had been carved. E heart M.

I giggled, unable to stop myself.

"What's so funny?" asked Gershom coming up behind me.

"Eran...He left his initials for me." I pointed to the carving.

Gershom leaned in to inspect them. "Sappy...but thoughtful," he commented blandly.

"Gershom, have you ever been in love?" I probed. "Ever had that tickle in your stomach or powerful explosion inside whenever a special someone was near?"

He thought about my question for several seconds before replying simply. "No."

I felt my shoulders fall. "We need to introduce you to a few girls," I said and turned back to the carvings. "We haven't always had these names. I wonder when he left them..."

"Well, since he's not here to ask, touch it and allow the memory to come."

"Touch-" I said, starting to repeat his sentence but discontinuing it because I knew I'd heard him correctly.

This place never ceased to surprise me.

It only took a few steps to reach the carving and then I placed my fingers gently over the initials.

Suddenly, as if a movie had started playing in my mind, I saw Eran in a hammock outside, his head tilted to stare across the water, his expression wistful. It gave me the impression that he was missing someone or something. Then, very slowly, a smile lifted his cheeks. He chuckled, stood, and entered the hut. Inside, he looked around to select the beam. Still grinning, he conjured a knife blade from thin air and carved the initials of our names for each lifetime. Standing back, he reviewed his work and then swept a hand in front of the beam, erasing them. In their place, he carved the marks I see now.

Although I couldn't hear his thoughts, throughout the entire duration of this scene I felt the overpowering sense of absolute love emanating from Eran. At the same time, I was aware of an absolute sense of peace as if I already had everything I needed.

Eran…he was all I needed, and being so close to him left an ache in my chest.

With his carving complete, he flipped the knife to close but upon snapping shut it disappeared completely. Then he strolled outside, his gorgeous trademark smirk in place. That was when the memory ended and I dropped my hand. "The carving was left during this lifetime, just before he fell to earth to protect me there. Incredible…"

"Yes, a little trick we use here," Gershom said. "Nearly anything you touch here has a memory which you can revisit at any time." Gershom glanced around, gripped by his own amazement. "This place…I'm constantly intrigued by it." His formal manner returned then and he said with an imposing presence, "All right. You have two more past lives to endure, correct?"

"Yes, that's right," I said wondering where his questioning was headed.

"When you've completed them, come find me we'll start your training. Agreed?"

"Agreed."

Gershom's wings unfolded outward and, flapping, lifted him off the ground. As he rose, his body shrunk to a dot in the sky and then moved like a bolt of lightning back from where we'd come.

I only had a few minutes left before morning would arrive on earth, I knew. Disappointed in the realization, I did my best to touch everything in sight – the coconut shells, the hammocks, the hut - and experience the memory or series of memories that came with them.

By the time I was pulled back to my bed in New Orleans, I couldn't have prevented the smile adhered to my face if I had tried.

13. THE PLAN

It had been a little over a week since Marco had arrived and warned of a coming battle. With Fallen Ones continuing to turn up throughout the city and invading the school campus, no one could deny that something was brewing even if no other signs were apparent.

This was on everyone's mind.

In fact, I found Eran on my balcony the next morning, a cup of coffee in hand, gazing across the rooftops. He was deep in thought so I did my best not to bother him.

The bed springs did that for me.

"You're up," he stated over his shoulder after hearing the sharp squeak. He stood to meet me and the full sight of him made my heart flutter. His hair was still windblown from last night's flight but he had changed into a new pair of jeans that hugged his massive thighs and a black sweater tight enough to accentuate the muscular curves of his torso.

"It looked like you were concentrating…" I said, avoiding the sight of him so I could recover. "Anything you'd like to share?"

He replied, "Actually there is something…" and my head snapped up.

He took a seat on the bed and I followed, wide-eyed. He hesitated and I was nervous he wouldn't go through with telling me. With his lips pursed closed and his brow creased, he certainly didn't like the thought of it. Then he began to speak.

"Magdalene, I debated myself on whether to disclose this information to you. The last thing I want is for you to be anxious or preoccupied by what I'm going to tell you. Please keep in mind that I have my army in place. You are well protected."

"I know that, Eran."

"Right…of course you do…I-I think I'm delaying…" He drew in a breath and ran his fingers through his hair.

"How about starting at the beginning?" I suggested, placing my hand on his bent knee and sucking in a breath at the excited jolt that ran through me.

He paused to notice it and then his smirk rose up, just enough to be seen. "Despite our situation, I like knowing you still react to me."

"Always…"

He allowed the smirk to linger and then it fell away when he began to speak again. "I've been traveling the streets each night in London, Germany, and France, listening to anyone talking. Alterums are well populated in those regions and they always keep themselves knowledgeable on what the Fallen Ones are doing."

"Really? Why is that?" I asked, surprised. I had gotten the impression from Campion that Alterums kept to themselves but Eran's answer erased that notion.

"Because they've also been attacked. Fallen Ones don't discriminate. If they can take something, be it from a human or an Alterum, they'll attempt it. So, Alterums watch their backs and each others, keeping a wary eye on the Fallen Ones."

"I didn't know they had a dog in this fight," I mused.

"They do. More than you know. It was for this reason, they've spoken openly to me about what they have heard was coming."

He paused then, still weighing whether to tell me.

"Which is?" I encouraged.

Staring intently at me, he continued though hesitantly. "You, of all others, have a right to know what is coming. I wish I had more to tell you...but what I do have is this...Abaddon's daughter, Sarai, you remember her..."

"How could I forget? She killed Gershom and nearly killed me."

"Yes," he replied uncomfortable and I knew this was because he felt that he'd failed me as a protector. Of course, that couldn't have been more wrong. "That's the one. She and Achan are preparing to release the Elsics from imprisonment."

That news made me sit straighter. "That would mean the entire world, everyone in it, would be in danger."

"Yes, it would," replied Eran soberly.

"When are they planning it? How?" I asked urgently.

"The actual details are not known yet, neither is the timeframe. That's what I'm working on."

I sat quietly tense, my eyes mindlessly tracing the folds of the comforter. "Do you think it was Sarai or Achan who we saw in the clouds that night? The one who chased us?"

Eran shook his head. "It wasn't Sarai...It was too large to be Sarai." He fell silent then and contemplated quietly before muttering, "But it also seemed too large to be Achan."

Having seen both Sarai and Achan from a distance and close up, I had to agree. Yet, without further evidence we had to assume it was either one of them.

"How would she help the Elsics escape? Aren't guards protecting the prison?" I asked. This measure of extra fortification couldn't have gone unnoticed when devising the prison layout.

"Guards are in place. I'm checking with them regularly and keeping them updated as well."

My head dipped in thought. "Abaddon…he's in the prison, isn't he? We put him there…"

"Yes, he's there," Eran responded. He then took my hand to turn my attention towards him. "Magdalene, what's on your mind?"

"I'm…" I searched for the right word. "Nervous. Nervous about the safety for my housemates. Nervous that with all the Fallen Ones here in the city a release of the Elsics would cause a frenzied slaughter. I'm nervous about you and the dangers you're encountering in collecting this information…" I sighed, disturbed by my thoughts. "I always seem to place others in danger, Eran, most all you, and I'm tired of it."

Slowly, he lifted his hand to cup my chin and forced me to raise it so that we sat face to face. The morning sun, glinting from some window nearby, penetrated his eyes, causing them to sparkle.

"You don't put anyone in harm's way, Magdalene."

I began to argue but he didn't allow for it. "The Fallen Ones do. Stop blaming yourself. No good comes from it."

Again, I tried to disagree and he cut me short. "It won't change our circumstances and you'll be left feeling distressed for no good reason. Let it go…"

His hand slid from my chin then, softly down my neck to rest gently just above my shoulder, leaving a trail of tingling skin in its wake.

He drew in a deep, shuddering breath. "I can feel your heartbeat," he whispered.

"Then you know it's sped up."

He nodded then, his lips pursed together, his eyes filled with longing.

Unable to refuse the tension mounting in me, I gave way to the moan caught in my throat. "Eran…" I murmured.

"I know…I feel it too."

The unbearable passion overcame us and our lips met. His hands were around my shoulders then, pulling me towards him. I leaned forward, moving into him. His lips pressed against mine feverishly, my own meeting his with the same intensity. We clung to one another, allowing ourselves the brief respite we needed, we deserved.

When Eran pulled away, he leaned his forehead delicately against mine, peering in to my eyes. I breathed in his earthy scent, a natural fragrance that always seemed to settle me down.

"Our two lives here, the brief blink of an eye that they are, challenges me more each time. My emotions for you, once again, test my resolve."

"I suppose telling you to give in to them won't make a difference…"

"It won't," he confirmed, using his most charming tone.

"Of course…" I sighed.

He pulled away entirely then. "Especially since I need to leave you alone now so you can get yourself ready for school."

Quicker than my mind could follow, he was on his feet and across the room, closing my French doors but not bothering to turn the lock. Instead, he strolled back across the room, using his innate power over mechanical objects to slide the lock into place without touching it, and boastfully winking at me as he reached the door.

"Café du Monde for breakfast?" he offered.

"Perfect," I responded, absorbed in his glory until he'd left the room. Then I sprang out of bed and headed for the closet to pull out my The Killers t-shirt and jeans.

After I showered and dressed, we said a quick goodbye to our housemates and stopped at Café du Monde before heading for school. Again, I felt the yo-yo reaction as the hair raised and settled at the back of my neck as we passed Fallen Ones on the street.

Classes and our house seemed to be the only place I didn't have to endure it.

The day passed uneventfully, which for us was just fine, and before I knew it I was standing on the back porch with Eran as he prepared for another night mission.

Our conversation from this morning still lingered in my mind as I reached for his hand, a gesture meant to comfort him as much as me.

"Where will you be going tonight?" I asked.

"Germany. An Alterum there has been very helpful."

"Okay…If-If you foresee any trouble, any sign of an Elsic-"

Eran smiled warmly. "Yes, Magdalene, I'll avoid trouble as much as possible. But your concerns are unfounded," he told me, his wings emerging from between his shoulder blades now. "All Elsics are safely imprisoned last I checked."

"It's the 'last I checked part' that worries me."

"I'll check with the guards again before I meet up with my contact. Will that make you happy?"

"Yes it will," I said bluntly.

"Then that's what I'll do," he replied, already lifting off the ground.

Our eyes remained on each other until he reached the trees when he was forced to turn and maneuver himself up and over them. He floated towards the sky, his wings barely needing to work, until he was far enough away to be undetectable by anyone stargazing. He then bolted across the city so fast that it left a blurred trail behind.

Campion, who I had learned, always adhered to etiquette, waited just inside the door. He opened it only when he was certain Eran was gone.

"Are you ready?" he asked.

"As I'll ever be," I replied.

We then took my bike across the city to Mr. Hamilton's house.

As was typical, Alfred led us to the underground training center where Ms. Beedinwigg waited. However, this time, he didn't leave, instead stepping aside and waiting with hands clasped behind his back.

I soon discovered why he stayed.

Ms. Beedinwigg, again in her skintight, black leather suit and hair flowing freely, asked me to run through each of the obstacle courses again. As she had predicted my timing was improving and I came through with less bumps and scratches this time.

Then she approached a tall wooden case, opening it to reveal it contained an array of weapons.

"As you know, Achan's favorite weapon is the bow and arrow," she mentioned, pointing to one. "Most Fallen Ones have a preference, even a fondness, for their specific weapon of choice. Rifles, shotguns, sabers, nooses, kamas, nunchucks, steel boomerangs, bokkens, metal stars, throwing knives, tonfas…" she continued on until she'd covered every piece of her inventory.

"Your preference is the rapier," she informed me.

My head jolted back in astonishment. "The rapier? My class last semester told me the exact opposite."

Still, she pulled the rapier from its mounted position in the case and handed it to me. "If you should ever remember your past, you will recall your expert level with this weapon and feel comfortable using it. If you don't, it's still a very good weapon to use. My particular preference is the sai."

She pulled a sword from the wall which had two curved, pointed prongs protruding from the handle, so that it was in effect three weapons in one. Another mounted to the wall behind it, which she also pulled down.

"These are commonly used in pairs," she explained.

I glanced at my slender rapier and wondered how I was ever going to avoid an attack with it.

"Now, the courses I've asked you to run through," she pointed to the contraptions she timed me on, "taught you to duck, roll, do what was necessary to avoid being injured, correct?"

"Correct."

"Good. Recall and use the steps you've learned in making it through the courses and you'll see that they've unwittingly taught yourself effective defensive maneuvers."

"Ah, so that's what those were for…"

"Thought they were meant for simple, mindless punishment, ha?" She smiled.

After showing me a few steps that, surprisingly, I recalled from my fencing class, we began to spar. Though she didn't go easy on me, she never made actual contact with my skin. She was clearly adept at using the blades and in the tactics used in the defensive arts. Watching her movements and having to defend against them gave me the chance to test and hone my new abilities.

Occasionally, she would call out, "Nice!" or "Again!" At the end of thirty minutes, I felt slightly winded but confident.

Then she changed the rules.

As I successfully pinned her against the wall, Alfred came up behind me. He'd selected a bamboo bo staff which he twirled skillfully in his hands and around his body.

I was now defending against multiple attackers.

Surveying my surroundings and my attackers weaknesses, I began to realize something change in me.

My senses heightened.

The roll in the carpet that could trip me came in to view. I noticed the way each held their weapon, offering me insight on how each would be used. I heard Ms. Beedinwigg's breathing coming now in short gasps and knew she was fighting exhaustion. I saw where the staff would hit long before it reached its destination and where the sword was aimed before she completed her step.

In the end, despite my abilities, I landed on the floor both weapons at my throat.

Alfred dropped his weapon and extended his hand, which I took. "You're the best I've ever seen," he said once I was on my feet.

"Really?" I was thrilled to hear it.

"Your mother was good with the rapier too," said Ms. Beedinwigg plainly, taking a towel to wipe her face. "But you're better."

I nodded, stunned.

"You did well tonight, Maggie," said Ms. Beedinwigg. "You're definitely improving but there's more to learn." She flung the towel over her shoulder.

Knowing where her comments were headed, I interjected, "I'll be back tomorrow night."

"Same time," Ms. Beedinwigg stated and headed for the stairs.

The rest of us followed her to the front door.

"Rest up," she suggested. "Tomorrow will be a big night."

"Oh really?" I said my curiosity piqued. "What am I in for?"

"Tomorrow," she replied, gently positioning me towards the door. "You'll find out tomorrow."

On the ride home, I wondered what awaited me when I returned to Mr. Hamilton's house but mostly I wondered how I could rest up when the emotional toll from visiting my past lives took so much out of me. Tonight I'd be visiting Paris which I couldn't deny was intriguing. It was just the prospect of encountering Marco and my other adversaries that left me uneasy.

Little did I know, it wouldn't be my enemies who would cause my emotions to unravel.

14. PARIS, FRANCE

After another session with Ms. Beedinwigg, falling asleep came easy. I immediately drew my scroll from its pocket in the Hall of Records and swept my finger over the name that would take me to my life in Paris:

Previously Marie Lafayette – Died Paris, France, July 14, 1789

I was transported into my body at the time, immediately noticing that I was crouching. I was startled inside to see my own face staring back at me. Then I understood that my likeness was being reflected in a still pond.

While I had just reached my teenage years, my hair was the same wavy, chestnut color it had been throughout each of my lives. I had the same nose, eyes, and petite build. The only difference this time was the scar running from the line of my jaw down my neck. Apparently, I had survived an altercation earlier in my life.

The hands of this body reached in to scoop the cool, refreshing water in to my cupped palms when a horse neighed nervously from behind me. The hairs on the back of my neck rose then and began twisting madly around one another.

I stood quickly and spun around to find the horse, which I quickly deduced was mine and which was now fleeing.

From behind it stood Abaddon.

His hair hung in its typical greasy disarray but that didn't seem to bother him. He sneered from beneath his long, beak-shaped nose. He wore a cloak embroidered with gold tassels, which he shrugged off as I came in to view, exposing his wings, inky black and grown to the length of his entire frame.

He appeared formidable.

"Tsk…tsk…tsk…" he clucked his tongue at me. "Marie, you've left yourself without protection…Shall I give you another scar so as to remind you not to do so again?"

Still grinning, he stepped forward, his feet crunching through the dead leaves of the forest floor.

"I don't see why," I said stoically in French. Though I'd never studied French in my classes on earth, I understood every word I spoke and I did it with undeniable fluency. "You won't leave me alive long enough to learn the lesson."

His head tilted back to release a long, cackling laugh. "I always have enjoyed your sense of humor. I'm going to miss it."

He continued his advance towards me while I remained still.

My wings had sprung, however, and were extended, ready for flight.

Then the ground shook and someone was suddenly standing in front of me, blocking Abaddon.

"Jacques," I heard myself calmly call out though I knew from the sight of him that it Eran standing between us and that I was using his name given during this lifetime. "I can handle this."

"Step away, Magdalene," he replied firmly, also in French.

"This is my fight," I insisted.

Abaddon sighed loudly then, halting our argument. "Must we go through this ever time? Every time..." he said wearily. "He is your guardian. It is his responsibility to defend you. You really must allow him to perform his duties. Of course...I'm inclined to honor your wish and send him off so that you and I may fight instead."

He was patronizing us and I had to forcefully subdue the anger that grew in me.

My eyes narrowed but I said nothing more.

"Or," he shrugged. "I'll fight you both."

"Agreed," I said and rose into the air, my body pivoting for attack.

Eran did the same and met Abaddon before me.

It was a pummeling, a fight that would have made Ms. Beedinwigg proud. Still, in the midst of it, I heard a hideous snigger from Abaddon just before he launched skyward, freeing himself.

He flew through the forest, winding around tree trunks with narrow but precise calculation, glancing back at us, leering, as we pursued him.

Reaching the forest's border, we entered a field populated with wildflowers. Despite the color, it wasn't what struck me.

I was focused on the chateau at the end of the field.

Apparently so was Abaddon as he aimed for it and flying directly through a window when reaching it, stained glass exploding into the room.

Eran, being faster than me, reached the window before I could and entered it. I followed and found that we'd entered a vacant but immaculately decorated hall.

Tapestries hung the length of one wall while a row of stained glass windows ran the opposite side. Leather chairs were positioned in groupings down the center.

Abaddon was nowhere in sight.

Eran was now hovering just inside the room, halfway between floor and ceiling, flapping his wings only when needed to stay aloft so as not to miss any sound Abaddon might make.

I lingered directly beside him. My hair was still on end so I knew that Abaddon was nearby.

The door at the end of the hall opened then and Marco stepped inside, his expression alert, cautious.

"H-Hello?" he called out.

This was not the conceited, aggressive man I remembered from school. He was meek, unsure of himself. The dagger he held at the end of his extended hand shook.

Eran and I waited until his head was turned and we dropped silently to the ground.

Slowly, Marco crept into the room.

"Hello?" he called out again.

He was the only sound or movement until Abaddon rose from behind a chair.

Wings sunk back into his body, he looked like nothing more than an intruder.

Marco swung his dagger in Abaddon's direction.

"Who are you?" he demanded though it came out more along the lines of a whimper.

"My name is Abaddon," he replied evenly. "I mean you no harm. I've simply lost my way."

Marco's brow furrowed. "Lost your way? Where were you going?"

Abaddon stepped forward.

"Don't come any closer…" he said in a rush of words, though to his credit they sounded stern. "I would be forced to use my weapon."

"And we wouldn't want that," said Abaddon, not the least bit threatened.

Eran spoke up then from the other side of the room. "Marco, leave the room," he commanded.

Marco's head snapped in our direction. He drew in a quick, troubled breath when seeing me. "No, I won't," he stated, a bit more firmly now. "Not until I see Mademoiselle Lafayette to safety."

Simply from his conduct, it was easy to discern that Marco had already become infatuated with me.

"She is safe…Leave now." Eran's tone left no room for argument, yet Marco did not budge.

Abaddon scoffed. "Marie, you really do have multiple admirers."

"Leave him be," I shouted, the vehemence in my voice echoing down the hall.

Abaddon tilted his head then as if he were figuring out something complex. Ignoring me and addressing Marco, he asked, "And who are you?"

"Marco LaRoche, Mademoiselle Lafayette's personal security here on the estate," he said with an air of superiority.

"It is a pleasure to make your acquaintance," said Abaddon cordially.

"Thank you, as it is for me. Now…I must require you to leave promptly or suffer the full weight of the law as it will surely be on my side."

Examining Marco, judging him and the demand he'd made, Abaddon replied, "No, I'm not inclined to obey your request."

Offended, Marco stated, "It is not a request, Monsieur."

"Marco," said Eran. "Leave the room…Now!"

Refusing, Marco stood his ground.

"Please, Marco," I heard my voice call to him, desperate. "Please leave."

"No, Mademoiselle Lafayette, I cannot oblige."

Eran had likely come to the same conclusion as me: Abaddon was far too close in proximity to Marco for us to deflect any attack. By the time we reached that side of the room, Marco would suffer mortal injury. Being without any knowledge of what he faced and without any training to contend against it, Marco was an easy target. The only solution would be for Marco to willingly leave the room before the tension escalated and a fight resulted. With Marco acting as security for me and his clear inexperience, Abaddon would not deter from taking his life first.

"Please, Marco!" I begged.

"I will not," Marco shouted back, bordering on insult.

Abaddon, enjoying this display of loyalty, asked, "Would you give your life for Mademoiselle Lafayette?"

"Yes," said Marco, tilting his chin up proudly.

"Are you in love with Mademoiselle Lafayette?"

Marco hesitated, glancing in my direction. "Yes," he said softly, submissively.

"Do you want to be with her until the end of time?"

"Yes."

Even from our place down the hall I could see the desperation in Marco's expression. He clearly had no idea what was coming next.

"Then allow me the honor of giving it to you…" said Abaddon, drawing a blade from behind his back, slicing it through the air and across Marco's throat.

"No!" I heard myself scream, long and in despair.

Instantly, Eran was darting across the hall, his wings moving with powerful intent, closing the gap as quickly as possible between himself and Abaddon.

"No," I said under my breath and fled across the room.

Wings now out, fluttering in the air, Abaddon spoke down to Marco who had collapsed to the ground. His instructions were simple and repulsive. "When you die, fall back to earth. Come find me, my friend, and we will make Mademoiselle Lafayette yours forever."

Abaddon turned then and fled through the window closest to him, disappearing across the field.

Eran reached Marco before me, kneeling at his side, unable to stem the blood streaming from Marco's wound.

Landing at his side my hand clasped around Marco's.

Gurgling against the blood now filling his lungs, he squeezed my fingers and shuddered. His eyes, locked on me, were filled with confusion as he drifted away and fell silent and still.

"No!" My scream released deep in my throat, leaving it raw from its fury, resounding against the walls again and again.

I was yanked then, away from this body, and dropped into it later in life.

Marco was gone but the scream still lingered in my mind, like the echo down a deep cavern.

I had truly appreciated him, I sensed, and I was melancholic in knowing that there was nothing that could be done now to avoid the way life had evolved.

Learn, I told myself. That is what you are here to do.

I refocused on my surroundings and found that I faced another row of windows. This one overlooked a city below. It was early morning and fires raged across the horizon, burning structures and sending hazy smoke into the darkness. Somehow, in the deep recesses of my memory, I understood what I was looking at to be the city of Paris.

From behind me, I heard the door open and turning I found it was a page boy.

"Madame Lafayette," he said in French, closing the door behind him, "your guests have been assembled. But…but not all of them stayed."

I felt my head tilt to the side. "Why is that?" I asked in the same language.

"They…Some of the nobles didn't feel they should wait in the same line as the bourgeois…the peasants is how they explained it."

My expression remained stoic and my voice did not waver when I answered. "That is their choice. Please begin sending them in one at a time. Thank you, Monsieur Desmoulins."

"I must warn you, Mademoiselle…you put yourself at great risk assembling so many on your estate and when chaos is at your doorstep."

"I am aware…and I thank you for your concern. They will stay."

Monsieur Desmoulins appeared fearful and in disagreement but his final comment on the subject was not contentious. It was in support. "I simply wish they knew all that you, as a noblewoman, have done to provide for them, to protect them."

My lips lifted in a kind smile. "What little I've done was not intended for reputation."

He turned to the door again but hesitated and looked back. "It was not little, Mademoiselle… and I would feel most comfortable if you at the least had your dogs by your side."

"That will be fine."

Appeased, he nodded. "I will fetch the dogs and begin sending them in."

My body moved then towards two chairs in the center of the room. They faced the door so that when I sat and the door opened I knew who was coming through.

Monsieur Desmoulins appeared again a few minutes later, releasing two French mastiffs into the room. Watching them from this body, I recognized them instantly and called out their names in silence. Annie and Charlie, tails wagging, bounded towards me to nudge their noses in my palms for a brief petting and then curled up at my feet.

For the next hour and a half, I took messages for the people who had come to the estate wishing to communicate to the dead. Some were thankful, others remorseful, and still others showed little emotion. Of this last kind, many of them were peasants suffering through the tumultuous time of what would become known as the French Revolution.

From inside this body, I desperately wanted to console them, tell them that all they were enduring would end soon and that the sacrifices they'd made would not be in vain. But, I had no control over this body.

I was simply a passenger.

When I had taken my last message, I walked to the window for another look at Paris, Annie and Charlie following loyally.

More fires burned now. A gathering of tricolored cockades marched through the streets, most carrying weapons.

The door behind me opened again but this time my body remained in position, my awareness was so tuned to the streets.

The dogs' tails began thumping the ground excitedly as I listened to someone cross the room. He stopped directly beside me.

An earthy scent reached my nose and I knew instantly who it was. Not a second went by and I began to calm down and feel the cocoon of safety that only Eran could bring.

"There is talk of storming the Bastille," he informed me quietly in French.

"It appears that is where they are headed now." I gestured towards the assemblage in the streets. "Is there anything we can do to stop it?"

"Nothing," said Eran wistfully. "Nothing at all."

Eran suddenly turned towards me, appearing restless, clearing his throat and straightening the jacket he wore. He then began to speak, hesitantly. "I-I have something to tell you. Admittedly, it may not be the best time but…that point…that point may never come." I was now facing him, drawn to him as he anxiously struggled through his words. I had never seen him in such emotional turmoil before. In an attempt to make it easier for him I intentionally kept my expression impassive as he continued. "When we met long ago in Germany I had a sense of the kind of person you were…a remedial sense. I can…I can liken it to spotting a rainbow but only seeing one color of the spectrum while knowing there are more. And then…then as I spent time with you, acting as your unwarranted guardian, I learned who you were and my respect for you grew. By the end of that brief life on earth, I had developed devotion…" He thought for a moment. "Not devotion, it is too pale a word. Honestly, I'm-I'm not sure I can sum it up in a single word. But what I felt for you then grew stronger in London when I became your appointed guardian. From then, I-I recognized that my feelings for you…" He appeared more uncertain now, nervous as to how I might react. "I knew my feelings for you had gone beyond that of a guardian." He swallowed hard, glanced out the window without seeing anything, and then refocused on me. "I'm not sure how it happened. I tried to prevent it; ignored myself, for the most part; dedicated myself to the single objective of protecting you. That dedication gave me purpose and…and alleviated some guilt in being your guardian while feeling the way I do…And still…" His gaze fell and for a moment he appeared defeated. "And still it is not enough. What I feel for you is not dissipating. It is growing, intensifying." He drew in a shuttered breath and ran his fingers through his hair. When he spoke again, it was quiet and tender. "What I'm trying to tell you, Magdalene, is that I am in love with you."

The tension that slowly built in me as he spoke exploded at his final words. A burning sensation coursed through my body, my breath caught, my skin prickled with excitement. The realization of what had just happened swept over me.

Eran had confessed his love for me. Against all rules, despite all obstacles, unforeseen by either of us, love had developed.

From this body, I knew that all I wanted was to throw my arms around him, pull him against me, and confess my love in return. But, this body of mine was unable to react because something or someone, more precisely, had activated my radar.

"I understand," he uttered mournfully, turning away to stare out the window. "You-You don't feel the same."

"No, it's-" I began but never had the chance to finish.

The hairs on the back of my neck had bristled and I shifted to watch the door. My senses were suddenly engorged, drawing in every part of my surroundings. The chants from the townspeople in the city below reached my ears. The fires from burning structures enflamed my nose. Most of all, I heard the footsteps approaching down the hallway outside and stopping at the door.

It blew open a second later.

Eran spun to face it, drawing his sword, his demeanor returning to vigilant defense.

Marco strolled into the room, his boyish mannerisms gone and now replaced with sinister arrogance. Wings now protruded behind his back, long enough to drag along the floor.

Annie and Charlie barked ferociously and sprinted towards the intruder.

"Come," Eran shouted, his voice reflecting the nervousness in allowing them too close to Marco. To my relief, they obeyed.

Behaving as if he owned the estate he'd now trespassed, Marco stopped in the center of the room, gripping the handles of two scythe-shaped kama weapons.

"Draw them and I will attack," Eran cautioned.

"Reserve your words. I am not here to speak with you," he said. His tone was defiant as he switched his concentrated interest to me. "It's good to see you again, my love."

"I am not your love," I seethed.

"That is not the welcome I deserve, not after giving my life to protect you…" Initially he seemed hurt but he quickly returned to leering.

"I did not ask that of you."

He shrugged, carelessly. "What is done…is done. I no longer fault you."

"Fault me?" I scoffed, offended at the insinuation.

Eran's hand moved to rest on my hip, intending to calm me.

Marco appeared not to care that he had insulted me, instead altering the course of discussion to center on him. "These years that have passed, I traveled far – the Orient, the colonies in America, throughout the Muslim territories – and I experienced many women. Some willing…others not as much. But, what I found was that my affection for you has not subdued. I still long for you, Mademoiselle. And with my new-found…abilities…Eran will need to step aside."

Now Eran was offended. He scoffed loudly which rolled in to mocking laughter. "That is not going to happen, Marco."

"Then I will kill you and she will come with me," he stated without any acknowledgment that he'd just iterated an absurd belief.

I opened my mouth to tell him just that but Eran beat me to it.

"Marco…she doesn't love you," he said sarcastically.

"That's right. I don't," I confirmed in a rush of words, which continued without any cognitive thought by me. "I'm in love with Jacques."

Eran turned to me and blinked. "But that's my name."

Clearly, I had no plan to speak those words. They came from the heart, uninhibited and honest. They had been waiting there all long until I had the courage to confess them. When I did, there was a release in admitting them, a burden that had lifted confirming that I too had been fighting the truth.

Still, I could not allow myself to validate that Eran was the one. Doing this would put Eran in far more jeopardy as the Fallen Ones would use him to get to me. That, I would not allow. Attempting to camouflage who my heart belong to, I reinforced my statement in a more imprecise way.

"I could never love you, Marco. My heart does not belong to you. It belongs to another."

None of this mattered to Marco, however. This became clear when he impatiently stated, "Simply having you by my side will do just as well."

As if he'd had enough of the delay, he drew both kamas from his waistband.

"I warned you," said Eran, unforgiving.

Before this body could react, Eran and Marco met in the air, their wings keeping them aloft, their weapons clashing, the dogs leaping to snatch at Marco's feet.

I shrugged the coat I wore to the ground and lifted into the air, the specially-designed petticoat opening in the back to allow my wings their freedom. I then closed in on them, my sword also drawn.

Eran grunted, deflecting Marco's sword.

The maneuver flung them apart.

Grinning wickedly, Marco informed us, "If I can't have her, no one will."

"Wishful thinking, Marco," said Eran before re-engaging.

They fought ferociously for several minutes, my body floating from side to side, looking for a way in, an opening to inflict Marco harm before he could harm Eran.

Eran's combat skills were evident as he moved effortlessly around Marco, often leaving him clueless as to where Eran had gone. It would have been comical to watch if Eran's life weren't in danger.

Minutes later, cut, bruised, and in disarray, Marco was visibly tiring. Knowing this, he ended the fight in one swift movement; oddly it did not come from the end of his sword.

He positioned himself in front of the windows, gestured to someone outside, and then fled out the door in which he'd come.

The moment he escaped the room, glass shattered behind me and my leading thought was that another Fallen One had come through it.

My body turned in flight to face the next attacker but it was a haphazard, lopsided turn.

Something was throwing off my balance.

With effort, I steadied myself and then Eran was at my side.

"Down," he was shouting.

Everything moved in slow motion then.

Something hit my torso, and then again, and then again.

As Eran forced me to the ground and just before the window ledge obstructed my view to the outside, I caught sight of a young man, immaculately dressed, hovering just beyond the edge of the property. I knew him instantly. Not only because of his clothing but because he held a bow, which had just released an arrow.

"Achan…" I breathed.

As Eran laid me gentle down, my eyes drifted across the floor where Annie and Charlie lay, both with arrows lodged just under their shoulder blades.

Fury raged in me and I released a scream that I was certain reached Achan's ears.

"Shhh, save your strength," Eran consoled me.

Strength? I thought. For what?

My head dropped farther and I found my answer. The stems of seven arrows protruded from my own body.

I was riddled with them.

He was bending over me now, his eyes running the course of my body to evaluate my injuries.

"They're-They're fatal," I verified softly.

Then the pain hit.

It felt as if my abdomen had been lit on fire.

I cringed against it, my teeth grinding, my breath coming in short gasps.

Unable to bear seeing me in pain, he took hold of the tip of one arrow, intending to break it off.

"No…" I rejected. "Leave them. There isn't much time."

Eran's head was shaking now, refusing to believe reality. Yet, the evidence was clear.

I was dying.

Cradling my head in his lap, he stared down at me, helpless.

"This can't be happening again," he muttered, subduing a sob.

I brought my hand up to his pressed against my cheek. I had something to tell him and I needed his full attention.

"The Jacques I was referring to…" I whispered.

"Yes," he muttered, confused and hopeless at the same time.

"That Jacques is you…"

The feelings that came across Eran's handsome features took my breath away. They were an evolution of shock, pride, relief, thrill, and ultimately fulfillment.

"Are you telling me that you love me?" he asked, astonished.

"Yes…" I breathed, able to release a laugh at his silliness. He should have known all along.

As if reading my thoughts, he said, "I was waiting for you to declare it."

"I'm-I'm sorry you had to wait…to wait centuries," I said, pushing back against the slowing pulsations rattling my body.

Eran smiled gently. "It was worth it."

"I'm…close…" I informed him.

He nodded and took hold of his sword, raising it over his head as he had done in London so many years ago.

A sob escaped. He choked back the rest of it and recovered. Then, in case didn't convey it already through the intensity of his expression, he declared, "My love does not end here."

Unable to watch his next action, his eyes closed and he brought the sword down on me, sinking it deep within my chest.

I kept my eyes open, calling out to him though my lips would not move. I too had final words for him and I was desperate to convey them. They were simple and direct, just as his had been.

"Neither does mine."

15. GETTYSBURG, PENNSYLVANIA

The following morning I awoke to a surreal reality.

Eran was slumped in the chair with his head dipped forward and his clothes disheveled. His chest moved slowly, habitually, a clear sign that he was dozing.

Strangely, only moments ago, it was me who appeared feeble.

Of course, Eran was not feeble. Far from it. It was his days of staying awake and alert to protect me and nights flying around the world to perform reconnaissance had caught up to him.

I couldn't blame him.

Realizing this was the first time I had seen Eran asleep – ever – I remained sitting in bed, studying him.

Gone was the horror at facing the taking of my life. In replace of it, was the calm, peaceful countenance that Eran traditionally exuded. His nose was chiseled to perfection, his jaw line was defined and powerful, his lips were swollen from sleep.

He was breathtaking.

Giving in to the urge of a closer look, I slipped my legs off the side of the bed and carefully placed my feet on the floor. Once standing, I turned and found him awake and staring at me.

He tilted his head to the side and, fighting an awkward smile, he asked, "Still trying to sneak out?"

Sneak out? I thought. Of course, he'd expect that. I had a history of it and I was currently in the motions of silently standing up.

I opened my mouth to respond but no words came out. How could I admit that I was about to approach him for a better stare? After all that I had seen of our past lives, after our confession of love, after the taking of my life, it felt trivial.

"I see," he said, deducing that he was correct. Standing also, he approached me to divulge, "Even when it may appear that I am sleeping…I am not. I hear every sound. You have little hope of escaping."

He was within arms reach, which as usual caused my heart to quicken and pleasant exhilaration to build in me. I opened my mouth again to answer and closed it when I realized that I had chosen no words to speak.

"I'll see you in the kitchen," he said, and left my room.

He was still smirking at me as I gulped down a cup of coffee and eggs made by Rufus. Felix was busy preparing a special dinner tonight – Pickled Pig's Snout – so he didn't acknowledge us much. Ezra and Campion were both reading the newspaper, heads bowed deep inside the fold. Eran and I agreed to be back in time for dinner and left for school, where I actively fought the reaction I had to Fallen Ones hidden throughout the streets. Nearly exhausted by that exercise I was thankful when we were able to take our seats in Biochemistry.

Again, Ms. Beedinwigg treated Eran and I like any other student, engaging us in conversation when the situation arose. It was a refreshing change considering that the students and remaining faculty either glared at us or snubbed us entirely.

Homework was becoming a problem for both of us – with nightly responsibilities consuming our time - so we spent much of the lunch hour in the library cramming in answers to questions and racing through required reading chapters.

At the end of the day, we made it home without incident involving any Fallen Ones, though I sensed them along the way.

Entering the house, our noses were assaulted with the smell of Pickled Pig's Snout which emitted the aroma of vinegar and rubber, a particularly unappetizing combination.

To our surprise, Felix agreed with the rest of us in our reluctance to dine on this newly-inspired dish and ordered pizzas instead. Someone turned on the transistor radio on a shelf in the kitchen to a melodic jazz station, another poured the drinks and we spent the next hour sitting around the table talking.

Eran and Campion were astonished to learn that Felix had grown up in foster care in Indianapolis and ended up studying with some of the world's most renowned chefs. In fact, it was one of these chefs that introduced him to his love for tarot cards and he joined the psychic circuit quickly after. He met Ezra on the circuit almost immediately and traveled with her from that point.

They were also intrigued to hear that Ezra had come from a wealthy family on the east coast and was handed off from one relative to the next when her parents died. As a teenager, she befriended juvenile delinquents and ran unchecked until she began to realize that she could change their lives for the better. From that point forward, she educated herself, earning multiple doctorate degrees while working the psychic circuit as well. She then dedicated her life to guiding those who needed it and counseling juveniles in trouble.

Rufus also grew up without parents. He had lived his life in an orphanage in Ireland until his teenage years. The tattoos he bore reflected something special and unique about each of his former orphanage mates. Alone and without much proper education, he had come to America, drawing sketches on the streets for dimes. He met Ezra not long after and began traveling the psychic circuit with her, picking up Felix sometime thereafter.

They had considered themselves a family from then on.

Then it came time for Eran to leave and we stepped out on to the back porch together.

"Germany again?" I asked nervously.

He nodded his head, sympathetic to my fear for him. Without me having to say so, he knew that my mind was more often on him than the dinner conversation. "I intend to find out more about Sarai and Achan's plan."

"All right," I muttered. "Just be-"

"Careful. I will…" he confirmed, drawing his shirt over his head and handing it to me. Then, with a powerful thrust of his wings, he spun and lifted into the inky black sky.

I waited, noting the elegant contours of his muscular back, until he was out of sight.

As always, Campion gave us our time and waited until Eran had gone before opening the door. He pulled my bike from the shed and we left for another session with Ms. Beedinwigg.

Just as the night before, I raced the obstacle courses and we practiced weaponry with multiple attackers. Although, this time Ms. Beedinwigg took each piece of artillery, described it, gave a brief history on which Fallen Ones were known to use it (recounting many names I'd never heard before), and finally showed me how to use it.

I memorized them and their uses on the way home and until my head met the pillow.

Seconds later, I was back in the Hall of Records.

Pulling my scroll from the wall, I unrolled it and moved my finger over my fourth and final past life:

Previously Margaret Talor – Died Gettysburg, Pennsylvania, July 3, 1863

I was dropped into my body sometime during my teenage years. I became aware of this after glancing at my reflection in a window across from me. My hair and face remained the same but my clothing was now a tight, itchy, sweltering dress and petticoat. My shoes were without cushion so my feet ached a little as I stood on a rutted dirt road.

Directly in front of me was Eran, also in his teenage years and wearing trousers, a cotton shirt, and an eagle feather behind his ear. A necklace dangled around his neck, lined with the teeth of different animals, ones that I figured he had killed as a test of courage and strength.

A line had been created in front of him of six boys, each restlessly shifting around as if they were itching for a fight.

"Injun lover," said one boy of the six standing before Eran.

He contemplated that and then nodded. "Yes, that would be accurate."

Another boy scoffed, "See…he doesn't even try to deny it."

A few others snickered.

One of Eran's shoulders shrugged and from the look on his face he couldn't have cared less. He then turned to leave.

Suddenly, the boy closest to him reached out and pulled him back by the shoulder.

To me, from my stance on the side of the road, that looked like a challenge. I stepped forward.

Noticing my movement, Eran put his hand up in my direction. "No."

Against my wishes, I stopped.

That gave the boys all the fodder they needed and the haranguing began.

"Letting a girl fight for you, eh Eran?"

"Scared? He's scared, boys!"

"Need a girl to do your dirty work?"

"Ignore them, Eran!"

Those last words came from my mouth, I realized.

A few of Eran's attackers glanced in my direction; the ones who didn't saw the first strike.

The boy closest to Eran pulled his arm back, curled his fist, and flung it forward.

The only problem for the boy was that Eran had seen it too.

As the fist came forward, Eran deftly stepped out of the way, sending the boy flying through the air, floundering to keep himself from falling forward.

Then a round of fists flew forward, all aimed at Eran.

He sidestepped them all, spinning, ducking and maneuvering himself away from contact.

I heard a commotion behind me and twisted to find a group of boys and girls of varying ages running towards us, clumps of dirt kicking up behind them. Most of them were yelling the same word: Fight!

Surrounding Eran and the other six boys, they watched with concentrated interest as the fists were hurled, none of which were Eran's.

"Isn't he heavenly?" said one girl beside me, not bothering to hide her wistfulness.

The girls next to her sighed, tilting their heads dreamily.

Who, I wondered, could these girls be stupid enough to be infatuated over when clearly none of them were able to defend themselves?

"His name is Eran, right?" asked one and the other shushed her, eyeing me warily.

Pride swelled in me then, coursing through my entire being. There was not a hint of jealousy with it. There shouldn't have been. Eran had already professed his love for me in Paris and, judging from this body's reaction to the girls, he'd already reinforced it in this life.

Eran pranced through the storm of attacks with ease, skillfully avoiding any injury. One by one the boys fell or tired and stepped to the side. In the end only one remained in the circle.

"Aren't you..." he huffed, "going to try to hit just once?"

"Why?" Eran asked confused. "You're doing a fine enough job beating yourself."

That spurred a brief rage in the boy and he took a swing, missed yet again, and, without the energy to keep himself up, fell to the ground in a puff of dust.

Eran waltzed to my side, took my hand, and led me through the crowd. But before leaving, he did land one jab. Glancing over his shoulder, he called out, his voice edged in sarcasm, "Thanks for the practice...boys."

We left the crowd at the roadside watching us walk into the forest surrounding us. We walked for several minutes with Eran courteously helping me over fallen logs and small boulders. We talked, though I didn't understand much of it as it dealt with people that I didn't recall in this life time.

Then we reached a cliff overlooking an awe-inspiring gorge and I wondered where we intended to go now.

Eran removed his shirt, his muscles still steaming from the fight and glinting off the sun, and tucked one end into his pants. Shockingly, I was removing my own clothing now. The stiff, tight dress I'd worn slipped down my body to my ankles and I stepped out. Beneath it was a pair of loose fitting cotton pants tightened around the waist and ankles. My torso was covered in a custom shirt with a gaping hole at my shoulder blades. The reason for it became clear to me when my wings sprouted from the hole and stretched admirably long. Eran also had his wings extended. They tucked under him, sprang out to their full length, and caught the air just as Eran tipped over the cliff's edge. He soared out into the gorge, the wind rippling the feathers along the base of his wings. Standing out in contrast against the green and blue backdrop of the gorge, his pale body and stark white wings carried him through the cool air with grace and agility.

I followed shortly behind him; tipping over the edge and allowing my wings to lift me back into the air. The wind caught under my wings and carried me effortlessly, whistling in my ears and carrying the smell of fresh earth across the breeze. My clothes fluttered wildly against my body and my hair, long and untied, snapped loudly behind me.

As I reached Eran, our wings just inches apart, he grinned and I knew he felt the very same way I did…absolutely free. Then his grin changed to a smirk just before he twirled and darted for the ground. I followed and we reached the treetops in seconds.

Eran came to a sharp stop just behind a boulder, where he pulled the shirt from his pants and slipped it on. I reached him and followed the same process, dropping the dress I'd worn over my head.

His grin returned as he took my hand and we walked around the boulder where a large cluster of teepees lay. Native Americans walked between them, carrying children, bowls, and clothing, going about their daily chores.

He led me to a larger but otherwise unremarkable teepee towards the edge of the village. Drawing back the animal skin doorway, he stepped inside, releasing my hand then so I could enter too.

An elderly man with graying, waist-length hair, braided and decorated with feathers sat inside. I assumed immediately that he was their chief.

He beckoned us.

In the Iroquoian language of the Susquehannock people, Eran stated, "I brought what you asked."

As in other past lives, I listened and, though I did not know the language, I understood the words.

The chief nodded and waited patiently as Eran drew a sack from his pocket and handed it to the chief.

The chief opened it, tilted the bag, and coins fell in to his hands.

"Was it a good trade?"

"Yes it was," replied Eran.

The chief nodded.

The entire process was extraordinarily unhurried and serene as if both men had the entire day to complete their business. I reasoned that the trade involving those coins must have been the purpose behind our trip in to the town where Eran had met his six rivals.

"When you came," said the chief, "to us as a child I saw courage in you. The teeth of animals you have collected hanging from your neck shows this. As our trade man, you have been good. Courageous and good. Your parents are happy too of your history. Now…it is time. Search out your own path."

Eran nodded once, showing respect and appreciation to the chief, and I deduced that this arrangement had been in process for some time.

Their discussion continued then but on less significant topics and when the meeting ended we left the tent. Stepping out, Eran looked up towards the sky. "Nearly dusk…Good," he muttered. Then he turned to me and with a glimmer in his eyes, he asked, "Will you fly with me?"

I agreed, we found our boulder, stripped down, ran through the forest and launched ourselves in to flight. Heading away from the village, we rose into the sky, lifting ourselves above the mountain range. There, in a spectrum of yellow, orange, and peach, Eran paused and I came to his side, as we watched the sunset together.

Just before the last of the sun's rays sunk below the horizon, Eran turned to me. His lips were pursed together as if he were trying not to smile, to hold back an influx of emotions. Then, a wave of peace came over him, his shoulders dropped, his expression grew quietly confident, and his eyes – his gorgeous blue-green eyes – radiated warmth and purpose.

"Magdalene," he said, using my eternal name. "I became your guardian in an effort to protect your life, your existence. I have done so to the very best of my ability and will continue to do so regardless of your answer tonight."

My brow creased and I asked suspiciously, "My answer?"

Without addressing it further, he continued on, unshaken and determined. "When I fell to earth and met you the first time…in Germany…I did so with the intention of finding you and learning about the messenger who had saved her kind from extinction by training them to defeat their enemies. But I learned so much more than I knew possible. I learned not about the messenger but the woman…who gave courage new meaning, who devoted her existence to saving everyone but herself, who defied the odds and endured agony beyond description at the hands of her enemies all to deliver messages for the distraught on earth to those in the afterlife. But it wasn't until London did I witness the awakening of your love for me. It was there in your eyes in your final moments…and it was undeniable…But you still hadn't spoken the words. Not until Paris did you confess your love for me. That was over two and a half centuries, Magdalene. Two and a half centuries is a long time to wait." He paused to chuckle at the understatement and I, recognizing the truth to those words, joined him. Then he grew serious again, though I noticed that the gleam in his handsome face never wavered. "I hope it won't take you as long to answer my question tonight…I promise to remain your loyal protector no matter how often you return to earth; I promise to remain dedicated to you beyond the realm of a protector; and I promise you that what I feel for you…this feeling that defies description and makes the word 'love' pale in comparison…what I feel for you will never end…" He paused briefly to emphasize his message, "…ever, Magdalene."

His head dipped then as he pulled something from his pocket. Holding it in a way that kept it hidden from my sight, he spoke again. Only then did he express any hint of awkwardness. "I'm aware that by custom, I should be bent on one knee. Given that there is no ground here to do so, please don't fear that my chivalry is at risk. I chose the sky for this proposal because it gave us privacy and peace."

"This proposal?" I mumbled.

Only then did I realize what Eran was doing. It became clearer when he reached for my hand and slipped a ring on my finger.

"I-I picked this up a while ago…on a trade for the chief. I-I hope you like it."

I didn't even bother to glance at it. Stunned, I asked, "You've been carrying this around with you? I had no idea…"

"That was my intention…" he said, laughing quietly.

He hadn't released my hand yet, still holding it gently in his own. "Magdalene, will you do me the momentous honor of being my wife?"

Beyond the lump in my throat and just before the tears came, I answered, "Yes…yes…for all eternity…yes…"

Eran sighed and pulled me into his arms, the hardness of his body meeting mine, causing my heart to leap. He moved his lips to mine and kissed me softly, tenderly but with deep, underlying passion. When he pulled away, I saw relief in him and it took me by surprise.

"You must have known I would say yes…Of course I would say yes…"

His head fell and shook back and forth. "I've seen you deny so many suitors…I couldn't be sure…"

Waiting until he lifted his head again and our gazes met, I responded pointedly, "None of them were you."

He drew in a staggered breath and subdued a quivering smile. He understood my meaning. "Then thank you for waiting for me too."

I was again yanked down the tunnel then and ended up in my body a short while later.

We were now standing on the edge of a crystal clear lake, surrounded by fragrant, towering pine trees. To our left was a wooden dock and, beyond it, a burbling brook ran across boulders and stones to reach the lake's edge. On the horizon, jagged red and brown mountain peaks cut through a layer of misty clouds.

I had been here before.

If I could turn around, if I had any control over this body, I would see a log cabin built at the base of the trees, chairs set on the front porch running the length of the structure and a dirt path carved from the porch steps to the dock down the hill.

Of course, I couldn't turn around and it didn't look like this body would do it any time soon. I was standing before the chief with Eran beside me. We were dressed in decorative Native American ceremonial clothes and as I listened to the chief I knew what we were doing.

"Oh, Great Spirit, whose voice I hear in the wind, I pray to you…look after the well being of these ones who are in love." The chief motioned to Eran and me, and I felt my head turn for a peek at Eran.

He was stunning.

The profile of his face; the strong slope of his nose; the eyelashes that brushed the top of his lids; the defined edge of his jaw line; the purposeful line of his lips, all made my knees go weak.

I looked back towards the chief before my body could collapse.

"Help them seek pure thoughts and act with the intention of helping each other and others. Let them learn the lessons you have hidden in every leaf and every rock. Make their hands respect the things you have made and their ears sharp to hear your voice. Make them wise so that they may understand the things you have taught my people. Help them to remain calm and strong in the face of all that comes towards them."

The chief ended the vows, his mouth falling closed, his hands clasped at his hips.

At the same time, Eran and I both realized that the ceremony had ended and we turned towards each other.

Eran was now the one staring, gratified and loving.

Behind us, the entire village had come to participate in our celebration. I did my best to catch sight of my parents in this life, these being the only ones I had come across while reviewing my past lives. They met me briefly, faces in a crowd but being the only white ones they were easy to distinguish. She was simple with a young beauty that challenged the passing of time. Her eyes were welcoming and proud and her voice was melodic, equal to that of an opera singer. He was tall and strong with wrinkles that defined the years he'd already spent on this earth. His smile was soft and supportive.

These were my parents...messengers in their own right...my family in more ways than one.

And then they were gone and I was unable to look for them as I was unable to control the body I was in now.

Food and dancing followed the ceremony and then dusk came and just Eran and I were left.

The air had grown cold so Eran built a fire in the hearth and we retreated inside. We weren't alone though. Not far away, owls screeched and wolf howls echoed through the trees.

The cabin was simple inside with just a table and two chairs for meals and a sofa and bookcase near the fireplace for relaxing.

I stood near the fire, holding my hands to it, rubbing them together. Eran moved around behind me, pulling blankets and pillows from their folded spot by the hearth and laying them on the floor.

A moment later he was beside me, standing close by.

"Are you nervous?" he asked tenderly, watching me for any sign of the emotion.

I realized then that through the centuries this would be the very first time I would be intimate with anyone at all. Without consciously intending to, I had saved myself for Eran. So, being completely inexperienced, I should have been nervous, unsure, but I wasn't. I felt at ease, loved and protected.

"No," I replied simply, openly.

"I'll be gentle."

"I know."

He was more than gentle. He was patient, moving over my body with his lips and hands slowly exploring, teasing me. His lips left warm, moist marks along their trail. His hands, roughly textured, felt like silk against my skin. At places along my body, he would squeeze, gently, seductively until I could no longer hold myself back.

"Eran," I breathed, drawing him to me.

The sharp intake of air told me that he had found his limit too.

Our lips met, moving feverishly, enticing, pulling me into him. Our hips pressed anxiously, our limbs wrapped around each other.

Then the room went black.

When I awoke, I found myself on my back against the blankets laid across the cabin floor.

"Please…" I whispered, "Please tell me that I didn't faint."

Eran laid beside me, his arm bent so he could prop his head against the palm of his hand. Various parts of our bodies touched, leaving warm connections between us. He was staring at me, almost smirking really.

He playfully pondered his answer before saying, "I don't believe lying to you on our day of marriage would set a good precedence."

I closed my eyes again and groaned, bringing my hand up to my eyes and covering them.

He took it lightly and guided it back down to my hip.

"You have nothing to be ashamed of. I'm thankful I have that affect on you," he declared, still on the brink of a smirk.

He then took his finger and traced the contours of my hand, up my arm, and along my collarbone. "You are so fragile…" he whispered. "And yet so strong…"

I reached up and took hold of his hand, lightly kissing the tips of each finger. Eran's breathing became staggered and on the last one, he fluidly lifted his body to lie delicately on top of me. The weight of him was comforting and exciting at the same time.

"Are you feeling better?" he asked, tentatively.

"Oh yes…" I said, noticing my body coming to life again.

His endurance was remarkable. He was cautious, ensuring my body wouldn't give out again, yet indulgent. In the end, it was me who begged for him.

The covers were left entangled around us, the pillows strewn aside, the fire simmered to just a flicker.

Once again lying beside me, Eran placed his hand against my cheek and turned me to him. I smiled weakly, incredibly content, intoxicated by him.

"You," he whispered his eyes warm and fixated on me, "hold my heart captive."

I nodded solemnly before murmuring my reply. "And I'll never let it go."

I wanted to stay there, beside Eran, immersed in his enchanting blue-green eyes and held firmly by his powerful arms, forever.

That was not going to happen.

I sensed that this dramatic event in the span of my life was coming to an end and, even as I fought against it, I was pulled away from Eran and into the tunnel that would take me to the next part of my life.

In direct contrast to the serenity and love I felt just seconds ago, my body was now in explosive pain.

I found myself bound between two trees, my arms and legs outstretched and tethered to the trunks. I had been pummeled with swelling already starting on my face and limbs. Blood ran down my body, saturating the dirt below. What I noticed most of all was the hair standing up on the back of my neck, so upset they were wrenching out of my skin.

My head hung to my chest with my eyes closed, cringing against the throbbing that vibrated through my body.

A fire crackled in front of me, filling the air with smoke and heating the already warm night.

Swallowing hard, I lifted my head with the little energy I had left. It felt like concrete against my weakened neck.

Against the firelight, I caught sight of a body just to my left, sprawled in the dirt at abstract angles, bones bent in places they shouldn't be. The wings, stark white, had been cut off and tossed against the body, as if they were frivolous and cheap. The head was turned towards me, his eyes were open but there was no life in them.

"Campion," my body whispered wracked with sorrow. A wave of guilt rose up in me causing a sob to escape, and I suddenly felt nauseous.

Mocking laughter filled the clearing which I faced, laughter that I recognized instantly.

Abaddon came in to view then, bending over so that he could peer up from underneath where my head was bowed. Instinctually, my eyes followed him as he stood straight.

"You are seeing clearly," he confirmed. "Campion, your dear old friend and your guardian's best man, is now dead."

"I know," I seethed. "I escorted him to the other side. He's safe now. You can't touch him."

"Ah yes…your talent in ushering your Alterum friends to the other side. I hadn't considered that when you passed out a moment ago." He brought a finger to his lips, pondering. "Maybe I should have eased up on my torture so that you weren't able to do so…I'll tell you what. I'll keep that in mind for next time."

Chuckles erupted and I noticed we weren't alone. Sarai, Achan, Elam, and those I didn't recall, although I'm sure I knew them at the time I lived through what I was now witnessing stood on the outskirts of the clearing, sneering and confident at the position I was now in. Their choice of weapons hung from their shoulders or their belt and they were bloodied and panting as if Campion had given them a good fight.

Achan, who was closest to Campion, stepped forward and kicked him in the leg. Campion's body rolled feebly to the side and back again.

He did not move otherwise.

"Leave him alone," my body screamed ferociously, surprising myself at the level of energy I could muster. For a fleeting moment, the pain was gone and I flapped my wings wildly to free myself, thinking only of hurting him as they had done to Campion.

"Or what?" he taunted. "Will you redeem your friend? I'd like to see that happen."

"I won't need to," I said with gritted teeth, breathing heavily from my exertion. "Eran will do that for me."

Even the mention of his name caused the others in the group to bristle and glance at each other apprehensively.

"That's right," this body told them, using their fear against them. "Eran's on his way. It may be a good time to flee and avoid his arrival."

Abaddon snickered even as his cohorts grew more concerned. "Dear Messenger…his arrival is what we await…Besides, leaving wouldn't allow us to watch the grand finale…" Abaddon paused to cogitate on his last thought. "And we certainly wouldn't want to miss that…"

He waited for me to question his plan, to beg for an understanding of what he meant by 'grand finale' but I wouldn't give in to his ego. I knew him too well. It would only incite him further. His face fell briefly when he found I wouldn't play his game and he skipped away, across the clearing.

"Who," he said, strolling in front of the others, "wishes to do the honors?" He withdrew a machete and grinned wickedly at me.

Each one stepped forward, calling out his name, eager for the opportunity to take my life, my eternal life.

Abaddon taunted me, and them, strolling around the circle again. "Who was it to draw the final blow to take Campion's life?"

Achan stepped forward again, his chin lifted in pride.

My nausea worsened.

"Then it is you, my friend," said Abaddon, handing him the machete, "who is befitting the honor…"

The satisfaction on Achan's face, in the dim light of dusk, could not be denied. He sauntered towards me, twirling the blade in his hand, intending to goad my panic.

It didn't work.

I stared him directly in the eye.

"You won't have that glare for long," he hinted, passing by me to standing directly behind my body. "Though I promise not to rush this…"

The blade found the base of my right wing first.

It started as a sting, as if a large bee had pierced my skin there. But this wasn't an insect. The sharpened edge of the machete began moving back and forth, sawing through what remained of my skin and into the bone.

I was able to keep my lips pursed. They broke their line once, quivering against the torture, but I forced them back in to place.

I would not allow them the glory of hearing me scream.

After several minutes, I felt my wing, its tendons and muscles no longer attached, dip down against its own weight.

The pain scorched through the entire right side of my body.

A sickening thud a second later told me that it had been dismembered from my torso.

The blade then began on the left wing.

Woozy and barely able to differentiate feeling from vision, I heard Abaddon approach, his feet crunching through the dead leaves towards me.

"Don't worry, dear," he whispered into my ear. "Not to let you down, the grand finale is yet to come."

He now had the machete in his hand, which he used to cut through the ropes binding me to the trees.

I fell forward, my knees, chest and face hitting the bloodied dirt with impact enough to leave bruises. Shaking, weak, I pushed myself up only to collapse.

The fire was snuffed out and I was consumed by the darkness.

It was humid and hot even without the fire, leaving me struggling for air.

A cloak landed on top of me, suffocating me further. I shrugged it off as best I could.

Then, just before I heard the sound of their wings lifting them away, I felt something drop beside me. Opening my eyes, I found it was the machete.

It was quieter now. No fire or mocking laughter and I could hear the bombs exploding in the distance, like firecrackers but with a deep resonance. Smaller cracking followed...which I knew could only be artillery fire.

The Battle of Gettysburg was raging in the midst of the forest and fields. Little did anyone of them know that another battle...of another kind...was being waged alongside them.

I lay in the dirt for what seemed to be a very long time, allowing my muscles to heal, wondering why the Fallen Ones hadn't taken my life as they had with all other messengers, wondering what Abaddon meant when he threatened the grand finale.

At some point, I attempted to stand and learned that...somehow...I had enough strength. Wobbling and with intense effort, I picked myself up and pulled the cloak over me.

I was losing too much blood. The chill in me told me so.

Pulling the hood over my head, I stumbled across the clearing, moving towards the flashes of light in the distance.

A battlefield would be safer than staying here.

Unfortunately, I didn't make it to the edge of the clearing before I found someone standing just beyond the outskirts.

They were playing with me. Allowing me the hope of escape only to return and finish me off.

In my daze, I couldn't identify which one had been chosen to kill me. My view had become distorted and this was a danger. I couldn't fight well without sight.

Blinking, I lifted the machete and prepared myself for what was to come.

My enemy had his weapon drawn but he didn't seem to be paying attention to mine. He was focused on the scene behind me...Campion's body and my dissected wings.

I imagined it was smiling, enjoying the sight of Eran's first lieutenant dead and his ward dismembered.

Then it released a roar so loud that I was momentarily deafened and it came at me with such force I didn't have time to react.

I didn't feel the blade cut through my neck. I didn't feel the moment my head was severed. I didn't feel any pain at all...any longer.

I was now outside my body, watching as my head spun into the air and dropped to the ground with a dull thump. It rolled across the leaves to land next to Campion while the remainder of my body fell to my knees, the cloak falling away to expose the gashes where my wings had once been.

My attacker stopped a few feet away but didn't move.

It appeared to be evaluating what it was seeing.

Then it ran towards Campion, haphazardly, without any sign of the poise it had used to attack me moments earlier.

Its cloak slide off its shoulders, left behind in its haste.

That was when I saw the wings.

They were stark white.

The face of the person who had just beheaded me came in to my view then.

It was distorted in to intense anguish.

If I hadn't known the contours of that face so well, I wouldn't have recognized it.

It was Eran and he had just realized that he had beheaded his eternal love.

Gripping my freed head in his hands, he lifted it to the air, tilted his chin back and released a tormented bellow that shook the earth.

Seconds later, from every direction, winged beings landed around the outskirts of the clearing.

Abaddon and his squad had returned.

Eran didn't react immediately. Quietly, tenderly, he laid my head on the ground next to Campion.

They watched attentively, not wanting to miss a single detail.

Eran stood slowly, almost clumsily, his heart in despair.

From where I stood, I was alarmed that his soul had been broken.

Then he bent and picked up his sword, giving me some hope.

Leaving it limp in his hand and resting against his leg, he addressed Abaddon. "You made me think she was one of you," he deduced, his voice no higher than a whisper.

"Clever game, wouldn't you say?" said Abaddon, teasing while still leaving his guard up.

Eran simply sighed.

Knowing he would need to provoke a brawl, need to resurrect the fighter in Eran, Abaddon persisted. "We considered ending her life all together. It would have been rather easy, actually. With your first lieutenant dead and you off doing your reconnaissance of us, she was left quite unprotected. But then we realized…mutually…that she'll return to earth again. This time…her death was simply for play. Next time…it'll be forever." He drew in a lazy breath and lifted his shoulders in a careless shrug. "It would have been more responsible to have simply killed her, yes. Thereby erasing any possibility of her taking our lives in the future…We just couldn't resist ourselves." He paused to snicker at Eran. "We'd just never seen a guardian take the life of their own ward before. It was just too…enticing to resist." Realizing he was not getting the response he wanted, Abaddon stepped closer to Eran then and landed a final blow. "Tell me…how did it feel to take the life of the one you are meant to protect?"

Those words conjured motivation in Eran again and he became a blur of motion, pausing only long enough to ensure his sword made a mortal blow before continuing on to his next victim.

The Fallen Ones, too, jolted in to motion, attacking Eran from all directions.

Even with the number of warriors on their side, they were no match.

One by one they fell, their own dismembered bodies collapsing as mine had.

In the end, only Eran was left. The bodies littering the ground didn't include Abaddon, Sarai, Achan, or Elam.

They had escaped, abandoning their comrades to their own fight.

Eran stopped in the middle of the clearing, his feet dangling, his wings barely pumping, his chest heaving from his efforts, as he seethed with astonishing fury. The sword he held was now hanging at his side, blood layered over it and dripping steadily from its end.

Clear that no one else remained, he slowly turned towards the remains of me and Campion.

"If you can hear me, Magdalene, I will avenge your death," he said firmly, with absolute dedication to his words. "For as long as this body breathes, until we are united again, for the rest of this life…I will hunt and destroy the Fallen Ones. Every…last…one."

With that promise lingering in the air, Eran collected the bodies of his first lieutenant and his eternal love and shot through the trees to disappear into the night sky.

16. ATTACK

Awakening the next morning in my bed in New Orleans made me appreciate life more than I ever had before. The morning sunlight filtered in through the windows of my French doors and spilled across floor, the birds chirped outside, the smell of bacon rose up from the kitchen below. Most precious of all, I was going to open my eyes to Eran.

It turned out that Campion was the one slouched in my chair instead.

He pushed himself to a sitting position and yawned loudly. "What time is it?"

I was already looking wearily at my French doors, which remained closed and locked. "Morning," I said. "And Eran's not back."

That made Campion perk up. He made three quick steps to the doors and swung them open, scanning the sky. I was at his side seconds later.

"This-This is the first time he hasn't come back," I said, trying to shove back the uncomfortable worries now nagging my consciousness.

My worry grew when Campion didn't reply. That, I knew, meant he had the same level of concern.

"Germany," I stated. "He said he was going to Germany."

"Yes, he had a meeting."

"A meeting?" My head snapped in his direction. "What meeting? With who?"

"Magnus...he's an Alterum who has been feeding Eran information."

"All right. What do we know about Magnus?"

Campion drew in a deep breath. "Not much I'm afraid...He has been one of the guards at the prison-"

My eyebrows rose. "The one holding the Fallen Ones...the Elsics captive?"

"Is there any other one?"

"Good point," I said.

"Magnus keeps in contact with the guards currently at the prison. He stays connected to others too, others who know things about the Fallen Ones. He's older, living the rest of his years in Berlin. He-There he is!"

Briefly I thought Campion, who had suddenly pointed to the sky, was referring to Magnus. But it wasn't an elderly Alterum coming through the clouds...it was Eran.

He was flying briskly, with a sense of urgency, and landed with the same intensity.

Breathless in his hurry to return, he apologized, "My meeting ran late."

"Did you learn anything?" Campion asked, without any sign of relief. Apparently, he overcame his worries quickly.

I didn't recover as easily.

"You terrified us," I snapped.

Eran glanced at me in insulted surprise. "I'm sorry."

"You should be," I said, drawing in a deep breath and finally relaxing.

Eran fought back a chuckle at my expense, clearly enjoying my public display of love. He chose to ignore me and let me settle down while he answered Campion.

"Magnus hasn't heard from the guards at the prison and that is suspicious. We're meeting tonight to discuss what should be done."

The three of us stood in silence, ill at ease with the news and the prospect of what news Magnus might bring back.

It was Eran who got us moving. "Campion, we'll meet you in the kitchen. Magdalene, get ready for school."

Campion did as he was instructed and I entered my room to pull clothes from my closet.

Eran paused at the door and cleared his throat. "I understand Ezra's rule about keeping the door open when a male is in your room, and personally I agree with it. But on this occasion I'm going to have to break her rule."

"Why?" I asked casually, dropping my clothes selection on the wingback chair.

"I don't want you alone in a room today."

"Well, I'm headed for the bathroom where I'll be taking a shower…"

"I won't peek," he replied politely.

"But if Ezra catches you…"

Eran smiled lightly at my teasing. "It's a chance I'll take."

True to his word, Eran stood at the door, his back to me the entire time. It must have been incredibly humbling considering that we were actually husband and wife. I wondered if Ezra knew that we'd been bound by marriage in our previous life whether she'd consider lifting her no-males-in-the-room-without-door-open rule. I suspected so but Eran, who knew we were married before, had never mentioned it to her. I wondered how he felt about it and decided to ask the moment we were alone and the shower wasn't thundering around my ears. I wanted to hear his answer clearly.

I showered in record time this morning. In fact, my mind was so concentrated on Eran and the remembrance of my life in Gettysburg that I didn't realize I'd forgotten to condition my hair until I'd stepped out of the shower and already blown it dry.

When Eran and I left the bathroom, the hallway was clear but there was one last hurdle to overcome in avoiding Ezra. My change of clothes was still in my room so I would need to dress there.

Eran apparently already took this factor in to consideration because he followed me into my room, closed the door, and faced it, just as he'd done in the bathroom.

This time, I didn't rush.

Eran stood stiffly in place though I couldn't tell if he was at all provoked. His breathing seemed to be even paced...

"I've been through my past lives," I announced, slowly unfolding my clothes.

"I see," he replied plainly.

"Including the one in Gettysburg, Pennsylvania..."

I didn't think it was possible but Eran stiffened further. "Which means you saw the end of your life...there."

This wasn't the direction I wanted the conversation to take.

"Yes, I also saw-"

"Then you saw what they did...what I..." He swallowed. "What I did."

"Eran," I stopped with my t-shirt nearly over my head and dropped it to my side. "I saw it and it wasn't your fault. You were...it was a deception. You were deceived. I was deceived. And now it's over."

"It'll never be over," he said quietly. "Not until they all suffer eternal death." He started to turn around, impulsively driven by the need to face me and show his sincerity, but realized what he was doing and turned back. "I made that promise to you, Magdalene. I will keep it."

"I'm not concerned about it," I said, noticing a muscle quiver beneath his taut t-shirt. He was growing angrier. Before he could go on, I changed the subject. "I also saw our wedding."

That did the trick. His breathing froze.

"Your proposal in the sky," I continued, "our ceremony outside the cabin you built…our wedding night…"

He drew in a shallow breath then and I knew his emotions were changing from anger to another type of physical response…lust.

I pulled my shirt over my head feeling slightly awkward about covering up while mentioning about a time when I had been uncovered in his presence. A single look at him made me overcome that way of thinking.

His broad shoulders were squared, his feet apart, his powerful hands hanging down his lean, lithe body. He was glorious.

"You touched me so lovingly…"

His hands clenched into fists and I guessed he was trying to quell the emotions running through him.

"The way your fingers…your lips…ran across my body…"

He drew in a slow, struggled breath and released it quickly.

"You captivated me…"

His jaw clenched tight and the muscles in his neck flexed.

"If we are still husband and wife, why won't you touch me like that again?"

He released a groan, one of pent up passion, spun around, and marched towards me. Two quick steps and he was in front of me, taking me in his arms. His kiss came down soft but commanding. I met him with the same enthusiasm, arching my body against his, grabbing his shirt and pulling me to him. He moaned. We pressed closer. It lasted another second, far too short, when a knock came at my door.

"Maggie?"

It was Ezra.

"Felix is wondering if you want breakfast."

Eran had already pulled his lips away but kept his arms locked around my waist.

"Uh, sure."

After a brief pause, she asked, "Don't you want to know what it is?"

"Umm, I'm hungry. I'll eat anything."

"Okay…" she replied forebodingly.

My eyes darted back to Eran and I whispered, "She's going to wonder where you are when she knocks on your door and you're not there."

As it turned out, Ezra already knew where to find him.

Still standing outside my door, she called through it. "Do you want breakfast too, Eran?"

He broke into a smile but was able to withhold his laughter. "Sure…Thanks, Ezra."

"Ummm hmmm," she replied, disapprovingly, through the door.

The floorboards creaked and we knew she was on her way downstairs.

"She's not going to be very happy with us," I whispered in case my voice carried.

"No…she won't be."

He hadn't released his hold on me yet and I wondered just what Ezra would do if she opened the door to find us in an embrace, me without my jeans on.

Eran was watching me, the passion in him still remaining. "For the record, I do want to touch you like that again…far more than you can imagine. But, being the gentleman that I am, I try to restrain myself as best I can. It

221

becomes quite challenging when you tease me like that, Mrs. Talor…"

My heart flipped at the sound of my married name.

"Now…" he collected my jeans and handed them to me. "It would be safest for both of us if you were to finish dressing or I don't believe we'll make it out your bedroom door until…well, most certainly, not until tomorrow."

"Tomorrow?" I asked, amazed.

"It has been a long time, Magdalene…and I like to take my time with you."

"I seem to recall that."

Grinning back at me, he returned to his place at the door…and turned to face it.

I slipped my jeans on quickly, so as not to tease Eran any further, and we headed downstairs to avoid Ezra's critical stare and suffer through Felix's homemade bacon and liver pastries.

It was Thursday, and only the second week at school, which meant pop quizzes. Everyone, including Ms. Beedinwigg, gave them. It was like a preplanned faculty assault.

Eran asked me how I'd done and my results were so poor I didn't want to tell him. He, however, missed only one question…just one out of four quizzes he'd been given. I told him that it was unfair that he, as an Alterum and with memory since the beginning of time, could recite the entire earth's history.

I sulked to my bike at the end of the day, gravely frustrated in my performance at school. Always having been a good student with impeccable grades, the late night training with Ms. Beedinwigg and the emotional toll of reliving my past life experiences were clearly having an impact on my life.

Still, after dinner was over that night and Eran had left for his mission, rather than opening my books, I headed for Mr. Hamilton's house for another session with Ms.

Beedinwigg. Even though I was frustrated with my grades, I knew that defeating the Fallen Ones was far more important in the scheme of it all. Ms. Beedinwigg didn't acknowledge my miserable pop quiz score so she'd apparently come to the same conclusion. Instead, she gave me another type of test.

"Maggie," she said, handing me a sword. "What have you learned when Fallen Ones were nearby?

At first this seemed to be another pop quiz, which didn't leave me thrilled.

"My radar goes off."

"Correct," she stated.

At least I got one question correct today.

"What did you learn about your radar while reliving segments of your past life?"

"That I was able to control it."

"Excellent," she said. "Do you know how?"

"No…" I said but unwilling to give up that easily I added, "By focusing on my surroundings."

"Yes, that's right," she said. "Although you don't remember this, you were able to control your reaction to them in every one of your past lives. You're going to learn how to focus on your surroundings again tonight."

"How?" I asked, leery. "Do you have a Fallen One stashed away?"

"As a matter of fact…" she replied, "we don't. But we don't need one. We're going to create a reaction similar to the way you feel when one is around."

With that announced, she approached me with a belt unlike anything I'd ever seen. It had small black boxes attached to it every half inch.

"This is a device we've created and used in the training of other messengers. It will send shock waves through you, bolts of electricity that distract you…exactly the same as what you feel in the presence of Fallen Ones."

I took it and buckled it to my waist, suspicious of how well it would work. I'd been experiencing these feelings for the last three months and most intensely since the hoards of the Fallen Ones began arriving in New Orleans. I was skeptical, to say the least, that it could simulate the precise feelings and intensity of my radar.

"Try it," I said.

She held a remote controlled switch in her hand that she flicked on.

Immediately, the hair on the back of my neck rose up, my palms went sweaty, and my heart raced.

She kept it on for only seconds but it felt like hours. Flicking off the switch, she waited for my confirmation.

"Yeah…that works."

Pleased, she walked to the beginning of the first obstacle course and pointed out, "You may have noticed that these two courses are meant to run together. You'll be running both courses tonight, starting here and stopping at the end of the second one. You will be timed and…I will be using the device."

I nodded though I was not quite sure of this exercise. My radar going off had always been a distraction. Yet, I figured if I could ignore it in previous lives, I could do it just the same here.

Stepping up to the beginning of the course, I waited for Ms. Beedinwigg's signal and then launched in to a sprint.

I felt her turn on the machine by the second step I made inside the contraption. The moment I felt the feeling of panic rising in me, I smelled the metal coming off the machines, something I'd never noticed before. I heard the grinding of the fourth mechanism and knew it needed oil. Looking ahead of me at the way each part of the obstacle course was laid to fall in a precise order…I knew what to avoid and when.

Being so alert to the course, I didn't feel the signal not once after it went off. At the end, as I stepped out of the last potential threat, I recognized the signal again.

Ms. Beedinwigg flicked it off.

Turning, I found Campion and Alfred staring at me, jaws fallen open.

Ms. Beedinwigg stood just to their left, smiling proudly.

"Was that good?" I asked. "It felt good."

"I think 'good' would be an extreme understatement," said Campion.

I smiled my appreciation at his flattery but Ms. Beedinwigg didn't allow me a moment of glory.

"Let's try it now with multiple attackers," she suggested, handing me a sword and collecting weapons for her and Alfred. "I saw you hone your reaction at our last session when Alfred came into the fight. Your senses were up. They were aggravated and you skillfully used them to defeat me and to fight Alfred. I want to see you use your panic again, dominate it, use it…and nothing will overpower you."

She and Alfred raised their weapons and then she flicked on the belt.

My body, having relaxed a little, sprang back in to action.

Then came the first strike.

I deflected Ms. Beedinwigg's weapon at the last second. Another glinting, silver shard came in to view – Alfred's weapon - and I was able to deflect it.

Then I saw it all. I knew where Ms. Beedinwigg was going to strike by the sway of her torso and the way she flexed her muscles. I saw Alfred's technique as if I was the one commanding the steps and because of it I could judge where he would land his weapon. The fight became a dance, one in which I saw every move before it happened. My body followed the speed and direction of their weapons so that they were unable to connect with me, taking aim and attacking when I saw a gap in their defense. In the end, Ms. Beedinwigg landed on the ground with Alfred on top of her, both necks against my sword.

Ms. Beedinwigg, panting, said, "You're better than I thought you'd be."

I smirked at her. "Happy to disappoint." I stood up, rolled my shoulders, and added, "That felt good. Let's go again."

Ms. Beedinwigg snickered. "I think the trainers have done all they can for the day."

Campion approached from his regular chair against the back wall. "It's a good day when you outlast the trainer."

"It certainly is," agreed Ms. Beedinwigg then she paused and assessed me openly. "You are almost ready."

"Almost?" I scoffed. "I believe I could have handled you and Alfred with one hand behind my back. How could I not be ready?"

Ms. Beedinwigg looked at me squarely. "Trust me…there will come a time when you are ready. You have not crossed that threshold. Not yet."

I rolled my eyes, spinning on my heels. Silent and disgruntled, I fit my weapon back in its place in the cabinet.

"I'll see you tomorrow," Ms. Beedinwigg called out.

"Right, right," I muttered, heading up the stairs.

Campion and I drove home, with me at the handlebars. I sped, while sensing strongly that Campion disagreed with my little display of anger.

I didn't care.

When we reached the driveway, I stopped and said over the rumble of my Harley Davidson, "I'd like some time on my own."

"Maggie," he called over the thundering motor, "don't you think you're taking this temper tantrum a bit far?"

That made me twist in my seat. My lips pinched in anger until I spoke. "I'm ready, Campion. I'm ready."

"Yes, but…" he sighed in frustration, "yes but she has generations of training experience. Don't you think you should listen to her?"

"She has generations of experience and yet I took her down tonight…she and Alfred…together," I pointed out.

"But she knows what you're up against with the Fallen Ones. She knows what to expect-"

"Campion," I cut him off. "I appreciate your input. I do. But I need some time on my own. Would you mind getting off my motorcycle?"

He disagreed. I could tell from his lack of movement. Eventually though, after several seconds of silent contemplation, he stepped off and moved to the edge of the driveway.

"Thanks," I said, though I wasn't sure if he heard me over the motor's roar.

The truth was…my mind was having an internal dialogue its self. While partly agreeing with Campion, I also trusted my instincts. I felt ready. I watched my past lives, reliving them so that my mind recalled the movements I'd used in defense. I had beaten the course and multiple-attacker training with Ms. Beedinwigg and Alfred landing on the floor at the edge of my blade.

I was good.

In the back of my mind I could hear Ms. Beedinwigg tell me, "Good isn't good enough. You are mankind's last hope. You are the last of the messengers. You need to be perfect."

Those words were lingering in my consciousness as I drove the bike into the shed. Still overwhelmingly annoyed, I kicked out the stand, leaned it, and swung my leg over to the ground. Pulling my key from the ignition, I strolled to the door and stopped.

Only then did I notice the hair on the back of my neck was going wild. I hadn't felt them rise up, being so preoccupied with anger.

Absentmindedly, I glanced down to my waist.

Yes, I'd remembered to take off Ms. Beedinwigg's device.

That was when I heard the growl.

It was nearly pitch black in the small shed where I stored my Harley Davidson with only a faint illumination from the street light several yards away. My eyes scanned the darkness.

There was only one place for the Fallen One to hide…in the shadows.

I hadn't moved since it let me know it was here. Instead, I concentrated on its sound, trying to determine where it stood from behind me.

It was breathing, slow and shallow, but the noise echoed off the metal inside, disrupting any potential at honing in on it. A rustling sound told me that it had just opened its wings…readying for attack.

I couldn't get a firm fix on the sounds until the very last second. Only when it had launched itself into the air did I know where it was hiding.

A scrapping, long and hideous, against the metal told me that it hadn't been standing in the shadows at all. It had been clinging on the main beam running from one end of the roof to the other.

It had been hiding from above.

That wasn't what threw me, however.

The scrapping sound came from claws and if my attacker had claws it wasn't a Fallen One.

I was now in the presence of an Elsic.

Although I attempted to turn, my body only made it halfway around before the collision came.

The force of it made my body flip, heels sweeping fully around towards the sky and back to the ground again.

Already in motion, I fell backwards, landing hard against the firm dirt.

My breath was gone. My mouth was open, my chest was moving, but no air was filling my lungs.

The wind had been knocked out of me.

Haggard, my breath drew in then, but the damage had been done. My attacker had me where it wanted me: On the ground, alone, and without a single weapon in sight.

Then my mind slowed, focusing. From its walk I knew it would attack from the right side.

Its muscles were tensing on that side of its body.

I, however, wasn't going to wait around for it.

Flipping my legs over my head again – this time with purpose – I rolled over and landed on my feet.

Its wings drew out, stretching longer than a man's body.

I couldn't see much of it in the darkness but I assumed it was sneering.

"Let's go," I hissed, not allowing my voice above a whisper or my housemates would hear and certainly be hurt in an attempt to rescue me.

It came at me then but it never touched me.

The influx of sensory perception when a Fallen One was present had now been controlled. Using it, I watched its attacks, diverting them, sweeping, hurling, and ducking out of its way.

It nicked my ear and slammed against my elbow but never came any closer.

Then it was on the ground, tumbling. Another body was on top of it, this one with white wings.

In one fluid motion, my savior rose up and sliced my attacker across the chest.

Blood spewed, it bent in pain only to snap back and spring towards the sky. Its wings flapping wildly, it disappeared a second later.

The one left on the ground, my guardian, turned to me. "Are you harmed?"

"No, Eran," I said quietly in awe of him.

He bent his knees then and launched himself upwards, his wings carrying him rapidly in the direction my attacker had gone.

Campion was beside me then, his own wings out and ready.

"Stay," Eran commanded with a holler over his shoulder and Campion's wings settled.

Campion and I watched the sky without a word spoken.

Minutes passed.

Everything was silent.

Then, in the distance…movement.

I held my breath, unblinking, watching the being approach.

It floated through the clouds, descending towards us, for what felt like hours until it was just beyond the tree tops.

"Eran," I breathed in relief.

He landed directly in front of us and stepped forward once, allowing his wings to settle against his back.

"I lost it in the lake," he said, all of us understanding that to be Lake Pontchartrain.

"I didn't know Elsics could swim," I replied.

Eran's head snapped in my direction. "Is that what you saw? An Elsic?"

"I'm-I'm really not sure," I admitted. "It was pretty dark out here."

Eran's eyes fell to the ground. "It definitely flew like one."

Campion, having remained silent this entire time, cut between us and headed for the shed. He stopped and dropped to one knee just outside it, picking up something from the ground. Carrying it back, he held it up for Eran and me to see.

"An Elsic feather?" Campion asked.

Eran's face tensed. "Magdalene, please go inside. Wait for me in the kitchen."

I was about to reject that idea until I realized I could simply listen to them through the door. Apparently, Eran knew this too because he spoke too low for me to hear, even with my ear to the door.

They entered a few minutes later, solemn. Campion left the kitchen almost immediately.

"Where did you learn to fight like that?" he asked.

"Was that an Elsic feather?" I countered.

He stared at me clearly not interested in playing a game of who could ask more questions before the other one caved.

"I believe so," he finally acknowledged.

"What does that mean?" I asked.

"Where did you learn to fight like that?" he repeated, unwavering now.

He'd answered me so I acquiesced to him. "Ms.Beedinwigg, of course."

He tilted his head forward, blinking. "Ms. Beedinwigg? Our biochemistry teacher?"

"Yes," I answered confused. "My nightly sessions...training with her..."

His brow creased. "Nightly sessions?"

"Yes," I stated. "Campion told you about it that morning on the balcony."

Eran brought his head back, perplexed and struggling to recall. Then his face loosened as understanding came over him. "That," he chuckled, "That was not a discussion about your training with Ms. Beedinwigg. He informed me that morning that you worry about my missions and that you've ask at times to be put to sleep for the night."

"What?"

"He never informed me-"

"I heard you."

We stared at each other for a moment and then I chuckled. "I wondered why you never asked about them…"

"Because I never knew about them to begin with…" he stated, not smiling but not upset. I figured his thoughts were still partly on the Elsic feather, which he held in his hand. "So…you're in training with Ms. Beedinwigg. Evidently she's training you to conquer Fallen Ones and has been doing so for a while now."

"Several days," I confirmed.

"Well, she's certainly good with her disguises." His shoulders lifted after a quick half-laugh. "I had no idea she was from the human families you hired to train you…" He stared back at me proudly. "She's taught you well."

"Retaught…retrained…whatever…" I shrugged, not knowing how to convey that I'd known it all before until I returned as a reborn and forgotten it. "She's a good teacher."

We were silent for a moment, an awkward silence, until I asked the question we both knew I would.

"You believe that was an Elsic out there tonight?"

He did not look like he wanted to answer. "I can't tell you one way or another, but I'm going to do my best to find out."

"How will you do that?"

"I'll be meeting with Magnus tonight and we'll need to determine who will go to the prison to ensure it hasn't been compromised."

"Not you," I nearly shouted.

There was no way I would go along with Eran stopping in at the place that held captive the Fallen Ones he had imprisoned, especially when the security could have been compromised.

Eran knew this and did the only thing he could at that moment.

"Magdalene, my love," he stated, "Forgive me for this." He then called out towards the living room. "Campion."

He came around the corner.

I began to oppose.

Even as I opened my mouth, the room slowly went black around the edges of my sight, closing in until the darkness consumed me.

The last thing I felt before waking up in the Hall of Records was Eran's arms coming around me, catching me as I collapsed in sleep.

Immediately upon waking up, I went looking for Gershom.

If Eran was going to the prison, on a reconnaissance mission unparalleled in the level of danger he'd already been facing, I needed all the training I could get.

17. MISSING

Gershom's training was just as perilous and tiring as Ms. Beedinwigg's, I learned. Unfortunately, he wasn't as disciplined in his constructive criticism.

"Do it again, Maggie."

"Faster, Maggie."

"Better, Maggie."

Setting all that aside, I trained hard in the afterlife. Knowing Eran could very well be on his way to the prison, I was going to exhaust myself in preparing to intervene if needed.

Being in the afterlife, I thought, might make training easier.

I was wrong.

Somehow, my training area was designed to be harder on the other side. My body felt weighted down, the temperatures were more extreme, and the terrain was more challenging than even Ms. Beedinwigg's obstacle courses.

The Fallen Ones – just figments that I had created to train against – were even tougher. They fought with more strength, screamed louder, and moved quicker.

I figured my logic had been to create an environment that was more demanding than what I would experience in a real fight against a Fallen One, to make it easier on me when I did encounter one.

After all the strenuous effort, I hoped I was right.

Gershom didn't show a single bead of perspiration or gasp for a deep breath once. He wouldn't. Having come here through the process of death, he was held to a different standard. As for me...I was simply visiting which lent me to a set of distinct limitations.

By the end of the practice, sweat dripped down my body and I was bent over in exhaustion, my palms braced against my shaking knees. Gershom stood beside me, waiting for me to recover.

"It's about time for me to go back," I said, glad for it.

"Then you'll be learning whether the prison has been compromised," he stated.

"I expect to."

"I truly hope that is not the case," he said warily, looking off in the distance.

"What are you remembering, Gershom?" I asked with the distinct feeling it had happened once before.

He was shaken from his thoughts then and turned to answer me, his expression ominous. "It happened during the 1300's. Only one Elsic escaped but that is a minor detail in comparison to the amount of damage, the number of deaths it caused. The destruction was almost incalculable. It was one of the first prisoners so there was no longer a single shred of humanity or human characteristics in it. It started in Germany and worked its way through Europe until it reached London. It fed off the dead, who were dying at an alarming rate due to a plague-"

"The Black Plague," I muttered.

He glanced at me with a quirky expression. "That's correct. Because of the plague, bodies were easy to find and still fresh. But then it became...bored, for lack of a better explanation, and it began to prey on the living. They, the Fallen Ones or the Elsics, don't need to eat. They enjoy it...the tearing of flesh." He shivered in memory of it. "And then it was killed on a London street by a single guardian."

I nodded. "Eran..."

Gershom's eyebrows lifted. "Eran was the guardian?"

"I saw it during a visit to my past life. The Elsic was hunting me in the streets and Eran intervened just before it attacked."

"I'm not surprised." He laughed to himself. "I always wondered which guardian had the technical aptitude to kill an Elsic on his own. Should have known it was Eran. No one else has ability equal to the task."

The very sound of his name made me wish for morning so I could see his striking face again. As if the universe had heard my wish, still harboring this longing, I felt the familiar tug back to my body on earth.

When I awoke, I noticed that a thick fog had rolled through the streets of downtown New Orleans. The peaks of rooftops across the street were gone. The tree tops had disappeared. In their place was a wall of grey mist.

Immediately, I sat up in bed looking for Eran.

"He's not back yet," informed Campion, tightlipped and irritable. He was slouched in my wingback chair; his elbow bent on the arm to prop his chin. He looked tired but far more worried.

I got up and went to the French doors, pulling them open.

"He's been late before," I called back attempting to be optimistic but my voice gave away my fears.

Campion was beside me in less than a second. Not bothering to answer, he simply stared across at the grey embankment surrounding our house.

Quietly then, he leaned forward, tilting his head so that one ear faced the fog in front of us. "I hear something," he stated quietly.

Then I heard it too.

Fluttering.

More importantly, I felt it: The hair rising up on the back of my neck.

Slowly, steadily the now familiar flap of wings grew louder.

Then Campion said the very words that I was thinking. "That's more than one set of wings."

"And Eran isn't with them."

Campion's head snapped in my direction, his eyes wide and alert. A second later he was back facing the fog.

The flapping grew closer and then slowed.

Out in the fog the moist air began to churn and the outline of dark figures appeared. There were a dozen of them, lingering just beyond the point of visibility. Careful to avoid stirring the fog further and clearing their concealment, their wing movements were so slight they were almost unnoticeable.

I wanted to tell them that their attempt at obscurity was unnecessary. It had failed. I already knew they were our enemies. The hair on the back of my neck told me so.

"Maggie, inside the house," Campion ordered.

I remained in place.

Instead, I squinted, peering in to the fog for a better look.

"Maggie," Campion warned.

Still, I didn't move.

In unison then, as if on command, their wings bolted to their full length. They were preparing to attack.

"MAGGIE," Campion shouted furiously, his own wings snapping out, tearing the shirt from his body, and preparing for flight.

He crouched and raised his arms, hands facing our attackers.

It was then that I noticed the change in me. While my radar, the hair at the base of my neck, danced in reaction to the attack now coming, the panic that usually accompanied it was dismal. I barely noticed it.

My training had paid off. I was no longer consumed by my fears and was now able to focus on handling the danger in front of me.

I was ready to fight.

Stepping forward, everything moved in slow motion then. Campion's head turned towards me, his mouth moving at a sluggish pace as he called for me to cower behind him; the beings in the mist curved forward in to a hunch and prepared to fulfill their attack; and then suddenly, without any warning, bright white lights fled in from every angle, the fog slowly swirling around them.

The figures scattered, darting off in varying directions, the white lights in pursuit. In an instant, I knew this was Eran's army leaving their posts to protect us.

Campion stepped back, now at a normal pace, his arms lowering and extending behind him to come around me as a form of shelter.

The fog was empty now, the morning quiet again, eerily quiet.

We waited, listening.

The fluttering returned.

Campion's wings stretched farther, forming a wall between me and the fog while again preparing for an assault.

I struggled to see over his massive wings, while hearing the other set approach.

A muffled sound and slight vibration told me that it had landed on the balcony.

The hair at the back of my neck was still bristled but was now slowly lying down. I couldn't be certain whether this was due to my ability to control my panic or because I no longer felt threatened by them.

Either way, I was already prepared for the attack.

Then Campion's wings fell, his defenses folding, and Eran stood on the other side.

"Eran," I sighed and raced around the tip of Campion's wing to launch myself into his arms. But it wasn't fear driving me there. It was relief.

"You didn't go," I stated enthusiastic.

"To the prison?" he said his chin on the top of my head, his arms around me. "No, I didn't get the chance."

Drawing back, ready to scold him for being too eager, I caught sight of his expression. It wasn't disappointed, it was leery.

Eran's voice was strained when he asked, "I felt your radar go off."

Campion's lips briefly tightened in anger. "I believe Maggie's life was in danger just now."

"By whom?" Eran asked, alarmed.

"I couldn't be sure. They were obscured by the fog." While Campion explained, Eran turned to face the balcony searching for any sign of danger. "There were twelve of them."

"That rules out Marco," said Eran contemplative and quietly furious at the same time.

"They were positioning for assault when the regiment stepped in."

Even with Eran's back to me, I was able to sense a smile from him, pride in his combat unit.

"Twelve..." Eran muttered, again deep in thought. "Could they have been Elsics?"

Campion didn't respond immediately so I instinctually turned my head towards him. He was deeply apprehensive. "I-I couldn't be certain." He stepped forward, hesitantly. "Sir...has the prison been compromised?"

"We'll have the answer to that shortly. Magnus made the decision to investigate the prison on his own…A courageous but irresponsible judgment for an older Alterum." He released a heavy sigh, clearly concerned for Magnus's well being. I, however greedy, was comforted by the fact it was not Eran who would be doing the investigation.

Eran pulled away from me then, his attention on Campion. "I'll need to check in with the regiment before classes start," he announced. "Will you watch over Magdalene?"

I rolled my eyes at that request. Despite the odds of the situation, I certainly felt capable of defending myself – especially after the training I'd been through.

"Magdalene," Eran cautioned, having seen the roll of my eyes. "I can focus better if I know you are safe."

I sighed. "Fine."

Eran, whose wings were still out, leaned forward and cupped my cheek with his hand. "Thank you," he whispered. He then stopped to stare intently in to my eyes before brushing his lips lightly against mine.

Then, in one fluid motion, he turned, crouched, sprang into the air, and flew into the grey fog.

"Magdalene," Campion shouted.

"What?" I spun around, aggravated and wondering why he was shouting. "What?"

"Sorry but you didn't answer me the first three times I said your name so I had to do something to get your attention."

He called my name three times? "I didn't hear you," I replied.

"I figured," he said, trying to keep from grinning at my fascination with Eran. "You should get ready for school."

"Right…" I said, peeking back over my shoulder. Already, I missed Eran.

Campion waited on the balcony as I changed, keeping an eye on the fog and any potential returning threats.

By the time I was strapping on my boots, I heard Eran's voice beyond the French doors.

"They couldn't be sure either. They moved like Elsics but…they couldn't get close enough."

Campion muttered something unintelligible to which Eran replied, "No, we'll wait to hear back from Magnus. In the meantime, the regiment is on alert."

I was standing by the time Eran pushed the French doors open and stepped into my bedroom. Although I knew he was waiting for me to ask about his plans, I didn't bother. They were already clear to me.

He would await news from Magnus before determining his next steps.

This was just what he did. For the next several days, we encountered no further attempted assaults. In the evenings, I practiced with Ms. Beedinwigg on earth and with Gershom in the afterlife while Eran left for Germany and any word from Magnus.

Each night passed without any sign from Magnus and Eran grew more worried with each hour.

The weekend came and I decided against taking messages in The Square. There was no time for them. I was too busy preparing for a battle that - now clear to all of us - would be arriving shortly.

Then came Monday morning.

I had spent the night being chased through my jungle training grounds by fabricated Fallen Ones and woke up feeling nearly as exhausted as when I'd gone to sleep. But it was nothing compared to Eran.

His polished image was gone, wrecked havoc during the nights he'd spent awake and the days staying alert in order to protect me. Now, he was hunched over the wingback chair, his hair disheveled, his clothes rumpled, and bags beneath his eyes.

My chest tightened when I saw him.

Slipping out of bed, I kept my eyes on him. He was breathing slowly, his eyes were closed, his lips slackened. I slid silently across the floor towards him to kneel at his feet.

Despite being unkempt, he smelled fresh and earthy. His face was still so handsome my breath caught in my throat and his body, firm even when at ease, still sent pleasure humming through me.

Usually it was him watching me sleep. This, I knew, was a rare treat.

We stayed this way for several minutes, each one I adored more than the next, and then his lips moved.

"Do you think you'll be finished staring any time soon?"

My mouth fell open in embarrassment…and annoyance. "How long were you aware I was here?"

"Since you woke up."

His eyes opened, glossy with fatigue, but lightening a little when they landed on me.

"Why didn't you tell me?" I demanded, still embarrassed.

"Because you needed it…and I needed the rest." He explained it with such blunt logic I didn't bother trying to dispute it.

Then he made an announcement I couldn't reject disagreeing.

"I needed the rest, Magdalene, because I'm going to the prison."

He then watched me for a reaction.

I felt my lips pinch closed, but this was very brief. My mind swirled with thoughts, gathering points to use in arguments against his decision but only one stuck out loud enough to be heard clearly. I said the words aloud without even realizing it.

"But you'll be exposing yourself to imminent danger."

He nodded. "That's possible."

"No," I whispered and then repeated it with far more force. "No." I stood up. "I forbid you."

His eyebrows immediately rose up but I didn't care if he was insulted.

"As my guardian, I demand that you stay."

"That's not how this works, Magdalene," he said in warning. "You know that."

"Your singular goal in existence is to protect me," I retorted. I realized, but quickly pushed it aside, that in any other situation I would have delivered those words with great affection. There was not a hint of it in my voice now. "I will not allow you to leave me without your protection."

His brow creased in confusion at me but he remained silent.

"Do you understand me?" I said, emphatic and absolutely unwavering even while deep inside I knew two things with equal clarity. One, I had never pulled this kind of authoritarian command before, and, two, it didn't matter. He wasn't going to listen anyways. His response confirmed it.

"I won't leave you without protection. You know this." He held up his hand just as I was about to cut him off. "You know this and so I'm reasoning that you are making this demand of me simply out of fear…fear for me and for what I might encounter. I respect and understand that but I cannot allow it to direct my actions."

"You don't have a choice," I retorted.

He was silent for only a brief moment and then he stood, his hands lifting from his sides to gently place them on both of my cheeks. "What would you have me do?" he asked quietly, filled with remorse I didn't understand until he went on. "I haven't heard from Magnus since he left for the prison…a mission I was meant to go on. He's clearly in trouble now. What would you have me do, Magdalene?"

I was torn and without a response. Stay, I wanted to tell him, beg him. There was only one problem with that request. It would mean that he would never forgive himself if Magnus was in danger, and without having to say so I knew we both believed that was the reality.

I stepped back, moving out and away from his hands. "Go…I mean it."

Eran nodded, not at all basking in the glory of winning this particular argument.

We stared at each other in silence then, neither one knowing what to say to comfort each other. There were too many words and not enough time.

Unable to condense all the emotions – dread, sadness, longing – in to a single sentence I settled on verbalizing something else entirely…something that had planted itself inside me long ago and had kept me full of life and hope throughout the centuries. It had given me inspiration to move forward during my bleakest moments and made me fight harder than I ever thought possible during battle.

It had given me purpose.

Despite it all, it was far more challenging to articulate than I ever thought it would be. Not because I had any inhibition in the meaning behind them but because the deepest part of my soul feared that it would be the last time I could ever tell him in person.

Because of that fear, every emotion I felt for him came through as I spoke the words.

"Eran…I'm in love with you."

His breathing stopped, he closed his eyes, and then he swallowed. "Say them again," he whispered.

"Eran, I am in love with you," I repeated with the same intensity.

He drew in a shaky breath.

Now it was me who placed my hands on his cheeks. They were firm and I could feel his jaw tightening as he struggled to hold back his emotions.

Leaning forward, I felt our lips meet. The touch was delicate at first but grew stronger, deeper. When we held each other, it was not like the times before. There was comfort in our embrace now and it told me that no matter what happened from this point forward we would be able to accept what came our way because the love that had grown from us had made us each stronger.

When we pulled apart, when our kiss had satiated us, we remained only inches apart.

"Those words from you...they always give me strength," he admitted.

I smiled gently. "They do the same for me...And that is why I am going with you."

Pulling away from him, I began collecting my clothes, selecting ones that were tight enough to allow ease of movement and loose enough to conceal weapons.

"Did I...I'm sorry...Did I hear you correctly?" he asked, thoroughly confused.

"Yes, I'm going with you."

"Magdalene," he began to oppose but I didn't let him finish.

"I'm not letting you go there alone. You need someone to watch your back."

"Magdalene," he stated again, grabbing my shoulders so that I couldn't finish collecting my clothes. "I appreciate your offer but-"

"I am perfectly capable of taking care of myself and I just might be of some use to you too," I nearly shouted.

"I realize that," said Eran calmly. "What I was going to say is that I can slip into the prison undetected. With you there, it would make it harder to do so."

"Then I'll wait at the entrance," I declared. "In case you do need my help."

He began to oppose me so I spoke more forcefully. "Let's calculate this...Magnus left for the prison alone and no one has heard from him. Now you're going to the prison alone. What happens when we don't hear from you?"

"That's not going to-"

"I'm going with you," I said, returning to my packing.

Eran's face settled in to a firm expression. "I won't let that happen."

"What?" I said, now furious. "Are you going to ask Campion to put me to sleep now? So that you can slip away? Is that your plan?"

He shook his head slowly. "I won't need to." He then turned towards the door and called out, "Campion."

Entering my room a moment later, he stood hands clasped behind him, feet apart, in a defiant stance.

"Campion, I'm leaving now. You will need to guard Maggie today. Keep her home. School is out of the question. And under no circumstances should you inform Magdalene of the prison location. Do you understand?"

"Yes, sir," he responded.

I sucked in a deep breath, never having been more offended. "You...You..." I couldn't finish my words, too embroiled in anger.

"That's right," Eran admitted. "Without knowing where to find the prison you won't be able to find me."

His wings snapped out from behind him then, both glorious and antagonizing. They would be the ones to carry him off, away from me, towards his impending peril.

He turned to race across the room and through the French doors, springing gracefully from the balcony and into the morning fog.

For the very first time, I didn't wait for him to disappear. There was no time to waste if my plan was going to work.

Spinning back around, I glared at Campion.

He slowly shook his head. "I will not tell you, Maggie. Do not ask it of me."

I already knew this to be true. My glare was simply to play along with the part I had been handed. It was imperative that he thought I was helpless.

"I'm going to get dressed now," I informed him, closing the French doors but not locking them.

Campion nodded and then stepped out into the hallway, leaving the door slightly ajar as a protective measure.

My clothes were on in seconds but I didn't bother to step into my boots. They would become a hindrance in just a moment. Instead, I tied the laces together and swung them over my shoulder.

After slipping out the French doors and quietly closing them behind me, I shimmied down the pillar between the balcony and the porch until I was on solid ground.

The fog was still thick but I saw no movement in it.

Only then did I realize what I was doing. As of now, I was completely exposed to any of the Fallen Ones interested in taking my life; including whomever it was that appeared off my balcony this morning. None of that mattered now. The only thing that did was getting to the one person who could tell me where to find the prison, the person who had trained me for this very mission, the one who had no concern sending me into danger:

Ms. Bronte Beedinwigg

18. HELP

I left my bike at the house and cut through the streets towards school. The motor, especially a Harley Davidson, would definitely alert Campion that I was sneaking out again. That, I could not afford.

Slowly, gradually I felt the hair at the base of my neck rise up until they were sticking straight out.

I was being followed.

Even though I glanced around several times to identify them, they remained hidden either by the fog or by some other structure.

Those Fallen Ones not already on school campus were now arriving there.

While I was able to control the panic that typically rose up in me, the hairs dancing at the back of my neck was a painful reminder that I was surrounded by my enemies. A few times I clapped my hand against my neck but it didn't help much. The hairs simply sprang back the moment I released them. Instead, I concentrated on calming them mentally and had nearly gotten them under control by the time I reached the school parking lot.

The lot was nearly empty, with only a few vehicles driven by faculty members parked in a line closest to the main entrance. I immediately recognized one vehicle in particular parked in a faculty slot, a military-inspired SUV called the Knight XV. It looked like an oversized toy but it wasn't. It was an ultra-secure, armored vehicle and it had been parked in the driveway of Mr. Hamilton's home every night I'd been there.

This meant Ms. Beedinwigg had arrived.

I hurried towards the main entrance, sensing the influx of ever more Fallen Ones. My being without protection must have sparked their curiosity, which didn't bother me in the least until I turned around.

There, emerging from the mist was a unified line of Fallen Ones, walking nearly shoulder to shoulder and stretching the length of the parking lot.

I nearly stumbled.

Fallen Ones rarely traveled together, Abaddon and Marco being the exception. Despite that fact, right now they looked like an army advancing on my school…and on me.

I slid inside the main door and raced down the hallway towards Microbiology. It was vacant and eerily quiet with just my footsteps echoing off the lockers and walls.

"No running," demanded a voice down the hall behind me.

I slowed to a fast-paced walk but didn't bother looking back. The voice belonged to Mr. Warden and if he knew who it was running in the hall he'd delay me just for spite.

I made it to the classroom door and had my hand on the knob before the warden called out to me again.

"Hold it."

I paused, still refusing to turn around.

"What's the rush, Ms…?" he asked, fishing for my name.

I sighed, feeling my shoulders fall in desperation.

The warden reached me, coming alongside me, and then scoffed. "I should have known."

Teeth clenched, I finally looked at him. My eyes were narrowed, conveying the loathing I felt for him.

A single thought ran through my mind: He was keeping me from getting to Eran.

"I really don't have time for this, Mr. Warden," I said, the words leaving my mouth before I even knew I'd thought them.

His jaw dropped in offense. "You have no respect for authority do you, Ms. Tanner?"

"Not your authority, Mr. Warden. Please excuse me." I was already turning the knob when the warden stepped closer to me in a move meant to be intimidating.

It wasn't.

His proximity to me didn't make me come to a halt. It was Marco. I'd been concentrating on subduing my reaction to the multitude of Fallen Ones assembling around the school that I had effectively blocked my reaction to Marco approaching from down the hall.

"Now...now, Maggie," he said, his tone leering. "What's the rush?"

The warden and I turned in unison to face him and to find him standing a few feet from us, arms crossed over his chest and flanked by his clan. His mock coyness, so commonly used in the warden's presence to project the image of obedience, was gone and he now exuded a confidence so potent that it seemed to fill the hallway and greatly overpowered the warden's.

He glanced around theatrically before asking, "Where's Eran? Where's your guardian, Maggie? Don't tell me that he left you alone?"

"Guardian?" asked the warden, befuddled.

Marco and I ignored him.

"Right behind me," I said defiantly.

Marco slowly shook his head. "I don't think so..."

My face fell to a glare, his slowly followed, and we stood silent and staring at one another, willing each other to make the first attempt at an attack. By this point, I was certain that the warden was suspiciously recognizing that something more than a casual conversation was taking place but to his credit he was smart enough to stay silent about it.

Finally, it was Marco who broke the glare. "You were headed for class, I noticed. A place of sanctuary? Where you feel protected by the presence of other students?" He paused to tilt his head to the side, mocking me. "There's no reason to rush now is there?" The hint of sneer rose up and then disappeared. "Or is there? Where is Eran…my dear Magdalene?"

"Don't call me that," I hissed.

There was only a brief gap before he retorted, "I'll call you whatever I want."

The warden, realizing the interaction between Marco and me was escalating, stepped in. "Hey now-" he declared, moving between us.

Marco immediately met the warden halfway, nearly slamming his chest into the warden's. "Leave us be," he commanded.

"I'll do no such-"

"Leave us or you will be hurt." The sincerity in Marco's tone left no question as to whether it was a veiled threat.

I had no doubt he would carry out his warning and actually prepared for it to happen when movement next to us caught all of us by surprise.

The first students of the day passed by, oblivious to the conflict they had just intruded on.

A quick glance around told us that more students were filtering into the hallway. Any attack by Marco or his men at this point would be detrimental to his objective at getting me alone.

Apparently, Marco deduced this to be the case too since he stepped back and reassembled his fake smile. "I'll be around," he said in warning to me.

"I'll count on it," I replied.

Marco and his men headed back down the hallway, resembling a small band of militia carving a path through the students now beginning to flood the hallway.

Only when Marco had nearly disappeared into the sea of wandering heads did the warden release his breath. He turned towards me, apparently wanting to rehash what had just happened but I didn't give him the chance.

I was already stepping through the door of my classroom in search of Ms. Beedinwigg.

The room was empty so I moved to the window in hopes I could catch sight of her outside. The fog had nearly dissipated by this point and I could see that her vehicle was still in the parking lot.

Then I heard her voice.

"Maggie?"

Twirling around, I ran through the maze of desks towards her, not waiting to reach her before trying to explain all she needed to know.

"Slow down," she instructed me. "You're not making any sense."

I struggled to stop myself and take a deep breath. "I need your help. I need to know where to find the prison holding the Fallen Ones captive."

She stared back at me, hesitant. "Why?"

"Because Eran has gone there and I'm afraid...I'm afraid for him." I groaned loudly in frustration. "I don't have time to explain everything in detail. Please...just tell me where to find the prison." I was becoming nauseous at the thought of Ms. Beedinwigg not helping me...because it certainly didn't look like she wanted to.

"Maggie, why do you need to know where to find the prison?" she asked carefully.

"Because I'm going there," I stated.

"No," she stepped back, shaking her head. "You're not ready."

"Not ready," I fumed. "You trained me. You've made me an expert in combat, weaponry, defensive strategy. I can control my reaction to Fallen Ones. I know the ways they fight…I'm ready."

"You are not," she replied simply.

Seething, I bent over; hands on my waist, trying frantically to come up with something, anything that would convince Ms. Beedinwigg that I could survive the mission. In the end, that didn't matter. There was only one thing that did.

"Eran is in a German prison surrounded by our enemies. I will not let him die there."

"Eran's in prison?" said a voice from the door. "In Germany?"

It was Bridgette Madison and her expression was both shocked and excited.

"Bridgette, class will start late," said Ms. Beedinwigg with a commanding tone she usually reserved for my training sessions. "Close the door."

She did but not before I heard her express, wide-eyed, to someone beside her, "Eran's in prison in Germany."

Those few words created a cataclysmic reaction that only I and Ms. Beedinwigg foresaw. There was just one thing to do with a wildfire, stymie it; and the only way to do that was to remove the elements that were passing on the fire.

Knowing this, Ms. Beedinwigg ran for the classroom door and flung it open, calling in the students waiting in the hallway. They filtered in but not quick enough, she nearly heaved a few through the door.

Still, the damage had been done. The gossip traveled down the hallway, from student to student until whispers of it diminished in the distance.

I approached Ms. Beedinwigg, slowly, uncertain what to do now. "Marco," I said quietly so that the other students couldn't overhear while still earning her attention as she ushered the last of the students inside. "He knows I'm here without protection."

She showed no sign of alarm and instead rapidly deduced the situation we were in. "Then the rest of them will know it too soon enough." A glimpse of concern surfaced and then fell away. "We need to get you out of here."

"To the prison," I insisted and before she could oppose I added, "It's far enough away and it's the last place they'll look for me."

Ms. Beedinwigg tilted her head to the side and nodded in a surprise gesture of agreement. Then she addressed the class.

"Students, I have to run to the main office for a moment. Please review your notes from last class and begin reading the next chapter on your syllabus."

She delivered the instructions with ease and patience that no one questioned her and a moment later their heads were down and reviewing their notes. All, that is, except for Bridgette. She continued to stare, inquiringly. It didn't matter. Ms. Beedinwigg and I left the room then, effectively ending any further information that she could turn in to juicy gossip.

The hallway was empty again, with students and faculty behind closed doors, steadily learning today's lessons. Ironically, my world, my existence had suddenly changed. Homework left undone had no meaning to me any longer. I didn't care that I was absent from class or that I didn't have a lunch to eat today.

My focus was on Eran and reaching him before our enemies could.

Apparently, so was Ms. Beedinwigg because she was already tearing the dress from her shoulders, revealing her black leather suit below it and the weapons attached to her waist which she secretly carried beneath it. With her free hand, she snapped the glass chain from her neck and pulled the pins from her hair, freeing herself as she had done during training. If any of the students had stepped out of the door at that moment, they would have wondered where Ms. Beedinwigg had gone.

She was ready for battle.

I followed her though she didn't head towards the warden's office. I didn't expect her to. Instead, she took the hallway leading towards the main exit, right where her vehicle was parked.

Unfortunately, it wouldn't be so easy to reach it.

Just as we turned the corner leading to the main hallway, my radar triggered, sending a concentrated wave of electricity from the back of my neck and down my spine. This, I had never felt before, neither the strength of it nor the extension of it through my body.

Unprepared for it, I moaned and bent over in pain, stumbling against Ms. Beedinwigg.

"Are you all right?" she asked nervously, taking my arm to support me but refusing to stop or slow her pace.

"The fight…" I said. "It's coming."

In reaction, Ms. Beedinwigg lifted her head to look around. Her voice was ominous when she spoke next.

"No…It's already here."

I looked up just in time to find a Fallen One collide with a blinding white light, directly ahead of us. They twisted and tumbled along the hallway, leaving slight dents in the concrete floor as they slammed each other down.

"Eran's army," I explained to Ms. Beedinwigg. "They're defending us."

"Good. We're going to need them," she replied, her pace remaining the same despite the number of fights we were starting to encounter.

To our left the boy's bathroom door swung open to reveal a Fallen One being tackled by two bright lights, its wings flapping madly to steady itself against the attack. To our right, down the staircase, a pair of Fallen Ones were approaching two bright white lights, wings up and arms forward, their bodies in a crouch.

"Why are the Fallen Ones fighting now?" I asked, my body still rattling from the intensity of my radar reacting.

"They were waiting for a fight, Maggie, one that evidently isn't coming. So they've started their own."

"It looks like they've worked themselves in to a frenzy over it."

We watched as a Fallen One swooped down the hallway towards us, a bright white light catching it before it could reach us. Still, just before the light yanked it backwards and down a side hall, it leaned forward towards me taking a swipe and coming dangerously close to my ribs. Ms. Beedinwigg spun around my body in a fluid move before I could even react. The movement ended with a moan and a brief stagger but she recovered and kept moving towards the doors.

"Are you hurt?" I asked, noticing her wince as she placed a hand to her own ribs.

"Not badly. Keep moving," she ordered. "They didn't expect you to be without your guardian and the opportunity to kill you is too great for them to pass up."

I blinked, the realization washing over me so great it made my breath catch in my chest. "Are you...Are you saying they're all going to try and kill me now?"

"Yes, that's what I'm saying," she replied flatly, keeping her eyes on the doors ahead in her unwavering attempt to reach them.

Once we did, I stopped and turned back.

"What?" she demanded impatiently.

"The students...and the faculty."

A few heads were already peering out from their doors and down the hall trying to source the reason for the commotion.

"They're safe if they stay in a group," she insisted quickly, already pushing the exit doors open.

"But they're not." I pointed to two faculty members stepping out in the hall, perplexed and surveying the damaged lockers and cracked floors left by the attack.

Ms. Beedinwigg heaved a sigh of frustration and in that fleeting second I saw why I had selected the Beedinwigg's as trainers so long ago. They had an inherent fervor that drove them towards a single objective and made them unwilling to be deterred by anything or anyone in their path.

Still, I wouldn't budge and, in this particular case, she knew it was best to compromise. She took a glimpse around for something to suffice and then smiled. "Perfect," she muttered just as she flipped up the fire alarm case and pulled down its lever, sending a piercing, screaming noise through the school.

"There," she yelled satisfied.

"Thanks," I said but it ended in a grunt as she yanked me out the door, again focused on her goal of removing me from harm's way.

Glancing over my shoulder, I found her ploy had worked. The students flooded into the hallways, heading for the exit doors.

Knowing that the Fallen Ones detested being exposed, preferring to do their evil work in obscurity, they would flee the campus. This was just what was happening. The alarm from inside alerted the Fallen Ones and they were now springing from the ground, rooftops, lampposts, car tops, virtually every solid, horizontal surface and into the sky. An onslaught of bright white lights followed close behind.

Ms. Beedinwigg and I made it to her SUV and headed out of the parking lot. A few Fallen Ones attempted to attack us as they left the campus but to her vehicle's credit we barely felt the chassis roll. Keeping a close eye on the sky, we were at her house in less than five minutes only to find that we weren't the only ones to reach it.

Campion stood on the lowest step from the porch, scanning the sky warily. Behind him stood Felix, Rufus, and Ezra. Also there, just stepping out the door and on to the porch was Mr. Hamilton with Alfred coming out behind him.

"Well, looks like the gang's all here," muttered Ms. Beedinwigg as she pulled her vehicle into the driveway.

"I won't be stopped from getting to Eran. I don't care what any of you say," I warned her.

"Oh…I don't believe they're here to stop you, Maggie." The way she said this made me wonder what I was missing.

"Well, it is a pleasure to finally meet you," said Ms. Beedinwigg taking the steps towards them, her smile both equally welcoming and in awe. Something told me that my housemates weren't a complete stranger to her. "I understand you've been in Maggie's life for some time now."

"We have," Felix said proudly, his usual flighty tone gone.

Ms. Beedinwigg nodded thoughtfully before addressing Ezra directly. "So you've been watching over…guiding Maggie since she's moved here?"

"That's correct," said Ezra.

"You've done a fine job."

Ezra declined the compliment. "It's all been Maggie's doing."

That was when I cut in. "I'm sorry. I don't mean to be rude but I'm on my way to Germany. I only stopped by for a few weapons."

Rufus stepped into my path but I didn't give him a chance to counter me. "I'll explain later. Right now, nothing you say will have any impact on me." I was already moving passed him.

My plan was to march into the house, down to the basement, gather the sword I'd been using during training, and to head to the airport for the first flight to Germany. How I was going to get my sword onboard the plane and find a prison so well hidden that no mortal had ever stumbled across it…well, I was still working all that out.

As it turned out, I didn't get very far with my plan.

Rufus's hand swung out and stopped me. I was about to oppose him when I saw what hung from his grip.

My sword.

"How-How…" I tried to finish my sentence but couldn't seem to formulate my thought.

"This what ya lookin' fer? Take it," he commanded softly in his thick Irish accent. When I did, he withdrew his own sword from a sleeve attached to his back. As he did, I heard metal grating around me and I rotated in time to see everyone else pull out their own weapons.

I stood back, speechless.

"We ain't lettin' ya go there alone," he informed me. "'Sides, I miss me travels in that part o' the world."

This was not a good idea, I concluded instantly. They were mere mortals walking into a battle against history's most notorious enemies. They didn't stand a chance. Of course, I was nothing more than a mortal and here I was doing exactly what I feared they planned to do. Still, at least I knew what I was getting myself in to.

"You don't know what you're up against," I said. Then I stopped, unable to describe what I meant. How did I tell them that we would be encountering enemies so evil there was not a hint of humanity left in them? How did I explain all that I had learned about their fighting skills, their motivations, and their lack of morality during the visits to my past lives in the few short sentences I had time for?

"Oh, I think we do," said Ezra confidently as she stepped forward.

Then something happened that I was absolutely unprepared to witness.

Ezra's clothing fluttered, as if a breeze had found its way down her back. At the very same time, something crept out from behind her, through an opening in the back of her dress. From over her shoulders, two appendages steadily expanded outward, reaching to their fullest length before unfolding. The wings behind Ezra, swathed in bright white feathers, trembled slightly and then settled down against her back.

My jaw dropped. "What?"

From beside Ezra, Rufus and Felix each expanded their own set of wings in the very same way. I was now standing before my housemates, ones that I had known only as mortals.

I stepped back, mumbling, "What the…" but only vaguely aware of saying it.

"Don't feel betrayed," Felix implored. "We each agreed it would be best not to tell you until it was necessary."

"'N goin' to the prison…it's necessary," added Rufus.

My hands lifting up in a sign of confusion but that was before I was honest with myself. It all made sense. They exhibited the typical signs of Alterums. They kept to themselves, a close knit group, a family who relied on each other and no one else. My thoughts briefly drifted back to just a few months ago when Abaddon and his clan had nearly taken my life. My housemates had interceded, stepping in against him, a formidable opponent, and they had survived. It was truly inexplicable as to how they had survived…until now.

"How could I have missed it all this time?" I muttered and then harshly demanded to Ms. Beedinwigg, "You knew about this didn't you?" You knew they were Alterums."

She tilted her head down, peering at me from beneath her lashes. "Is that really what you want to discuss right now?" she asked pointedly.

Eran.

It was the single thought, the fleeting memory of his face that realigned my motives.

"We need to get to Germany," I said.

"Well, you can't drive there," Alfred noted. "I'll see what flights are available." He was already pulling his phone from its belt clip when Ezra stopped him.

She held up a hand and said, "That won't be necessary. I think we have a quicker method." Then she turned to me and offered, "Maggie, would you like a lift? I imagine you have quite a few questions by this point."

I laughed through my nose. "That's an understatement…Yes, I'll go with you."

Campion suggested he take Ms. Beedinwigg and she stepped up next to him in agreement.

Leaving Mr. Hamilton and Alfred behind, Felix, Rufus, Campion, and Ms. Beedinwigg lifted into the air just as Ezra took my elbow. Her wings gently flapped and a moment later I found my surroundings slowly moving downward as I was lifted higher. I no longer felt the hard feeling of concrete beneath my feet. A soft breeze picked up, ruffling the hair around my face. We drifted higher, through the fog bank, Ezra's wings moving smoothly inward and outward generating enough speed to raise us steadily in to the sky.

Up ahead I could see the rest of our small group, their wings moving in waves of beauty and power, their legs dangling behind them.

Still in a surreal state over finding my housemates, my family, were Alterums, my mind swirled with questions, just as Ezra had predicted with only a single clear thought coming to the surface.

We were headed towards the most dangerous beings this world had ever known and, because of that, my anger over discovering they had hid their true identities had now been replaced with appreciation. At least they now had a fighting chance.

Seconds later, we broke through the fog and found the sun, strong and warm, on the other side. Using it for direction, we turned and fled towards Germany.

19. DEATH

We were too far above the ground for me to pinpoint where we were flying over until reaching the Atlantic seaboard. Thankfully, we hadn't encountered any Fallen Ones, not even a commercial airliner. The sky seemed to belong to us. It was peaceful too. Somehow Ezra had positioned herself so that no force of air was touching me. It was so quiet within the span of her wings that I could hear my own heart beat. I may have even enjoyed the ride if it weren't for the intention of rescuing Eran, the constant realization of that purpose settling like an unwelcomed guest in the forefront of my consciousness. In an attempt to settle my nervousness over Eran's safety, I asked Ezra the questions that lingered since she announced my housemates' secret.

"Ms. Beedinwigg," I said, positioning my head so that I could easily see Ezra. "I feel like you two know each other…"

She nodded thoughtfully.

"We have never met in person until now," she explained. "Rufus, Felix, and I knew of her, or rather her family, for some time. There were whisperings, tales of them throughout the Alterums."

"But she knew who you were? That you were Alterums?" I reasoned.

"Yes, she knew of us. The Beedinwigg's, and to a lesser extent because of their role as financial investors, the Hamilton's, have kept excellent records on Alterums and Fallen Ones."

I recalled Ms. Beedinwigg mentioned that on our very first meeting when she'd shown me the book of faded images of my past lives.

"So why is it that I was never told who you were? Was there some kind of plan to keep me in the dark?"

"Plan? No, there was no strategy in place, only a simple request. And only because it came from your mother did I respect it."

"My mother?" I asked, shocked.

"Yes, after meeting her and after her guidance in my journey, my life's pursuit in helping others, it was the least I could do. She wanted you to grow up innocent, Maggie, without the conundrum of dealing with Fallen Ones or Alterums. She wanted to give you a real life, one that you've never had."

"So much for that..." I muttered.

Then something occurred to me. "How did she know that I wouldn't remember? She died when I was born, Ezra. We never spoke to each other. She couldn't have known that when I died alongside her that I would return as a reborn...unable to remember anything at all."

"Your relationship didn't start there, Maggie. Your mother...she was a friend of yours on the other side. They all were."

Instantly I felt the muscles in my body tighten in reaction to that announcement. "I was...I was friends with the other messengers?"

"Yes, of course. You trained them...remember?"

My breath caught. I had never considered it before but it was logical that the messengers would form friendships. We were unified by a common bond, an ability to deliver messages that set us apart from the rest, a gift and a curse - one that had made us capable of bringing peace to those on earth with the delivery of messages to their deceased and one that left us so vulnerable as to suffer eternal death upon our fatality at the hands of a Fallen One.

"Friends…" I said to myself. "I wish I could remember them."

Ezra smiled at me sympathetically. I imagined that under any other circumstance she may have reassured me that I would remember them at some point, when my existence on this earth had ended and I returned to the afterlife. But we were getting closer to our enemies, a great number of them, and the outcome was uncertain as to whether any of us would survive. It was as if we were about to jump in a lake without an ability to swim. The realization was sobering.

Being the only mortal in this small group it made me wonder, as I had throughout my life, my purpose for being here. Glancing at Ezra, I wondered if she may have some clue as to why I had come.

"Did she ever tell you why I returned as a reborn? Why I had returned to earth without any memory of my past and without any supernatural powers to protect me?"

"She told me that you had always wondered what it felt like to be human, to come not for the sole purpose of delivering messages but for the experience. This was the reasoning behind her request to keep you from knowing about Alterums or Fallen Ones." She paused and smiled subtly at some resurfaced memory. "She was adamant about it too. You had always returned as an Alterum and during unstable times, helping to calm fears of that era through the delivery of your messages. This time, you chose to return as a mortal and during a time of peace, and you chose this time because it was believed that all Fallen Ones had been either imprisoned or killed. It wasn't until we learned that the Fallen Ones still existed that we intervened in your life."

"Because you learned it was no longer safe," I summed it up for her.

"That's right. We did," said Ezra, remorse underlying her tone.

"I appreciate that."

"We thought you might," she replied with a grin.

"So how is it that I intended to return as a mortal but I'm still able to visit the afterlife between waking hours. Mortals aren't supposed to be able to do that, right?"

"Because that is your gift, Maggie," she said, noticeably frank. "We all have one and it's there whether we choose to accept it or not."

I fell silent for several minutes, registering everything she had just told me. It was a lot to understand, to piece together. So much of it had happened with my direct involvement and I couldn't recall a single word said about it. Once again, I internally harangued myself for not having the ability to recall my past. Somehow it didn't make it any easier knowing I had intentionally put myself in this position.

"What a mess," I muttered.

Ezra heard and replied, "Could be worse. Your mother taught me that when I first met her. Your mother taught me a lot of things."

"That's right...You said that you were in a rough crowd before meeting my mother, before she tutored you and changed your way of thinking."

She smiled mischievously down at me. "I'm an Alterum, Maggie. I'm not perfect."

That quirk of fate made us giggle for a few seconds before we fell silent.

We were now somewhere over the Atlantic Ocean with no sign of land in sight. Moving as fast as my human body would allow, we seemed to be making good time judging from how quickly we had reached the Atlantic seaboard from New Orleans. Still, it wasn't fast enough. A supersonic jet wouldn't be fast enough.

Ezra must have sensed my impatience because she said, "Eran's the best warrior in history. Keep that in mind, Maggie."

"I know," I said, still nervous. "But I also know that he's in trouble."

"How?" she tested me.

"Because this morning…in the hallway at school…my radar went off more painful than it has ever been…and Eran didn't come to my rescue."

She nodded pensively in return.

"He's in trouble, Ezra. I'm certain of it."

She didn't say another word until we reached land. The sky was clear on this side of the Atlantic but there was a chill to the air. I knew Ezra must have been emitting heat somehow in order to maintain my body temperature while at this altitude but it seemed unable to compete with late winter weather in Western Europe.

"We'll be there soon," she reassured me.

My teeth chattered a little but I was able to respond with a quick one word. "Good."

Our flight path took us over towns and roadways, rivers and rolling hills until we reached a mountain range covered in snow, exposed rock faces, and towering over deep valleys of emerald pastures and evergreen forests. We dipped lower then, lining up with the mountain peaks, a seemingly more stealth route.

"Where…Where…are we?" I asked through my teeth.

"The Bavarian Alps," she replied.

It felt surreal. I had just been in New Orleans this morning and was now in the Bavarian Alps. I had read about them, seen pictures, and discussed them in classes but none of it had prepared me for their rugged beauty. Flying passed a waterfall of water so clear it could have been liquefied crystals I wondered how something as terrible as a prison for sinful immortals could be found here.

Yet, strategically, I couldn't think of a better place to build it. I had seen no roads, the rock appearing to be impervious to any attempted gouging, and certainly I had seen no people in these rugged mountains. I was thankful for those with me now. It would have been impossible to find this place.

Just as we flew over a peak Ezra pointed her shoulders slightly downward and we began to descend, following the others in front of us. A moment later we were diving straight downward against the face of the mountain. Nearly midway, they slowly turned up so that our feet were pointed towards the ground and we faced a small opening, a cave carved into the side of the mountain.

It was small, dark, and inconspicuous, a perfect entrance to a prison intending to be obscured.

We each floated to the edge and settled on to the ground.

Standing silent, instinctually, we listened for any sign of danger.

After several seconds, there was nothing but the sound of the wind softly howling through the cave ahead of us.

Then the sound of grating metal filled the air. Each of them around me withdrew their weapons in unison, the sound an eerie reminder of why we were here.

My sword had never left my hand.

"We'll go in together in pairs," said Ezra. "Maggie and Ms. Beedinwigg, you two will go in last."

Ezra and Rufus paired up and stepped into the cave, being swallowed by the darkness within three steps. Campion and Felix followed. Finally, it was just me and

Ms. Beedinwigg on the outside peering in. She looked at me firmly. "You are the most important one here. Do not sacrifice yourself."

It was odd how well she knew me when I had only just met her.

I looked back towards the mouth of the cave. Somewhere inside was the only man I had ever loved. If it came down to sacrificing myself there was nothing that would stop me.

I took the first step and she came up behind me so that we entered the darkness together.

The light inside had been a minor concern for me, not knowing how we would be able to fight without seeing, but it was erased with each step farther in. Oddly, we could see the walls, the rock path where we stepped, the ceiling and its varying heights of stalactites. I couldn't identify where the light came from and could only assume that it came from all around us. Every rock inside glowed, dimly but it glowed.

We headed deeper into the cave, coming across alternate corridors that led us in varying directions. Ezra, who seemed to have an innate sense for the direction each led, knew which one to take and guided us farther into the mountain's core.

"We're getting close," I said quietly.

The group stopped and turned in my direction.

"How do you know?" asked Ms. Beedinwigg.

"Just as Eran can sense my emotions, I can sense his," I explained to her. "I figured you already knew that."

"Nope, that's something I hadn't come across yet."

"What are his emotions?" asked Felix, tentatively.

"Right now…" I drew in a shaky breath. "He's angry."

There were no comments on my announcement but I could guarantee we were each thinking the same thing: If Eran was angry, that meant trouble ahead.

We started walking again, each one lifting their weapon a little higher.

No more than a hundred feet farther in it started to happen.

The pain began at the base of my neck, along my hairline. It rapidly intensified, stretching beyond my neck to run through my spine. Within seconds it was shooting out to ever nerve ending in my body. For a split second, I wondered if I'd just been struck by lightning. Then I thought nothing at all. My awareness was completely immersed on the pain now absorbed in every part of my body. My radar, meant to warn me against danger, to protect me from it, had become the source of my danger.

Control it, said the voice in my head. You've done it before. Concentrate. Do it before they find you because if you feel them, they feel you.

I was on the ground now, my knees digging into the sharp, rocky earth, hands on my back attempting to comfort me. My breath was caught in my chest, my body was shaking uncontrollably. I think I released a moan.

Then something broke through the pain.

Someone was giggling.

The laughter was at my expense and that meant one thing.

A Fallen One was watching me.

Focusing on it, using it as a distraction from the pain, I lifted my head.

There, directly in front of us was Sarai, her face beaming, unable to contain her enthusiasm over my pain. Behind her stood Achan who couldn't hold back his grin either.

The sight of them gave me the strength to overcome the pain and stand up, though it was a struggle.

In the midst of my alarm sounding off, my senses magnified and I could hear everyone's heart beat quicken, a commotion of celebration coming through the walls, and most of all I could feel Eran seething with rage.

"Leave her alone," I heard Felix growl.

Ezra put a hand on his arm to steady his emotions, knowing an angry fighter was a dead one.

"It's not…" I took a deep, stifled breath. "It's not them… causing the pain."

"You're right, Magdalene," she said, drawing out my name and finishing with a sneer. "It's not me…It's not Achan…It's everyone. They're all here, for the most part. Some left," she admitted without care, "after we released them-"

"You did release them," I stated, furious to almost a dizzying level.

"Them? Who's them?" asked Felix, bewildered.

I could barely gather the control to tell him, sapped of energy, filled with terror for the first time in my life. I felt my lips quiver when I answered him. "The Elsics. They released the Elsics."

Horror moved across their expression, to Sarai and Achan's satisfaction.

"We did," she replied plainly. "Achan killed the guards, I opened the gates. But don't worry your pretty little head," she mocked. "The majority of them are here, ready for the grand finale."

Grand finale, I thought. Those were the same words Abaddon had used in my past lives when he'd planned a destructive climactic ending.

"Abaddon…" I sighed, realizing for the first time why we were here. Sarai's next words confirmed it.

She nodded, her sneer turning to a proud grin as she declared, "Eran's pitiful diminutive army imprisoned him here to rot but I wasn't about to let my father live through that."

"Should have simply killed him when they had the chance," Achan added from behind, chuckling.

"But that's not the only reason you came here," I said, already piecing together her plan. "You left a trail for us. You led us here for another reason."

"To kill you," she confirmed, flatly. "Of course, I did release the Elsics on the presumption they might do it for me. Something told me, however, that they would take their time with you. Tease you, taunt you. Keep an eye on you." She inhaled, excited. "And they did, didn't they? I can see it in your face."

She was right. I thought back to the Elsic feather left in the cemetery, the one who attacked me in the shed, the dozen waiting in the fog just off my balcony. They had been around me all along.

"Then Eran's loyal confidant, Magnus, went missing. I found him in the rocks..." she whispered as if she were confiding a secret. "And I kept him there, appearing only when he gained the courage to escape, and he'd scamper back into his hiding place. And then Eran arrived," she went on coyly. "Eran, ever the brave savior, came in search of his loyal confidante, Magnus. Alas, Magnus fled. Slipped out from under my nose as I dealt with Eran. Gone was the little troll only to leave Eran himself to be caught."

"Magnus left Eran?" Campion fumed.

"He did. But that's not the most intriguing part." She smiled wickedly before continuing. "Magnus's disappearance brought Eran to us. And now Eran's disappearance brought you to us. You, the last of the messengers...here, surrounded by your enemies. The final battle..."

"Well, rumor had it one was coming," I said trying to appear indifferent. I would not give her the pleasure of interpreting my responses as fearful even if I did feel a hint of it.

"Unfortunately, the battle won't be much of one." She pinched her lips together in a frown. "There's so few of you and so many of us I'm afraid it'll be over so quickly."

She twisted around then and said to Achan, "Would you like to call in the cavalry?"

Achan spun around into a crouch, preparing to take flight and announce our arrival, but Rufus didn't give him the chance.

The behemoth Irish man I knew to be heavy and languid sprang lithely over Sarai and landed with a thud on Achan's back. Felix and Ezra were at his side instantly, pummeling every side of Achan's body.

Campion, Ms. Beedinwigg, and I took on Sarai.

She saw us coming and immediately used the only supernatural power she'd brought with her. "Campion, I've missed you," she said in a rush. Despite the insincerity of her words, Campion collapsed to the ground, tears already flowing, groveling like someone begging for his lover to return.

"Fight it, Campion," I urged. "You aren't in love with her."

She smiled impishly, already drawing her sword. "He doesn't know that…"

I spun to face her, doing my best to restrain the anger swelling in me. My senses were still heightened and I could hear Eran grunting against his restraints. He was close by and that gave me hope.

Yet, it wasn't my sword that wounded Sarai. Ms. Beedinwigg spun across the ground, fluidly slicing her sai through the air. It connected with Sarai's torso, leaving a gash across her waist, blood quickly flowing from the cut.

Sarai released a raspy growl and heaved her own sword up to plunge it forward.

My senses, still heightened, allowed me to see where it would land…directly in Ms. Beedinwigg's back. I leapt forward, coming down on Sarai. Her distraction in countering Ms. Beedinwigg left her an open target. She was completely vulnerable, allowing me the opportunity to strike where it would do the most damage.

The tip of my sword slid across her neck in a single swipe, taking with it the chance that she could ever again use her voice to debilitate another man in her presence.

"You'll never convince anyone else they are in love with you ever again," I told her, standing over her body which now lay sprawled on the ground.

Chocking against the blood filling her airways, she could only convey her wrath through action. She sat up, reaching for me, her blade extending out in hopes of connecting with any part of my body that would take me to eternal death with her.

"You missed," I told her as she closed her eyes for the very last time.

Stepping away, I turned my attention to Achan. He was now in pieces strewn across the cave's opening.

Ezra, Felix, and Rufus stood in a cluster, now turning towards us. They were winded but alive.

"Achan's claim to distinction is his strength," I said. "Nice job." I stopped and shook my head in amazement. "I didn't know you all were good fighters."

Felix chuckled, still bent over, hands on his knees. "We should be…you trained us."

My head jolted back just as soon as I comprehended those words. How could that be? I thought. They…They were just my housemates. I had met them only a few months ago.

"He's right," Ezra confirmed, walking towards me. "You probably don't recall it."

"No…I don't."

"You trained more than messengers, Maggie," said Ezra, nodding. "And we are a few of those Alterums who participated."

I briefly stared back towards Achan's dismembered body, frowning. It was increasingly frustrating not to remember such important details of my past. Conceding that there wasn't much I could do about it now, I simply replied, "I'm glad you did."

Everyone's breathing was slower now but we didn't have much more time to recuperate. We realized this when a screech resounded through the cave, echoing off the wall towards us.

"Elsics…They know we're here," said Felix.

"Then we need to leave," Ms. Beedinwigg insisted.

"Not without Eran," I said, already starting to walk again, farther into the cave.

With Sarai gone, Campion was standing again, furiously wiping the tears from his face. "No, not without Eran," he agreed.

Ms. Beedinwigg came up beside me and then stepped in front. "Stay hidden," she commanded before turning towards the others. "Let's move."

The screeching continued, building to hysteria inside the cave's corridors. The sound came from a centralized room in the heart of the mountain, where we followed it to an opening overlooking the cavern inside.

Below us, hundreds of black, winged creatures moved in waves across the room, some leaping into the air and landing on the backs of others, some crawling up the cave walls to leap into the mass below. All of them excitable beyond measure.

Only one body was not moving. He was bound to the wall, arms and legs in shackles, high above for all Elsics to see. He was swollen and bloodied but his head was lifted and he stared back at them with unshakeable determination.

"Eran," I sighed and instantly stepped forward.

Ms. Beedinwigg held up her arm, stopping me. "A distraction," she instructed, "will create the leverage we need in getting both of you out of here safely."

"I agree," said Ezra attentively. "What do you have in mind?"

"I'll find my way to the side farthest from Eran and call their attention. With their backs turned and their interest on me, you can unbind Eran and lift him to safety."

Ever fearless, Ms. Beedinwigg moved towards the entrance.

"Just a second," said Rufus in his uncompromising Irish voice. "Doncha go thinkin' ya'll be takin' all the glory. Been a while since I had me a good fight. I'm overdue. 'Sides, how'd ya plan on getting' down there without these?" He shook the wings behind him. "I'm the fastest one here. Leave the commotion upta me."

Without permitting anyone the chance to oppose him, he dove through the opening and soared into the cavern below. Roars suddenly vibrated off the walls, telling us that Rufus's entrance had been noticed.

Peeking in to the cavern, we saw him circle the room and then flee through another opening across from us, into another corridor. The Elsics, spun into a circle following him like a string of bees following an intruder in the hive, and shortly afterwards the room was vacant.

"That was a better idea," Ms. Beedinwigg pointed out.

I didn't really care. I was now worried about two things: Rufus's safety and Eran's escape.

Unable to do much about the first one, I acted on the second.

"Will someone lift me and Ms. Beedinwigg down there? And Campion, Felix will you untie Eran?"

We didn't hesitate and a moment later we entered the cavern.

Eran was already looking for us by that point. Having recognized Rufus, he knew the rest of us were close behind. Although, he didn't count on me being there. That much was evident when his eyes landed on me.

Ezra had hold of my elbow, allowing me the opportunity to hover directly in front of him as Campion and Felix went about untying his bindings.

Every part of my being ached to hold him, to clean the blood from him, to nurse his wounds. I couldn't believe what they had done to him.

Something itched running down my cheek and I realized I was crying. I brushed it away, enraged.

"Stay calm," said Ezra, noticing my breath quickening. "He'll recover."

"Ezra," said Eran, barely able to speak against the swelling in his face. "Get her out of here."

"I won't leave…I won't leave without you." I felt my head shaking back and forth though I didn't feel like I had any control over it.

"Ezra," he warned again and when she didn't move he tried to reason with me. "Magdalene, you…" His voice cracked and he swallowed hard, the terror he felt showing through. "You cannot be here. There are too many of them. I cannot protect you. Leave."

His pleading did no good. "No," I replied flatly.

"My army?" he inquired, nervously addressing Ms. Beedinwigg.

She shook her head, her face tense. "Back in New Orleans… restraining the Fallen Ones there."

Furious, Eran refocused his efforts. His hands now untied, he worked on the bindings at his feet. Felix and Campion worked with fervor too, loosening them as quickly as possible.

"You'll be free soon and we'll leave here together," I said.

"Listen to me, Magdalene," he said, not bothering to look up, his breath coming in short gasps now. "It's a complex system of caves. There are multiple entrances and exits. If you go, you can find a way out now… before they return."

Ms. Beedinwigg had been deposited on the floor below, keeping an eye on the cavern's entrances and any sign of returning Elsics. She was silent until now, until she made the announcement we all hoped she wouldn't.

"They're coming back."

"Go! NOW!" Eran roared.

"There's no time," said Ms. Beedinwigg. "There's no time."

Just as she released the words, a stream of black entered the cave and raced towards us.

Ezra had already placed me on the ground and lifted herself into the air. She now blocked me from above while Ms. Beedinwigg blocked me from the floor.

"Protect Magdalene," Eran ordered, causing Felix and Campion to abort their attempt at untying him. Eran feverishly began the process of releasing himself as they came to hover on the sides of me. Rufus, still in front of the wave of black creatures, swooped in and landed a few feet from me, forming a shield with his body.

Through the white wings stretched out in front of me, I saw nothing now but a sea of black. Tainted teeth or the whites of eyes glinted in the midst of them but for the most part it was simply a chaotic inky black wave of creatures eager to tear us apart.

Something, however, seemed to be stopping them.

"Welcome…welcome, my dear captor."

The voice of the winged being now floating down in to my view could not be mistaken but it was Eran who addressed him.

"Abaddon, you will regret anything that happens to her."

Abaddon came in to full sight then, hovering just beyond Ezra, Felix, and Campion and in front of the Elsics as if he had somehow tamed and taken leadership over them.

"I don't think you're in any state to be threatening me," Abaddon said before snidely chuckling to himself. "None of you are."

I shifted for a better view of the prisoners, attempting to use my engaged senses to predetermine their next actions. I could foresee the next steps each one would take three deep in the group. After that, their preconceived actions became a blur.

"Don't worry, Magdalene. They won't make a move without my say so."

"And how did you get them to agree to that?" I asked, trying to buy us some time.

He seemed surprised by the question. "They still have their logic. And being the logical person that I am, I explained to them if they were to attack you all at once many of them would be left out of the opportunity to take a piece off the very person who brought them here. You, my dear, are a very hot commodity. And with some Elsics having all the fun and others being left out of it…well, that leaves those who didn't participate in the entertainment of your death with a vindictive side. And we wouldn't want the Elsics fighting amongst themselves, now would we? Not when I have a perfectly fine plan in which we can each take a piece of you."

"And what does this plan of yours entail?" I wondered if Eran was close to freeing himself. He wasn't at my side yet so I was certain the bindings still held him captive. An image rose up from the back of my mind in which the Elsics attacked him as he struggled against his bindings to avoid the assault. It nauseated me and I shoved it back down.

"I can tell you that it involves the very same bindings Eran is now struggling to unleash," Abaddon was explaining, "but don't you worry. I'm sure you still recall my ability to control your movement. I promise not to use it on you." He said this as if he were doing me a favor. "No, I won't. I think they'd like to actually watch you struggle."

Rufus groaned then. "I've heard enough o' this," he muttered, launching himself into the air.

Abaddon made several gestures and two Elsics rose up from the crowd to tackle Rufus.

"Don't you hurt him!" I screamed and the wave of black grew more agitated, more excited.

"Now don't fret. There's enough of them to go around," said Abaddon before again making several gestures.

Several more Elsics leapt up and collided with Ezra, Felix and Campion. They were dragged off to the side, held down by their limbs and winged appendages.

Ms. Beedinwigg and I now faced Abaddon and the Elsics alone. Nothing separated us but empty space.

"NO!" Eran bellowed from behind me, still fighting against his restraints. The panic in him was evident as he was about to witness me, his soul mate, be committed to eternal death, slowly and by each one of the Elsics lined up before me.

Abaddon approached first, a hideous leer rising up along with the tip of his sword. "On the contrary...oh yes."

Ms. Beedinwigg, who had clearly been discounted as nothing more than a mere human and thus no threat at all, was the one who they least expected to bring their plan to a halt.

She turned to me and, with incredible fortitude, said, "As I told you before, I'm sorry but you are not ready for this mission."

I felt my brow furrow in confusion as she lifted her sai high above my chest. It came down into me with amazing precision, shattering my chest bone and striking my heart directly through its center.

There was no pain. I felt no fear or animosity. There was only surprise and the lingering thought of what would happen to my loved ones now.

My body, controlled by gravity now, spun around and fell to the hard, cold rock floor, the force of it releasing my breath in a slow hiss, my lungs no longer working and frozen in exhalation.

Only my eyes worked any longer and as my head rolled to the side, I caught sight of Eran.

He was no longer focused on his bindings. Now, he was watching me, grasping for me, unable to reach me as his hands gripped only empty air. His face contorted in shock and anger and then fell to deep sorrow. Finally, his eyes emptied and he went limp. His head lolled back and his jaw fell open and the last thing I heard was his deafening howl of sorrow…just before my soul left this body.

20. THE RETURN

I was now dead, or in the process of dying, and trying to mentally prepare myself for the ultimate death that was to come when a force pulled me upward, an undeniable one that insisted I follow it.

In the next moment I was weightless and hovering beside my body. Campion had been right on, I realized. Our bodies did weigh us down. I found that I had again been given the ability to move my arms and legs, my head and torso, but this time they were without restriction. Was this what eternal death allowed, I wondered. Instinctually, I turned towards Eran, his head was level now. His eyes were glistening as he mouthed something to me.

"Go…" he was saying, the horror in him gone now. He was calm and accepting. "Go…" he insisted.

I was stunned. He seemed so composed about my passing now. He had come to terms with it, I reasoned, and therefore so should I.

In all my time on this earth as I visited the other side night after night, I never witnessed a bright light leading me through a tunnel, leading me home. Finally, for the very first time, I looked up and found it waiting for me.

As Eran had urged, I took it without looking back, agreeing to face whatever destiny had in store for me. Yet, even as I felt the tug pulling me onward and despite Eran's reassuring enthusiasm, I was hesitant.

I wasn't ready for eternal death. There was so much more I wanted to experience; children, old age, traveling, learning different cultures, conversations with Eran that had been left unfinished or never started in the first place. I already missed him, everything about him; his charm, his wit, his courage, the way he looked at me, the way he touched me.

I imagined a dark, empty place, void of any living thing. Alone for the rest of eternity.

But the tunnel did not end where I thought it would.

It opened to a gathering of people, old and young, of varying ethnicities, and both genders. They were smiling, laughing, opening their arms to welcome me. Amidst them, animals of all types, roamed through the throng and, oddly enough, I knew them.

This was eternal death? Confused, I searched the crowd for some understanding. Then someone approached me, his face so familiar I couldn't have mistaken him. He was someone who could explain this to me, as he had done on so many other occasions.

"Gershom?" I said in awe.

"Welcome back."

He was gleaming, taking my hand now and leading me through the group, all of whom I somehow recognized.

That was when it happened.

As my eyes landed on each one of them, the memories returned. I remembered each life, every movement, every person, every good memory and every bad one. I recognized my sister from my life in Germany and recalled skipping stones with her across the water; Monsieur Desmoulins stepped up, grinning, and telling me that I had finally gotten the peace I deserved; and there were others who I had met in the afterlife, those who I never interacted with on earth but whom I could recall visiting and holding hearty discussions.

"Gershom?" I asked, in a surreal state by this point. "Is this…Is this eternal death?"

He half-smiled and then fought the urge to laugh. "No, this is the same place you've been coming every night for your entire life on earth."

"I'm on the other side? But…I was killed…" I muttered.

"By a Fallen One?" asked Gershom, puzzled.

"No…"

"By Eran?" he asked.

"No," I said, dazed.

"By whom?"

Then I realized what she had done. She had killed me before a Fallen One could do it. She hadn't sent me to eternal death; she had given me another chance at life.

"Ms. Beedinwigg…my trainer."

My memory drifted back to Eran's explanation in the school hallway. He had explained what would happen if I were killed by a Fallen One or by himself, but he didn't explain what would happen if I died at the hands of anyone else, including a mortal…such as Ms. Beedinwigg.

Although Eran had been unable to do it himself, he recognized what she intended before I had. He had urged me to take the tunnel because he already knew that she had saved me from eternal death.

Here I was now…on the other side…safe.

Glancing around, I saw ornate steps, waterfalls, towering buildings, a place of tranquil beauty beyond anything I'd ever come across on earth. I wanted to stay and celebrate with everyone here, to ask how they've been and to tell them about my excursion to earth. But, far more important to me, was Eran and the others I'd left behind.

Eran. His name screamed through my thoughts. My eternal soul mate, bound to a wall, mauled and now facing eternal death by a mass of our strongest enemies. Despite the deep peace presiding here, anger began to swell inside me as the memory of him was conjured. He was going to endure incredible pain and here I was, standing safely among my loved ones.

Then something came to me, as if it had been spoken directly in to my thoughts, and my anger turned to relief and then to elation.

"Gershom," I said with enough excitement to make his eyebrows lift.

"Yes?" he replied slowly, hesitant, already knowing something was on my mind.

"I wasn't killed by my guardian. Do you know what that means?"

"No..."

"It means I can return...immediately...right now."

"Why would you want to do that?" He looked at me as if I hadn't contemplated the benefits of staying.

I had, and this beautiful, peaceful place was empty without those whom I loved, those who I'd left behind.

"I'm going back. Tell everyone I'm sorry for the quick departure," I said, motioning to the group behind us.

"I will...and don't worry. They'll understand...They know you."

Without hesitation, I turned and knew exactly what to do. I had done it many times before. I also knew the pain I was about to bear and while leaning forward I braced myself for the impact of it.

I fell forward, remaining rigid, arms against my side, my chin tucked under. The tunic I wore fluttered madly against the sides of my body, against the wind now rushing by. Only a few seconds passed before the pain set in.

Minutes prior, I had fallen to my knees in excruciating agony as my body reacted to the multitude of Elsics nearby. This torment…the kind I felt on my fall back to earth was indescribably worse.

It felt as if my skin was tearing off; my finger nails were peeling back; my limbs were bending in the reverse direction; and the pain was simultaneous and unrelenting. Heat surrounded me, penetrating me, searing my exposed skin.

Finally, I heard myself release the scream that had been building in me, one so deep it came from the depths of my stomach, clenching my muscles, and causing my torso to curl against it.

A moment later I was tumbling through the air; my body now curled in to the fetal position. There was no sound, including the wind rushing by me.

Then I opened my eyes and found I was falling through the clouds. The pain was ebbing away and best of all I had control over my movements again. Straightening out, I steadied my flight. My skin healed rapidly then, fresh and unblemished. With the pain nearly gone, I could concentrate on something beyond what it was doing to my body. It was then I noticed below me mountains topped with snow and revealing colorful textured rock faces.

The Alps, I thought, and smiled.

I was hurling towards the earth faster now but that didn't bother me. It only meant I was getting closer to Eran, to my housemates, and my trainer, the ones who needed me. Faster, at this point, was better.

Without realizing it and without true intention, I felt my shoulders roll up and forward, lifting towards my chin. My shoulder blades opened across my back and gave way to the appendages waiting beneath the surface of my skin. An aching tickle in two places across my upper back told me that my appendages were breaking through, as if my bones were slivering through my body, out through my skin, and moving against the momentum of the wind. Vaguely, I noticed them emerging from the open slit in the back of my tunic, feathers lifting, fluttering against the force of my fall.

No longer a reborn, having died today, I once again had my appendages and the power it took to fight the Elsics.

I consciously flapped my wings once and my descent accelerated. Another flap and I was able to steer. By the third flap, I remembered what it felt like to fly.

The mouth of the cave I had entered with Ms. Beedinwigg only minutes earlier was now directly in front of me. I soared through it, along the corridors, passing Sarai and Achan's bodies.

As I raced through the system of tunnels towards the cavern, my body grew in strength and agility, easily avoiding stalactites and fallen boulders, the very ones I had struggled through in my mortal body.

I felt powerful.

Reaching the cavern, I didn't stop at the mouth of it. I entered, full force, angling myself directly towards Eran.

He was free now, standing over my dead body, my sword in his hands. Only he and Ms. Beedinwigg were left standing. My housemates, Campion included, were still pinned to the ground.

Eran saw me first, just before I landed. His expression was exactly as I'd expected it to be: aggravated. He confirmed his feelings as I stepped up beside him, my wings remaining open and ready for battle.

He heaved a heavy, frustrated sigh at me and returned his attention to Abaddon. Yet, it was Ms. Beedinwigg who voiced her astonishment.

"I gave you an escape, Maggie," she said furious.

"And I did with it what I thought was best," I replied, my eyes now forward and focused on Abaddon.

"What is that?" she demanded. "Returning to danger?"

"To those who need me," I said through clenched teeth.

She gave up on me then and asked to Eran, "Does she ever choose the reasonable path?"

"No," he and I replied in unison.

She threw up her hands. "It's almost as if you crave eternal death," she mumbled.

Abaddon snickered then, drawing our attention. "Well…she won't need to wait long for that," he said, moving forward, his face lifting in a sneer. To the Elsics behind him, he suddenly called out, "Prepare for retribution."

The wave of creatures followed him, closing the distance between us and the sea of our immortal enemies, fangs out, claws extended, eager for revenge.

Then the wave stopped and each one tilted an ear towards the cavern's entrances above.

They heard the whistle before I did; the sound of something approaching, something enormous and powerfully fast. They shuddered in unison, their wings spreading out quickly, knocking against those closest to them.

All of this happened just as winged beings streamed through the tunnels and into the cavern's mouth, circling once in open surveillance, and then pointing themselves downward in attack.

Eran released an amazed chuckle, watching in awe as the army of Alterums collided with the Elsics, now struggling to free themselves from their neighbor's wings.

His plan destroyed, Abaddon's face twisted in to a snarl and he lunged himself forward. He and Eran collided, swords clashing, their bodies spinning upward.

Instantly, I was in search of a weapon but this only lasted a moment. Ms. Beedinwigg stepped forward, her sword extended towards me.

I gave her a smile of appreciation, took it, and launched myself into the air.

The following minutes were a blur. Swords clashed, limbs were severed, bodies hurled through the air only to stop short at the edge of a blade.

My own blade moved with incomprehensible speed, lashing at the Elsics, carving a path through them, refusing to wait for one to fall before attacking the next. My housemates, Eran, and Ms. Beedinwigg did the same and at those times when they came into my view I was proud.

In the end, the bodies of dismembered Elsics lay piled across the ground, from one end of the cavern to the other, hundreds of them intertwined with the bodies of nearly the same number of Alterums.

Ezra, Felix, and Rufus settled down beside Eran and me, surveying the damage.

The cavern had been replaced with an eerie quiet, shattered only by the intermittent gasps and aching moans of those still fighting death.

"No…" I muttered. "No."

Suddenly I was moving through the bodies, heaving aside Elsics in search of living Alterums. "It's not supposed to be this way," I heard myself saying. "They can't die this way. We can't let them die this way…"

Then I felt Eran's hand on my shoulder. Spinning around, I said, "Help me find the living. I can escort them. I can bring them to the other side. Help me!"

I was now frantic, searching for the lift of a chest, the inhale of a single breath, the flicker of an eyelid…Anything…

Then I came across Campion.

Eran drew in a sharp breath and immediately lifted his first lieutenant over his shoulder. He brought him back and laid him against the outcropping where we now stood.

Kneeling at his side, Eran watched Campion draw his last breaths as I stepped up beside him.

"Eran," I said quiet but firm. I was calmer now, realizing my job, my purpose in existing was being called on. "Eran, you need to step aside now. Time is running out."

"Running out?" Ms. Beedinwigg asked quietly, bewildered.

I didn't bother to address her so it was Ezra who explained.

"Maggie has the ability to deliver not only messages but souls into the afterlife."

Eran, who understood my unique ability, was already shifting away from Campion.

"And this will be the second time I've escorted him," I recalled. "Remember Gettysburg, Campion?"

I didn't expect an answer but he mustered the strength to nod; it was slight but detectable.

"Ready?" I asked him, taking his hand.

This time no nod came. His last breath released in a hiss and his body went still.

It was the last sound I heard before my own body became lethargic, before my eye lids grew heavy, and finally I fell still.

There was no bright light, no tunnel, nor was there any rushing wind or need to pump my wings and lift into the air.

As was always the case when delivering messages, I simply awoke on the other side, the one who I'd carried there already beside me.

"Maggie," Campion urged me awake. "Maggie…"

I opened my eyes to find him standing over me, once again grinning.

I sat up and brushed off the sleep. "Where are we?"

"The other side," he said, sarcastically.

"I realize that but where exactly?"

His hand swooped out, gesturing for me to look for myself.

We were at the base of the very same steps I'd just left. My circle of family and friends were no longer present. In their place were Campion's loved ones, eagerly approaching him with open arms.

I didn't bother to stand, already knowing that my time here would be short. Campion, knowing it also, simply knelt beside me.

"Thanks again for the escort," he said, confirming he had remembered my assistance in Gettysburg. "Tell Eran that if he calls on me again, I'll be ready."

"I will," I replied warmly.

"Now go," he insisted, standing.

No sooner were the words out of his mouth did I end up back in the prison, directly beside Campion's now vacant body.

Others were now being laid next to him. Alterums, each struggling for life. My housemates, Eran, and others, anyone who was able moved quietly and quickly to sift through the bodies, carrying those still moving to the outcropping. I didn't hesitate. Without addressing anyone nearby me, Eran included, I found the ones closest to death and escorted each to the other side, one by one, until I returned the last time and found no other Alterums living.

"Welcome back," Eran said, stepping towards me to tenderly brush the hair from my cheek.

I smiled my thanks at him and delivered Campion's message, my eyes making one final sweep of the bodies to ensure I hadn't missed any.

"They're all gone," Eran said gently. "Your job here is done. You can rest now. They are all safe."

"And we have you to thank." The statement came from a man behind us, one with a thick German accent. Turning, I found him to more closely resemble a Greek god than an Alterum. His face twitched as the flicker of a smile crossed over it. "Because of you, they will live to fight another day."

"Well, let's hope that won't be necessary," said Ezra, pointedly from a few feet away.

The man's lips pinched closed briefly before acknowledging, "This battle...It won't be the last."

With that ominous statement, we stood in silence, absorbing all that had just taken place. When Eran could take no more of it, he turned and said to the Greek god, "Magnus, I would like you to meet Magdalene."

My heart flipped at the way he said my name.

"It is an honor," said Magnus with unquestionable sincerity.

"Thank you for coming back," I replied, surprising him a little. He hadn't expected me to be so forthright, I assumed.

"Took me a while to gather them," he slowly motioned towards the Alterums, some of whom were alive and trying to recover from their battle wounds. "Wasn't sure we'd get here in time."

"We are glad you did," said Felix, his face lifting in a shaky smile of appreciation.

No one else smiled.

We studied the cavern and realized how close we'd come to being annihilated.

Movement from the Elsics, all of whom still lived despite their injuries, caught my eye. Among them, I did not see Abaddon.

"We have one more thing to do…" They each rotated their heads towards me. "Seal the cave."

21. GOODBYE

We reached New Orleans just as the sun set over the horizon. The fact that it was the end of the day took on a different meaning then. Deep down, I'm not certain I believed we would ever see another sun set.

Eran and I had flown back as close to each other as possible, so close the tips of our wings brushed against each other at times. Each touch sent a thrill through me and lifted my face in a smile. His response was his signature smirk and I wondered at times if he wasn't doing it on purpose. Not that it mattered. I adored the moments when we touched and those moments would come to an end soon.

His wounds were rapidly healing now. The swelling was gone and his eyelids could open fully. Bruising still showed but rather than the greenish-purple hue they had been, his damaged skin was now a pale yellow. He would still need a shower to wash off the blood caked to him.

The streetlight went on just as our feet touched the gravel driveway at the side of our house. A hazy, yellow illumination stretched across the side and over the shed, giving us enough light to see where we landed.

The kitchen light was on, making most of us bristle.

Ezra, who had brought Ms. Beedinwigg back with her, stepped up to the door and peered inside without much concern.

"Looks like cornbread and chicken," she muttered before glancing over her shoulder at us. "Comfort food...Don't know about you but I could use some right about now."

She opened the door and Alfred stepped into view, his butler uniform untouched by a single morsel of food. Mr. Hamilton followed, covered in flour and paste from head to toe.

It didn't matter much what they looked like. We were just glad to see them.

Dinner was soothing, as much as it could be. Neither Mr. Hamilton nor Alfred asked about the mission. The state of Eran's face and Campion's absence told them enough. Mr. Hamilton informed us that the local news channel had covered the disturbance at the school and an investigation was being launched into the prank that left the school nearly destroyed. Students and faculty were safe and, in their panic, had apparently not seen any Fallen Ones since none were reported. Conversation from that point on was kept to safer topics such as Mr. Hamilton's attempt to drive Ms. Beedinwigg's SUV and Alfred's questionable choices in cologne.

We all helped with the dishes and when the evening was over, I walked Ms. Beedinwigg, Mr. Hamilton, and Alfred to the front porch where the SUV waited, one wheel parked up on the curb.

As Mr. Hamilton and Alfred waited by the vehicle, Ms. Beedinwigg paused at the bottom of the steps. "See you in class on Monday?" The way she asked her question made me think she already knew the answer.

I smiled back at her, unable to lie. She would have seen through it anyways. I had the feeling that even my silence told her with certainty that she should expect me to be absent.

Smiling sadly to herself, she started down the path again.

"Ms. Beedinwigg," I stopped her and she slowly turned. "When you said I wasn't ready…for the mission against the Elsics…I now know what you meant."

She nodded once, resolutely.

"Thank you…" I paused and looked her directly in the eye, hoping she would understand what I was about to say. "Because of you…because of my death, I believe I am ready now."

She briefly hung her head wistfully and then looked up. "You are, Maggie. There is no doubt about that." Her lips lifted in a soft smile. "I'm going to miss you." It was the first and only time she'd ever admitted that she thought of me as anything more than a responsibility, a student.

She gave me one last, lingering look, as if she were capturing my image in her memory, and then headed for the vehicle.

I watched as she drove away, feeling a loss, a vacancy inside. It was the same kind of emptiness that I imagined a fighter feels entering the rink without his trainer or a captain feels taking over the vessel for the very first time.

I was now on my own. Whether I won or lost, survived or died, I would do it alone.

Later that night, as Eran showered, I stood on my balcony, watching over the rooftops of the city I had come to love. Cherishing it, I breathed in the salty sea air; listened to the melodic jazz music playing down the street; feeling the humidity envelope and comfort my skin, wondering if all the Fallen Ones had been scared off by today's incident.

This would be the last peaceful night I would allow myself.

Eran entered my room behind me, wrapping his arms around my waist, stepping into my world for a moment and silently appreciating it alongside me.

His arms were strong and firm, forming a protective barrier. The warmth of his body, still moist from the shower, pressed against my back, settling against me.

I was going to miss him so much.

Not long after, we left the balcony and he made his way to the door.

"Stay with me," I whispered.

Something in my voice made him listen and he came quietly to my bedside. We slipped in and he pulled the covers over us, our eyes adjusting to the darkness.

I found him watching me, his expression filled with love…and appreciation that we were both still here. Then his lids closed and his breathing deepened and I knew it was time.

Still, I couldn't bring myself to move. I couldn't free myself from our entwined hands. I couldn't roll to the side, put my feet on the ground, and walk away. I could envision it, but I couldn't do it. My entire being refused. Doing so meant putting distance between me and Eran and the very thought of it sickened me. We'd endured enough distance, we had the right to be together.

Yet, it was exactly what I was about to do. He could not come with me. I wouldn't allow it. Doing so meant putting him at risk again. No, I said silently to him. You'll remain here, out of harm's way. Only this will give me the peace of mind to do what must be done.

My eyes landed on the scars left behind from the Elsics' beatings in the prison and my resolve was reinforced.

It took the full measure of my will power to pull away from him, to end our touch, the action making me feel as if my chest were caving in.

Still, I carefully slipped out of bed and stood over him. Now deep asleep, he had no idea that I had left him. I didn't blame him. After everything he had been through, the weeks of sleepless nights, the emotional turmoil, the fear of losing me, he deserved peace.

My eyes traced the contours of his chiseled face. He was handsome even in exhaustion. The very sight of him comforted me, making me feel as if everything would be all right. That, I knew, was not true.

Not only were his wounds still visible, so many Alterums had endured incredible pain to save us...to save me. Everyone I loved had again been placed in grave danger...because of me.

Ironically, Eran rarely rested in order to ensure I was protected. Now I would forgo sleep to ensure he and all others were protected. Although he didn't know it yet, our roles had now been reversed.

Quietly, I redressed and, choosing my wardrobe selectively, packed what few belongings I needed into my backpack. From the same pocket, I withdrew a note I'd written just as Eran had left for the shower. It was brief, since I had little time to write it, but it was to the point.

My eyes scanned it once before setting it down.

Eran, I am in love with you. When you wake and find me gone, please don't take it as any sign to the contrary. Leaving is unavoidable. I can't put you or any more of those I love at risk any longer. As odd as it may seem, I am doing this for you. I will miss you – all of you. I realize you know this – but I'm going to mention it anyways – there won't be a second that goes by without my heart aching to be with you. With all of my eternal love, Magdalene Talor.

My heart broke as I left the note on my pillow.

When I left my room, closing my door behind me, I never took my eyes off Eran, locking in the memory of him as Ms. Beedinwigg had done with me.

After I made my way down the stairs and out the back door, I pushed my Harley Davidson down the driveway and, for extra measure, halfway down the street. Kick starting it, I then made my way through the now familiar route across the city towards Mr. Hamilton's house.

Stopping there, I parked my bike at the path leading to the front door. It was midnight now. The streets were silent. Not even the crickets called out. My knock on her door will wake the neighborhood, I thought. But as it turned out, I never found the need to knock.

Taking the steps two at a time, I found that what I had come for was already there.

Leaned against the door, hidden in the shadows, was the book of notes the Beedinwigg's had collected over the years. Picking it up, I realized the importance of this tome of information. All the Fallen Ones were listed inside, their descriptions, their acquaintances, their strengths, their weaknesses, and most importantly their common residences.

I remembered the warning Magnus had left us with inside the prison cavern. The fight was not over, he'd said, and I knew just what he meant. So long as the Fallen Ones existed we would always be in peril.

That was exactly what I was going to change.

Beware Fallen Ones, I thought while gazing out into the night, you asked for a fight and I'll be bringing it to you.

Opening the book, I flipped to the first dossier. "Marilyn Hauser...Fort Lauderdale..." I muttered to myself. Quickly committing the rest of the Fallen One's profile to memory, I closed the book and walked it back to my bike.

After securing it inside my backpack, I slipped on my bike and started the engine.

I would have to hurry if I was going to make it to Florida by morning...

ABOUT THE AUTHOR

∞

LAURY FALTER graduated with a Bachelor's degree from Pepperdine University and a Master's degree from Michigan State University. She lives with her husband and two stray dogs in Las Vegas. Her website is www.lauryfalter.com.

Made in the USA
Lexington, KY
25 June 2012